Heather BURNSIDE

Born Bad

HEAD
of ZEUS

First published in the UK in 2017 by Aria, an imprint of Head of Zeus Ltd
First published in print in the UK in 2019

9 7 5 3 1 2 4 6 8

A catalogue record for this book is available from
the British Library.

ISBN (PBO): 9781789541847
ISBN (E): 9781786692542

Typeset by Divaddict Publishing Solutions Ltd

Printed and bound in Great Britain by
CPI Group (UK) Ltd, Croydon CR0 4YY

Head of Zeus Ltd
First Floor East
5–8 Hardwick Street
London EC1R 4RG

WWW.HEADOFZEUS.COM

BORN BAD

HEATHER BURNSIDE spent her teenage years on one of the toughest estates in Manchester and she draws heavily on this background as the setting for many of her novels. After taking a career break to raise two children, Heather enrolled on a creative writing course. Heather now works full-time on her novels from her home in Manchester, which she shares with her two grown-up children.

Also by Heather Burnside

Born Bad
Blood Ties
Slur
A Gangster's Grip
Danger by Association
Vendetta

Coming soon

The Mark
Ruby
Crystal

For Ellen,

who would have been so proud

Prologue – 1994

Steve Anthony, clinical psychologist, looked at the attractive young woman sitting across from him. Despite her attempts at composure, she bore all the signs of stress. Her face was flushed and she continually dabbed at it with the tissue that she clasped in her sweat-drenched hand. With her other hand she was twisting her forefinger around a lock of her dark, glossy hair.

He could see that the tissue was becoming sodden so he offered her a fresh one and passed her the wastepaper basket. She uncrossed her legs, which she had been clenching tightly, while she dropped the tissue into the bin and grabbed another.

'So, what do you think prompted this disagreement?' he asked.

The disagreement had, in fact, been a major row with her partner, but it was part of Steve's job to play it down. He didn't want to add to her stress. Instead, he wanted her to analyse the row calmly so she could perhaps find a way to handle similar situations better in the future.

Adele was visiting him as a private patient and he respected her decision to seek help. In many aspects of her life she was a successful young lady. That was obvious from her appearance. The clothing she wore and the way she presented herself showed that she was an intelligent, sophisticated and savvy woman.

But there was one area of her life in which she wasn't successful. It concerned her ability to maintain loving relationships. Instead of ignoring the problem however, she had chosen to confront it, and had therefore sought his help.

'It started over something trivial,' she said. 'I found some hairs in my brush. I knew they weren't mine because they were blonde. There was only one person it could have been so I asked him. He'd used it without my permission and I got really annoyed because he'd gone behind my back.'

'I see. Do you think you were annoyed because he used something of yours or because he did it behind your back?'

'Both. But mainly because he used my brush.'

Despite his thoughts about this, Steve was careful in the wording of his next question. 'Would you have let him use it if he had asked?'

'No!'

'Really? I'm surprised,' Steve replied, keeping his voice deliberately calm so his response wouldn't sound like a challenge.

He allowed Adele to digest his words for a few moments, remaining silent so she would feel pressed to respond.

'Don't get me wrong; I'm not selfish,' she added, when she realised the implications of her sharp retort. 'It's just that I look after my things. It might sound daft but I always wanted a nice brush, comb and mirror set. It's silver-plated. I saved for ages to buy it, and I don't really like anyone touching it.'

Steve noted the awkward expression on her face and knew that the importance she attached to the brush was nothing to do with selfishness.

'So, what happened next?' he asked.

'Well, he started going on about me being selfish, then about my jealousy, and then things just escalated.'

With a little probing, Adele went on to describe what had happened during this latest argument with her boyfriend. Steve was convinced that her inability to maintain relationships was rooted in her difficult childhood. Her reaction concerning the hairbrush, and other facts she had divulged in a previous session, hinted at this.

In order to move forward, Steve would have to explore what would have been a traumatic period in Adele's life. But she was ready to go to the next stage, and Steve had already decided that this was where they would venture during today's session.

When they had finished discussing the row with her boyfriend, Steve said, 'Adele, I would like to find out a bit more about your family relationships. Let's start with your brother, as you've referred to him quite a bit during our sessions. Did you have a good relationship with him when you were a child?'

'At first, but then things changed. When we were kids we got on most of the time. He was always up to mischief though and some of the things he did were bad, even as a young kid. But I tried to look out for him, being his older sister.'

'OK, do you know what caused the change in your relationship with your brother?'

Adele sighed heavily and rolled her eyes, 'It's a long story.'

'OK, well perhaps you'd like to start at the beginning. I'd like you to take me back to your childhood and tell me about

your relationship with Peter when you were children. Think about when things may have started to go wrong between you, and try to focus on that. Then we can gradually move onto the present.'

Adele took a sip of water followed by a deep breath to compose herself. Then, hesitantly at first, but gaining momentum as the memories resurfaced, she began to recount her troubled childhood.

PART ONE

1973-1974

1

As soon as Adele walked into the back garden of her home in the Manchester suburbs, she was horrified by the sight that met her. Among the overgrown bushes and weed-filled borders was an assortment of cracked and mossy flagstones that acted as a path. There, her ten-year-old brother, Peter, stood facing her. He was wielding a large twig which he had stripped bare. For him it now represented a whip; flexible enough to slash rapidly through the air, yet strong enough to inflict damage.

He chuckled as he repeatedly thrashed his whip onto the paving slabs in front of him. His target was several squirming caterpillars of differing sizes and various shades of green and brown, which he had lined up. Adele could see their tiny bodies writhing as savage blows from the hand-made weapon assailed them, causing their oozing entrails to spill out onto the path.

'Stop it!' she yelled.

Peter paused briefly to reply, 'They're only insects.' He laughed and lashed the whip once more.

'I don't care. It's cruel and disgusting,' Adele shouted, becoming annoyed.

'You're stupid, you are. I'm not doing any harm. Go and mither someone else, Miss Goody-goody.' His impish laughter had now disappeared, transforming his face into an unwelcoming sneer.

'At least I'm not like you!' said Adele.

'What do you mean?' he asked, staring at Adele while the caterpillars wriggled around on the paving slabs.

Adele could sense his change in tone but, despite her unease, she refused to give way. 'You're always up to no good, you are. You're gonna get in trouble again if you don't watch it.'

'Oh shut up, you crybaby! Go and play with your dolls.' And ignoring her pleas, he went back to meting out his vicious punishment.

Adele felt her stomach lurch at the sickening sight and cried out to him, 'Peter, stop it; it's horrible!'

Unfortunately, her cries soon reached the ears of their father who sped through the back door, pushing her aside. She noticed that he was still in his shabby vest, and knew that he hadn't been out of bed long, even though it was midday. He was a menacing sight. The scruffy vest emphasised his bulky muscles, and his rugged features were set in a hard expression. She knew that he wouldn't take kindly to having his Sunday disturbed.

'What the bleedin' hell's going on here?' he demanded.

Peter dropped the whip and looked up guiltily at his father. His jaw hung loose but he failed to utter any words of defence.

Their father didn't need a reply, however, as his eyes took in the revolting sight. In one stride, he was on Peter, grabbing at his shirt collar and thrusting upwards until his feet left the ground.

'You dirty little get!' he yelled. 'Look at the bleedin' state of that path.' He released his hold, allowing Peter to drop shakily to the ground. Then, prodding his forefinger into Peter's face, he ordered, 'Get it cleaned up… NOW!'

Peter hung his head in shame and approached the house in search of something with which to clean up the mess.

'Where the bleedin' hell do you think you're going?' roared his father. 'I told you to clean them up.'

'I'm going for some newspaper to wipe them up with,' Peter replied.

'No you're bleedin' not! You weren't bothered about newspaper when you put the bleedin' things there, so why bother now? You can get them shifted with yer hands. And I want every bit cleared up, including that slimy shit that's come out of 'em. That'll teach you, you dirty little bastard!'

He turned and pushed Adele aside again as he trundled back indoors. Just before stepping into the house, he turned his head back and added, 'And you can get your bleedin' hands washed when you've finished as well.'

For a few moments, Adele stood still, her eyes fixed on Peter, awaiting his reaction.

'What you looking at, you bitch?' he muttered. 'It's all your fault! If you hadn't started carrying on, he wouldn't have known.' As he murmured these few words, he made a show of wiping up the slimy mess with his fingers, as though deliberately trying to antagonise her.

Adele couldn't take any more. She ran into the house retching, and headed straight for her bedroom where she threw herself onto the bed. But the tears didn't come. At eleven years of age, she'd suppressed her tears so often that it had become an automatic defence mechanism that helped her get through life.

Adele felt bad. She shouldn't have carried on so much at Peter, then her father wouldn't have known. It was bound to annoy him, especially on a Sunday. He was always in a mood on a Sunday. In fact, he was always in a mood any day, but Sundays were particularly bad. It was only recently, as she was growing up, that Adele realised why; it was because of the skinful he had had on a Saturday night. All he wanted to do on Sundays was sleep it off. Then he would sit and pore through the papers whilst their mother, Shirley, made a pretence of cleaning the house, and cooked the traditional Sunday dinner in an effort to please him.

This was usually the first attempt at cleaning that Shirley had made all week. She spent most of her days gossiping with the neighbours, sleeping or watching TV. Her evenings were spent in a similar fashion, except for the few nights a week in which she tore herself away from the street to go and play bingo.

Adele got up off the bed and drifted towards the window. She avoided the sight of Peter but looked out instead at the other houses, watching people go about their business. Allowing her mind to drift, she contemplated, for the umpteenth time, her miserable existence.

Lately she was realising that although this way of life was commonplace within these four walls, there was a different world out there. Talking to her friends had made her understand that her circumstances weren't the norm, and other parents were different from her own. Other children went out with their families to the cinema or country parks. They had holidays at the seaside and expensive presents for their birthdays.

The only advantage she had over other children was her freedom. Her father was hardly ever home, so that gave her and Peter a chance to roam the streets and do whatever they pleased as long as news of their mischief didn't get back to him. Their mother scarcely showed any interest in where they were going or what time they would be back.

Adele often consoled herself by imagining that one day things would be different. When she was old enough she would get a good job and a rich husband, and she would escape her domineering father and slovenly mother. She would have a beautiful home and children who would never want for anything. It was this dream that kept her going.

Just then Adele was jolted back to reality by the sound of raised voices downstairs.

'Don't go, Tommy, I was gonna do you a nice dinner later,' pleaded her mother.

'Bugger off, I'm going for a pint. There's nowt to stay in this bloody pigsty for. I'm sick of you, you lazy cow, and those two scruffy little gets!'

This was followed by a loud slamming of the front door and Shirley muttering something to herself. Adele couldn't quite hear her mother's words, but she gathered that she wasn't happy about him going out.

Adele had had enough of home for one day, so she decided that she would go outside for a while too. She was heading downstairs when she heard the sound of the door knocker. Worried it was her father coming back, she scuttled back to the top of the stairs. It was only after her mother had answered the door that Adele realised it was her grandma, Joyce.

She entered loudly and, appearing as bumptious as ever, declared, 'I've just passed His Lordship in the street. He's got a right face on him, as usual. It took him all his time to say hello. What the bleedin' hell's up with him this time?'

The soft features of her plump face had tightened to form an expression of scorn.

Shirley said nothing, but shook her head from side to side as she led her mother into the living room, leaving the door ajar. Adele would normally have raced down the stairs to greet her grandma, who she thought the world of. Although loud and opinionated, Joyce had a kind heart and was full of good intentions. But the look of resignation on her mother's face, and the tired way she dragged her feet, stopped Adele from following them. She had guessed that they were about to have one of their chats, and overcome by curiosity, she crept down the stairs so she could listen in. She could just about see them both through the gap of the open door.

'Jesus, Shirley love, what the bloody hell's happened to this place? It looks like a bomb's hit it and smells bloody awful! It's worse than last time. I thought you were going to try and get on top of things!'

'Oh don't start, Mam. Don't you think I'm sick of it? It's not me that makes it a tip you know, and what's the use of tidying it anyway when they only mess it up again?'

'I'm worried about you, love. Every time I come you've let yourself go more. You're just not happy, are you? Has he been at you again?'

'Not really. It's Peter he's pissed off with, because he made a mess on the garden path, squashing some caterpillars or summat. I wish he'd leave him alone; he's not a bad lad really.'

'I don't know, I worry about our Peter, always up to mischief and getting into fights. I've told you, he takes after his side of the family.'

Their conversation then became much quieter, and Adele had to strain to hear them. Without getting too close, and risking being caught out, she managed to catch snippets of her grandma's words.

'Bad lot... told you before... bad blood... mad... great-uncle... always fighting... ended up in an asylum.'

A few moments of silence followed until Shirley said, 'I don't know what I'm gonna do, Mam. I've no idea what our Peter will turn out like. I'm just glad our Adele's all right.'

'Aye, she's a good girl,' replied Joyce whose voice had returned to its normal level. 'Keep encouraging her to do well at school so she can bugger off to university or summat. She'll be bloody better off out of it.' Joyce's voice then adopted a sympathetic tone. 'I do worry about you, Shirley love. You've changed so much over the years, ever since you met Tommy. You don't seem to care anymore and you were never like this when you were younger. Did you go to the doctor's like I told you to?'

'Yeah, he's given me these for the daytime on top of the ones I take at night,' she said, passing something to her mother.

'Let's have a look,' said Joyce, who then tried to read the words on the bottle of pills. 'Dia... ze... pam. What are they supposed to do?'

'I don't know,' said Shirley. 'But I feel more knackered than ever. I've not got the energy I was born with, honestly, Mam.'

'Well, I don't know what the bloody hell to make of it all. I wish to God you'd never married him in the first place. I tried to warn you, but you wouldn't be told. I'd take you and the kids round to my house, but I've just not got the room.'

'I know that, Mam. I've just got to put up with it, haven't I? Besides, I love Tommy. I just wish he wasn't so angry all the time.'

Joyce looked exasperated, but didn't continue. It was a topic which she had already covered many times before, so she moved onto something else. When Adele had grown tired of hearing about what Joyce's neighbours were up to, she returned to her bedroom. There she mulled over the conversation in her young mind.

She knew her grandmother had been referring to her father and his family. She was used to her grandma Joyce talking about them, but she had never heard her mention the word 'mad' before. Maybe it just meant they had bad tempers. She wondered about the word asylum. It wasn't one she was familiar with, but she decided to check it in her dictionary.

Adele took her dictionary off the row of books on the shelf. She opened it up, and scanned the words under the letter 'a' until she reached asylum. She found two meanings; the first of them referred to a place of refuge, but the second related to a mental institution. She wondered which of these her grandma could have been talking about but she daren't ask.

Adele stared at the dictionary for a few moments but when the words 'mental institution' seemed to leap out from the page, she quickly shut it. Those words frightened her. She knew her dad had a temper, but surely that couldn't mean he was mental. She'd heard kids at school use the words 'mad' and 'mental' when they were trying to put down someone who was a bit stupid. They weren't nice words and she didn't like to think of them being linked to her family.

She was curious about the tablets her mother was taking as well; something called diazepam, her grandma had said. Adele opened her dictionary again and flicked over the pages, checking whether diazepam was listed, but she couldn't find anything.

Her thoughts flitted back to the words 'mad' and 'mental'. Adele was confused. She couldn't understand why her grandma would use such words about her family. Grandma

Joyce didn't usually say nasty things. Grandma Joyce was nice. So if she was saying bad things about her dad, then maybe they were true. Maybe he really was mad. And, if Peter took after their dad's side of the family, did that mean he was mad too?

2

The school holidays had been over for several weeks. It was now autumn, and winter was fast approaching. Adele's school teacher, Mr Parry, had been summoned to see the head teacher in relation to an incident. Full of curiosity, he tapped lightly on the office door and stepped inside when beckoned.

'Oh hello Mr Parry, do take a seat!' ordered the head teacher, Miss Marchant.

Hardly giving Mr Parry a chance to settle in the seat, she straightaway began to address the matter in hand in her usual authoritarian manner.

'I have received a report from one of the dinner ladies about an incident involving two girls in your class. I thought I might get some background information from you before dealing with the matter.'

Mr Parry nodded his head and allowed Miss Marchant to continue.

'The two girls involved were Deborah Clare and Adele Robinson.'

Mr Parry pricked his ears on hearing the name of one of his star pupils, Adele.

'Apparently,' continued Miss Marchant, 'there was a fight between the two girls, but a rather one-sided affair, with Deborah Clare on the receiving end of quite a beating, from what I am told.'

'Really?' asked Mr Parry, shocked at this news.

'You seem surprised, Mr Parry.'

'Yes, I am. Are you sure there hasn't been a mistake?'

'No, no mistake. I trust the member of staff involved, and she knew both girls by name. I must admit I was surprised to hear Adele Robinson's name when she had such a glowing report last year.'

'Me too. But not only that, she's very quiet in the classroom. I wouldn't have thought her capable of giving someone a beating. I would have thought it was more likely she'd be the victim, to be honest. Are you sure the dinner lady hasn't got things the wrong way round?'

'No, Mr Parry, it was definitely as described.'

'Well, I do have to say, I'm very surprised.'

'What about the other girl, Deborah Clare? How do they get along together?'

'Deborah's a real trier. She's above average, a likeable girl but a bit mischievous at times. Oh, nothing serious. She just gets a little cheeky, but once I give her a ticking off she usually toes the line. They seem to get along well together, no major problems in the past.'

'Well thank you for your help, Mr Parry. In view of what you've told me, I'll regard it as a one-off. Can you send both girls to see me after the lunch break please, and I'll give them a stern talking-to? That should do the trick.'

'Certainly, Miss Marchant,' he replied, and as he left

her office, he couldn't help but feel troubled by Adele's behaviour.

Adele felt sick with worry. The dinner lady had just gone to see the head teacher, leaving her and Deboran in the playground. Adele knew that there would be repercussions from the fight. She wished that she hadn't done what she had, but she couldn't help herself; something in her had just snapped. As she stood in a corner of the playground, she replayed the incident in her mind.

She and Deborah were having a laugh, giving each other donkey rides. Adele's ride was just coming to an end and Deborah had walked over to the wall with Adele on her back. The wire mesh paper bin was attached to the wall, protruding in an arc shape with the lid slanting downwards away from the wall. It formed a welcoming seat, but one that you couldn't sit on for too long, because of the slope.

'Put me down on the bin!' she said to Deborah, which Deborah did.

But instead of letting go of her legs so that Adele could ease herself off the bin and down onto the ground, Deborah began to pull her legs away from the bin.

'What are you doing?' asked Adele, alarmed.

Deborah didn't answer but Adele could hear her giggle as she pulled her legs further away from the bin until Adele was horizontal.

Adele gripped the wire mesh with her fingers, 'Put me down!' she yelled.

When Deborah wouldn't put her down, she yelled louder. It seemed that the louder she yelled, the harder Deborah pulled.

Adele's arms had now become fully stretched behind her, and her fingers clung perilously to the wire mesh to prevent herself falling. She felt the metal digging into her flesh, and had visions of her body slamming to the ground, with her head crashing against the concrete.

'Let go of my legs! Put me down!' she yelled.

But still Deborah pulled.

When Adele felt her fingers loosening their grip, panic seized her. With a strength that she seemed to muster from nowhere, she tore one of her legs away from Deborah. Her back then slumped towards the bin, dragging Deborah with her. Using her newfound strength, Adele pulled her other leg away from Deborah, releasing her hold, and her buttocks met the top of the bin. By now Adele's panic had turned to fury and she kicked repeatedly at Deborah's back.

'You bitch, I hate you!' Adele cursed.

Oblivious to Deborah's agonised screams, Adele continued to kick as rage overtook her. It was only the sight of the dinner lady running towards her that brought her to her senses.

Now, as she thought about the incident, she felt remorseful. If only Debby hadn't decided to do something so daft. If only she could have persuaded her to stop without losing her temper. But Debby hadn't stopped. She shouted at her a few times, and she still didn't stop. That's what she would say in her defence. She had to pull her legs away; it was her only chance.

But did she have to kick her?

Adele was feeling desperate. *Oh God, it's no good*, she thought, *I'm gonna be in trouble no matter what.*

She thought about what her father's reaction would be if he found out. She dreaded that even more than she dreaded being summoned to see the head teacher.

The sound of the bell interrupted her thoughts. It was the end of the lunch period and Adele entered the school building in a state of trepidation, to the sound of taunting.

'You're gonna be in trouble, Adele Robinson, for what you did to Debby.'

'Yeah,' added another girl, 'Miss Goody Two Shoes is gonna get done, ha ha.'

When Mr Parry announced that she and Debby were to see the head teacher straightaway, Adele felt her stomach sink.

Mr Parry led the two girls down the long corridor towards the head teacher's office, and told them to wait outside while he knocked on the door. After he had been inside for a few minutes, he came back out, and asked Debby to go inside. He then lowered his eyes towards Adele and told her to wait there until she was called for. She noticed the look of disappointment on his face and felt ashamed. Then, with nothing further to say, he left her standing outside the head teacher's office, trembling with fear.

After what seemed like an endless wait, Debby came out of the office, and looked away from Adele as she walked past her.

'Next!' shouted Miss Marchant.

Adele was already in tears by the time she entered the office and presented herself at the other side of the head teacher's large desk.

'Now then, what have you been up to?' asked Miss Marchant.

'I... I... I didn't mean it,' muttered Adele.

'Didn't mean what? And for heaven's sake, speak up, young lady.'

'I didn't mean to hurt Debby,' Adele sobbed.

'Well, from what I've been told, you've got a bit of a temper, haven't you, young lady?'

Adele, by now very tearful, nodded in response.

'I can't hear you!' thundered Miss Marchant.

'Yes,' Adele replied.

'Yes, what?'

'Yes, Miss Marchant.'

Adele was so worked up that she thought she would vomit at any minute. To her surprise, just when she reached the point where she felt she might faint, the head teacher seemed to relent.

'Well, Miss Robinson, although I don't condone your behaviour in the playground, I have received glowing reports from your class teacher. So, I'm going to let the matter rest on this occasion. However, I would suggest that in future you keep that temper of yours well under wraps.'

'Yes, Miss,' answered Adele.

'You may go.'

Adele quickly made for the door, feeling a mixture of relief and shame, but before she could get to the other side, she was stopped by Miss Marchant's stern tones.

'And if I ever hear of any repeat of this behaviour, you will be punished severely!'

'Yes, Miss,' Adele replied as she dashed from the office.

Anxious to be away from the head teacher's office as soon as possible, Adele rushed down the corridor and into her classroom.

Mr Parry raised his eyes from the papers on his desk and abruptly ordered Adele to sit down in the vacant seat next to Tony Lord, who had a reputation for being the best fighter in the school.

As Adele felt everyone's eyes on her, a tear escaped from

her eye. She was greeted by a barrage of questions from the other children sitting at the table. Adele's feelings of guilt and shame made her shy away from their questions, even though she could tell they were impressed that she'd beaten Debby up.

'Why are you crying if you won the fight?' asked Tony, puzzled.

'Don't know,' muttered Adele, dipping her head.

How could she explain to somebody as insensitive as Tony Lord that she was upset at hurting her friend, and ashamed by her own display of temper? Adele hated violence; she'd seen enough of it at home. It also hurt her to think that she may have gone down in Mr Parry's estimation.

For the rest of the afternoon, Adele tried to concentrate on her classwork, but she couldn't shake off the feelings of guilt and shame. As thoughts whirled around in her head, she tried to suppress her sobbing, but still the tears tumbled down her face.

When the bell rang at the end of the day, Adele ran out of the classroom and headed directly for home. She was glad to put the incident behind her. Little did she know that this wasn't the only time she would be made to feel ashamed.

3

Adele arrived home to find the house empty, as usual. Her mother, Shirley, could spend an age in the corner shop, chatting to the shopkeeper and other customers. Adele always found the front door unlocked. It was a habit of her mother's, as well as many of their neighbours.

It wasn't that there weren't any burglaries in the Gorton area, but rather that they were all so poor that a potential burglar would be hard-pushed finding something worth taking. Adele's grandmother, Joyce, had once commented that if somebody was to attempt to burgle Shirley's home, they would probably run straight back out, screaming about the state of the place.

Adele was also used to the stench and the untidiness. It was so much a part of her life that she hadn't even realised there was anything wrong in it until she had begun to visit her friends' homes. She knew her grandma often complained about the state of the place, but that was just Grandma Joyce having a moan. Adele's mother said that it was all right for

Grandma Joyce who had nothing better to do than tidy up all day.

She took off her shoes and put them in the corner of the living room. Picking up her old shabby slippers, she swatted at the fly that flew off them. As she turned to make her way towards the settee, she heard the sound of the front door being opened. Then Peter walked into the living room shortly afterwards. He nodded at her in his usual way, saying nothing. For a moment they both sat in silence, until Peter spoke.

'Are you coming out?' he asked.

Adele didn't see any reason not to. She would only be bored at home, and going out with Peter was always a bit of an adventure. He might be bad at times, but he was never boring. So she put her shoes back on and they made their way outside.

As they approached the top of the street, they passed their mother, Shirley, on her way home.

'Hiya, Mam,' they both chorused.

'Where are you two off to?' she asked.

They gave a cursory response and continued on their way, Shirley not seeming particularly interested in what they were up to.

'Make sure you're home for tea,' she shouted after them, before they were out of hearing range. Then she continued shuffling her way down the street. She was a pitiful sight in her lopsided and stained coat with buttons that strained against her ample breasts and stomach. Her hair was greasy, and her legs bare despite the chill in the air.

Adele and Peter turned the corner and saw a group of boys. Anthony Hampson, the brother of Adele's friend, Janet, was amongst them. As they approached the boys, Adele noticed that they were carrying a football, and heading towards them.

'We're going for a game of footie. You coming?' Anthony asked Peter when they had drawn closer.

'Sure,' said Peter, turning to join the boys as they passed by on their way to the park. Adele remained on the spot, ignored by the boys and hurt because Peter had chosen to abandon her so soon. She couldn't understand why he was so willing to go off with Anthony when they were always falling out and getting into trouble.

Adele tried to shrug off her disappointment. 'Is your Janet in?' she shouted to Anthony, but he didn't reply.

Feeling deflated, she called at Janet's house, but Janet had gone to Gorton Cross Street, shopping with her mam. Adele called for another two of her friends but when she found neither of them was in, she gave up and returned home.

The smell hit her as soon as she walked in. Her mother was cooking something in the oven. Something with meat. Cheap cuts of meat. Fatty, gristly meat. *Oh no*, she thought. She had lost her appetite well before the meal was served up.

Later, Peter sidled up to the table just in time for tea, but their father still wasn't home. Adele knew that he would have called into the pub straight from work. An air of expectancy hung over them. Tommy might arrive home at any moment, and none of them could anticipate what mood he would be in.

Normally Adele would make the most of the time while he was out. This was usually the period when it was still relatively peaceful, before the trouble started. But tonight Peter was in a mood. He had slammed down onto his chair and was banging his cutlery noisily onto his plate as he ate his food. Something must have upset him after he had left her to go and play football. *I bet it's that Anthony*, thought Adele. *I knew Peter shouldn't have gone off with him.*

'Stop making so much bloody noise, will yer?' said Shirley.

Peter responded by banging his cutlery even louder until Shirley gave him a perfunctory slap to the side of his head.

'Belt up or I'll tell yer dad when he gets home,' she said.

The meal was a struggle. Adele cut through the fatty stewing steak which was swimming in watery gravy, and covered with a layer of overcooked slimy onions. The colour of the steak was somewhere between brown and grey, and the texture was rubbery. She stabbed at it with her fork. As she raised a morsel to her mouth, it gave off a powerful, unpleasant stench that made her gag. But she knew she had to eat it. She'd get in trouble otherwise.

Adele grappled with pieces of the steak in between swallowing the bland cabbage and lumpy potatoes that covered the rest of her plate. She willed her mother to leave the table so she could get rid of it before her father came home.

When Shirley eventually retired to the living room, relief flooded through Adele, who sneaked out through the back door and dumped the remainder of her tea in the dustbin. Peter followed her into the garden and did the same. She covered the food with some empty tin cans so that it wouldn't be spotted, then returned to the kitchen and washed the dishes.

'What's wrong with you?' she asked Peter as she passed him a plate to wipe dry.

'That Anthony's a cheat,' he muttered.

'Why, what's he done?'

'He cheats at football. The ball went outside the line but he wouldn't have it. Then he went off in a huff and took his ball home. I'm gonna get him.'

'What are you gonna do to him?'

'I'm gonna batter him. He called me a liar!'

'Don't! You'll get in trouble again and you know what will happen if Dad finds out.'

'I don't care. He deserves it.'

Adele tried and tried to dissuade Peter from fighting with Anthony Hampson and by the time they'd finished their chores, she thought she had succeeded. For a while they stayed indoors watching TV, but when the news programmes came on, Adele grew bored and read a book. She was a few pages in when she noticed that Peter had sneaked out of the house. That could only mean he was up to no good. Knowing that anything could happen when Peter was in a bad mood, she threw down her book and dashed out of the house after him.

4

Tommy was having a bad day. His boss had sent him to work on a house in Cheadle where they were building an extension. It was in a tree-lined street of large, detached properties, which were in contrast to Tommy's modest council house in Gorton. As soon as Tommy arrived, the householder made it clear that she resented his presence.

'Go round the back,' she instructed, when she answered the door. Then, eyeing him from head to toe with a look of unconcealed contempt across her face, she added, 'I won't have you traipsing your muck all over my nice clean carpets.'

She opened the side gate of her substantial property and directed Tommy to the area at the back where the extension was being built. Then she left him to it after issuing strict instructions that he wasn't to enter the rest of the house under any circumstances. The stuck-up bitch! She hadn't even offered him a cuppa.

Throughout the day he noticed her hovering close to the kitchen window as she watched him working. Every so often she would come to the back door to complain about something she wasn't happy with. He could still hear her shrill, nagging voice echoing in his ears, *'Don't put that there!'* *'I hope you haven't damaged the azaleas.'* *'Keep the noise levels down!'*

She even refused to let him use her toilet and told him to go elsewhere. So he went to the pub at dinner, sank a couple of pints and used the toilet there. When he arrived back at the house, she came to the back door to speak to him.

'Where do you think you've been till this time?' she asked.

'Having my dinner,' he grumbled. 'Why, what's wrong?'

'You've been gone almost two hours! Does your manager mind you taking so long for your lunch break?'

'As long as the job gets done, what's the problem?' he asked, annoyed at having to kowtow to a woman.

'We'll see about that. I shall be keeping a close eye on you to make sure the work does get done! And I want it completed to my satisfaction, otherwise there will be repercussions.'

Snobby cow! If it wasn't for the fact that he needed the work, he would have told her where to shove her extension. And to make matters worse, he had to go there again tomorrow, and every day after that until the job was finished. He couldn't ask to be put on another job either. He was lucky to have this one after he had upset his boss a few weeks previously.

Taking flak from people like Mrs Heston, and not being able to retaliate, didn't suit Tommy at all. As he worked in silence, his resentment grew. To add to his woes, the two pints he'd drunk at dinner had worked their way through to his bladder and he was bursting to have another piss.

When Mrs Heston declared in a self-important manner that she was nipping out to do some errands, Tommy saw it as an opportunity to exact some revenge. He waited till she was well away from the house. Then he unzipped his flies and pointed his penis towards her herbaceous border, sending a spray of urine all over one of Mrs Heston's precious azalea bushes. He'd have a go at the heather tomorrow.

Despite this act of defiance, he was still annoyed when he stepped off the bus on Hyde Road, so he decided to stop off at his local. A couple of beers before tea should help, he thought.

The dusty cement had given him a thirst and it wasn't long before he'd sunk a few pints. He was sitting with two of his cronies, who listened patiently while he let off steam about the shit job he'd been given. They even bought him a couple of drinks to cheer him up. But Tommy Robinson always stood his round. So he got up and made his way over to the bar to return the favour.

'Three pints of bitter, Rosie, and one for yourself,' he said to the barmaid.

When she served him, he grabbed hold of the three pint glasses with his large, calloused hands, wedging the third pint between the other two to hold it in place and gripping it with his fingertips. Men like Tommy didn't take two trips to the bar to collect one round of drinks. He could comfortably manage three pints at once.

Well he could when he hadn't already drunk a few. He swung around, eager to return to his friends and get started on his beer, but before he could complete the turn, his arm connected with another customer, and one of the pints slipped from his grasp. It crashed to the ground, showering the grimy pub carpet with fragments of glass. The spilt beer soaked through Tommy's work boots and jeans as well as those of the other man.

Tommy slammed the remaining two pints back down on the bar and swivelled to face the man. 'You clumsy bastard!' he shouted as he jabbed the man sharply in his shoulder, 'Why don't you watch what you're fuckin' doing?'

The man had a reputation to rival Tommy's and he immediately retaliated, landing a punch squarely on Tommy's chin. Tommy didn't have a chance to hit back. Customers dashed between them to stop a full-on fight.

'Turn it in or you'll be out the door!' shouted the landlord.

For several seconds, both men tried to reach beyond the customers who were holding them back. When Tommy's adversary realised it was a waste of time, he gave up and stepped back.

But Tommy wasn't so easily pacified.

Unable to reach the other man, he aimed blows at anybody who tried to hold him back. 'Let me at the bastard!' he yelled.

'I'm warning you, Tommy! Turn it in or you're out on your arse,' shouted the landlord.

Tommy's drinking buddies tried to calm him down but Tommy was past caring. All the frustrations of his day spilled out of him in a stream of profanity and wanton punches.

'Right, that's it. Get him out!' ordered the landlord.

Tommy took one last swipe at the two pints of beer that stood on the bar. The glasses flew past the landlord before striking the back of the bar area then ricocheting and finally shattering on the ground, drenching the landlord with beer and spraying him with broken glass.

'I'll fuckin' have you!' shouted Tommy as several men hauled him through the crowded pub. He glared at the customers who sank their heads into their pints, aware of Tommy's reputation as a fighter. 'If anyone else wants a go, just step outside and I'll sort the fuckin' lot of you!'

Tommy landed outside on the pavement and heard the bolt sliding across the pub door. He kicked the door in frustration before spending a few minutes hurling abuse at all those inside. Eventually, he gave up and went home.

*

While Tommy was causing upset in his local pub, his son was also letting his temper get the better of him. All through tea he thought about what had happened earlier. Anthony Hampson was in the wrong and he knew it. But he was also the owner of a leather Casey football, which put the balance of power in his favour.

Peter was sick of Anthony getting all his own way just because he had a Casey. If he had one of his own then things would have been different but, despite pleading with his mother to buy him one, he always received the same answer: 'We can't afford it.'

As Peter thought about the injustice of it all, he became increasingly angry. Finally, determined to confront Anthony Hampson and have things out with him, Peter sneaked out of the house.

He couldn't see anybody outside at first so he walked to the top of the street to have a look around. Once there he scoured the adjacent street, looking to the left and right. Nothing. So he decided to venture further. He crossed the road and made his way towards the pathway which ran down the back of Anthony's home.

When Peter reached the top of the path, he saw Anthony up ahead. He began to approach him, but Anthony walked further away, towards his back garden. Peter continued in Anthony's direction. Then Anthony spotted him and increased his speed, so Peter sped up too, determined to catch up with him before he reached his home.

When they were a few metres away from Anthony's back garden, Peter finally caught up with him, grabbing the back of his coat and forcing Anthony to turn around.

'Gotcha, you dirty cheat!' announced Peter in triumph as he saw the look of fear on Anthony's face.

'Get off me!' shouted Anthony.

'No, I won't. You're a dirty cheat, and I don't like cheats. Now you're gonna pay for it.'

While clutching Anthony's coat to stop him running away, Peter gave him a sharp kick in the shins. He was set to continue. But, unknown to Peter, Anthony had been playing in his back garden with two of his friends. On hearing the commotion, the two friends ran out of the garden and jumped to Anthony's defence, punching and kicking at Peter. Although Peter was two years older than them, he was outnumbered. Within seconds they had him on the ground and had surrounded him, ready to take revenge.

5

Adele was eager to stop Peter getting into trouble. Once outside she spotted him in the distance, turning into the pathway that ran along the back of the adjacent street and heading in the direction of the Hampsons' home. When he was out of sight, she sprinted to catch up with him.

As she approached the path, she called out his name but he didn't seem to hear her. Undeterred, she carried on running until she saw something up ahead. Before she could stop to catch her breath she spotted a group of boys kicking someone who was lying on the ground, hunched up trying to protect himself.

It was only as she drew nearer and spotted the vivid blue of Peter's coat that she knew for sure the boy on the ground was him.

'Get off him!' she yelled. 'Or I'll batter you.'

The boys ignored her but the sight of her brother being set upon made Adele so furious that she acted without caution and raced up to them. She pushed the first boy she reached, sending him sprawling onto the ground. The shock halted him temporarily, giving her chance to set about the next boy: Anthony Hampson.

Adele towered above him and she grasped the back of his hair, tugging him away from Peter who got up off the ground. Not content with merely stopping Anthony, with her free hand Adele punched and slapped him repeatedly.

Witnessing her fury, the third boy didn't want to be next, and he ran away. Meanwhile, the boy who Adele had pushed was still trying to stand back up but Peter lunged at him before he had a chance to gain his balance. Being bigger, Peter was easily able to overpower the boy and he soon left him with a bloody nose and his face red and swollen.

'Leave him!' ordered Adele. 'He's had enough.'

'It's not him I came for anyway,' said Peter, petulantly.

He turned towards Anthony Hampson who Adele was still holding onto. Despite the hiding that he had already received from Adele, Peter aimed a few last punches at Anthony to 'teach him a lesson' before they walked away triumphantly.

But Anthony Hampson hadn't learnt his lesson from the hiding he had received and he called out to them from the safety of his garden gate. 'I'm gonna tell my mam and dad what you've done,' he sobbed. 'And I'll tell our Janet about you too, Adele Robinson. She won't want a big bully for a friend.'

Adele ignored him but she was worried. Janet was her best friend, and she loved going around with her. Apart from acting a bit spoilt at times, Janet was a good friend. She often let Adele come round to her house. There, Adele would spend hours engrossed in Janet's Spirograph, Etch-a-Sketch and other art materials. She also enjoyed playing in Janet's bedroom. It was in complete contrast to hers, which had lino on the floor and an old shabby wardrobe, and was always cold. Janet's bedroom was tidy with a plush carpet and matching furniture, including her own dressing table. Taking pride of place on the dressing table was a beautiful brush, comb and mirror set which Janet said was silver-plated. It had roses carved into the metal and, although Janet wouldn't let Adele use that set, she did let her use her older, plastic one.

'Take no notice of him,' said Peter. 'He won't tell his mam and dad.'

But Adele was as annoyed with Peter for putting her in that position as she was with the boys for setting about her brother.

'You don't know that, Peter! We'll be in loads of trouble if Dad finds out. You should have left it! I told you to leave it, didn't I?'

'Don't be daft. Even if he tells his mam and dad, they wouldn't dare come round to our house. They're all too scared of Dad. Anthony's just narked 'cos we beat him. Serves himself right, haha. Did you see his face when I smacked him one?'

'It might be funny for you but what about me? Janet's my friend.'

'I don't know what you're worried about. You've got loads of other friends. Anyway, she's boring. She never goes climbing or anything. She's too scared of ruining her nice clothes.'

'Shut it, Peter!' shouted Adele and, to her surprise, he did.

For the remainder of the walk home Peter didn't say another word. Adele didn't know whether it was out of guilt for putting her in this position or gratitude that she had rescued him from a beating, but nevertheless she was glad he kept quiet. Her temper was still raging, and she didn't know how she would react if he continued to goad her.

Eventually they arrived at their front door, which stood out from the rest of the street because of the dent two thirds of the way up and the faded, peeling paint. Adele could hear her father shouting even before they got inside the house. As they walked into the lounge, they heard his voice coming from the kitchen.

'Do you honestly expect me to eat this fuckin' shite? I come home after a hard day's work, and this is all you can fuckin' manage!'

Adele then heard the sound of crockery being slammed.

Peter was just about to switch on the TV when their mother rushed into the living room.

'Go upstairs while I try to calm him down,' she whispered before dashing back into the kitchen.

Adele and Peter did as they were told. Although Adele was curious about what had prompted her father's current rage, she was too frightened to go against her mother's instructions.

'Wonder what's wrong with *him*,' muttered Peter as they mounted the stairs.

'Shush, he might hear you.'

The sound of their father's shouting continued. Adele could also hear the faint sound of her mother's voice, but it was drowned out by her father's angry cursing. A torrent of abuse and profanities carried up the stairs. As his voice increased in volume, she could also hear more crockery being smashed and the scraping of furniture on the floor as though it was being pushed about the room.

Then, all went quiet.

A few seconds later, she heard her mother speak – the sound a mere murmur, pleading with him. 'Do you want some toast, Tommy love? I can soon make you some toast if you don't fancy your tea.'

'Fuck off! You stupid bitch.'

Again his cursing was accompanied by the sound of crashing furniture, and Adele thought she heard her mother let out a suppressed yelp. But it was so slight that she couldn't be sure.

Adele's earlier feelings of anger had now turned to fear; her adrenalin redirected to serve this new purpose. As her heart thundered in her chest, Adele wrestled with her conscience, unsure whether to go to help her mother. She wanted to. She really did. But she was scared. Scared of her father's wrath. Scared she might make matters worse.

But what if her mother was hurt?

'Should we do something?' she asked Peter.

'No chance. I'm keeping away from him while he's like that.'

'But what if our Mam's hurt?'

'Nah, she'll be all right. They're always at it.'

Adele wished she could be so sure. She stayed for a while longer, her hands clammy and the muscles in her shoulders tense. Each time her father shouted, and every time she heard the clatter of crockery and furniture, her heart beat even faster. She also had a strange feeling in her head, which felt like her scalp was prickling as the blood surged in response to her increased heartbeat.

When she heard the heavy tread of her father's work boots at the bottom of the stairs, she felt as though her heart would burst through her ribcage. She breathed in sharply, anticipating his approach. But his footsteps became fainter. He was heading back towards the living room. The sound of the living room door bouncing forcefully back on its hinges verified this. Then she heard the television.

For several minutes she remained listening, but all seemed

to have gone calm. The only noise she could hear was coming from the TV.

'Sounds like it's over,' said Peter.

'Shhh, I'm listening.'

'For what?'

'I want to make sure before I go downstairs.'

'What d'you want to go down there for? You must be mad!' said Peter. 'I'm staying here till the morning.'

Normally Adele would have stayed where she was but as she was getting older, she was becoming more concerned about her father's behaviour and how it affected her mother. Adele continued waiting. She wanted to give her father a chance to calm down. Eventually she gathered her courage and made her way downstairs, tentatively, listening all the while. But it seemed that the only sound she could hear was her own pounding heartbeat.

She drew nearer the bottom step, her hands leaving sweaty imprints on the banister. Once she was downstairs she peeped into the living room where she saw her father asleep in the armchair. *Thank God*, she thought, letting out a deep breath, which she had been subconsciously holding. The tension in her wired muscles also eased.

Turning, she then made her way to the kitchen and stepped inside. Her relief was short-lived. The room was almost unrecognisable. Adele was used to living in a messy home but the sight before her surpassed even her dismal expectations.

The table, which stood against the wall, was littered with broken crockery. Part of it was from the plate that had contained her father's tea, but there was more, much more. Adele surveyed the damage. A variety of shapes, colours and sizes, and a broken cup handle attached to part of a cup, hovered precariously on the tabletop. The remainder was on the floor.

Gravy flooded the table, spilling over the sides in a constant drip, drip, drip. It streamed down the wall, flowing past the slimy onions and lumps of potato, which clung to the outdated wallpaper. On the table, remnants of potato and cabbage sat amongst the gravy and formed unappetising clusters on the broken crockery.

Most of the kitchen chairs were upended and scattered about the room, and the table itself had switched position. Amongst this devastation sat Adele's mother, her head sunk low, grasping a ragged and bloody handkerchief to her face as she wept silent tears.

Adele approached her, hesitantly.

'Mam,' she whispered.

Her mother raised her head, but the sight of her bruised and bloodied face unsettled Adele, and for a moment she didn't know what to say.

Quickly recovering, she said, 'He's asleep.'

Her mother didn't reply. Instead she gazed at Adele, her eyes full of sadness.

'I'll help you clear up,' Adele offered.

'Thanks love, you're a good girl,' her mother said, her voice trembling, but she remained seated as though she had neither the energy nor the will to deal with the mess.

Adele crept towards the pantry where the used newspapers were kept. Pulling out a few sheets of newspaper, she placed several on top of each other to form a thick layer then began to scoop broken crockery onto them. Her mother stayed still.

Stopping to look at her mother, Adele asked, 'Do you want me to get the flannel for your face?'

Her words seemed to spur her mother into action. She rose from her chair, saying, 'It's all right, love; I'll sort it out. You carry on doing what you're doing, but be careful not to make too much noise. We don't want him to wake up.'

By the time Shirley had taken care of her face and rejoined her daughter, Adele had already cleared up most of the broken crockery and spilt food. Together they cleaned the wall and table, swept and mopped the floor and put the furniture back in place.

'Thanks, love. Let's get to bed now,' said Shirley.

Adele nodded then looked towards the living room.

'We'll leave him till the morning. He'll sleep it off.'

Adele wasn't sure whether 'it' referred to his mood or the excessive amount of alcohol he had obviously consumed. She watched from the door as her mother tiptoed across the living room and switched off the TV before tiptoeing back again.

'He won't like it if it's still on when he wakes up,' she muttered. 'He hates us wasting electricity.'

Adele and her mother then went up to bed while Tommy lay sprawled in his armchair, snoring. She hoped he'd be in a better mood the next day, but there were no guarantees. None of them could ever predict what sort of mood her father would be in or how far he would go the next time he lost his temper.

6

Following the fight with Anthony Hampson, Adele waited for her friend, Janet, to call for her, but she didn't show. Perhaps Janet didn't want to go around with her anymore or maybe she had gone out somewhere with her parents. Eventually, after two days of missing her best friend, and overcome by curiosity, Adele couldn't wait any more. As soon as Mrs Hampson answered the door however, it was obvious to Adele she knew all about the fight.

'Go away! We can do without your sort here. I never did approve of our Janet going around with the likes of you, and what you did to our Anthony proves I was right.'

Feeling ashamed and humiliated, Adele turned away as Mrs Hampson continued to berate her, 'Girls fighting in the street; it's disgusting! Girls don't fight. Not decent girls, anyway. I've a good mind to tell your parents if I thought it would do any good.'

When Adele was a safe distance from the house, she peered up towards Janet's bedroom to see if there was any sign of her. She spotted her at the window just before Janet gave her a scornful look then ducked out of sight.

Adele returned home deflated. Mrs Hampson's words had stung, and they confirmed what Adele had always felt; that the Hampsons thought she wasn't good enough. She'd always felt that way. It was in the sly little comments she'd put up with over the years as Mrs Hampson had made unfavourable comparisons between Janet's possessions and hers. *'Don't you have one of those at your house?' 'You should be wearing stouter shoes on a day like today, like the ones Janet has.' 'Don't let Adele use your new brush and comb, Janet; she can use the old ones.'*

When she got back inside her own home, she told Peter what had happened. His view of things was different to hers.

'I don't know what you want to go around with her for, anyway,' he said. 'Those Hampsons are a load of snobs.'

But Adele did want to go around with Janet. She missed her company, and Peter was partly to blame. His words irritated her. She might have other friends but none of them let her use their things like Janet did. And Janet had such lovely things, which Adele could only dream of owning.

She might have fun and excitement with her brother but her friendship with Janet fed her desire for a better life. It fuelled her dreams that one day she would have nice things of her own. And now that friendship had been taken away from her.

The next day Adele was outside with Peter who was spending a lot of time with her since the local boys wouldn't have anything to do with him.

'I'm going to call for Wendy,' said Adele.

'No, don't. You'll only take off with her. Stay with me. We can go somewhere.'

'It's all right. You can still hang around with us,' said Adele.

Disappointingly, Wendy wasn't at home.

'She went to Janet's,' said Wendy's mother who had no idea of the trouble that had taken place three days previously. 'They're probably still in the garden. I'm sure they won't mind you joining them if you call round.'

'Thanks,' muttered Adele, her eyes downcast.

'Ah well, where d'you fancy going?' asked Peter.

But Adele was undeterred. 'I'm going to Janet's to see if Wendy's there.'

'But what if Mrs Hampson's there?'

'I'm not calling for Janet. I just want to see if Wendy's there. They can't stop me standing outside.'

Peter followed Adele up the street while she strode purposefully in the direction of the Hampsons' back garden. As they approached, they could hear the sound of voices. Adele turned to Peter, giving him a knowing look.

'You stay here while I walk up to the gate,' she whispered, 'just in case Anthony and his friends are there.'

When Adele reached the gate, she saw that Anthony and his friends were indeed in the garden as well as Janet, Wendy and, another friend, Susan. They all stopped what they were doing as soon as they saw Adele.

After a few uncomfortable moments, Janet said, 'My mum says I'm not to go around with you anymore.'

'I've not called for you,' said Adele, trying to mask her feelings of hurt and rejection. She then directed her gaze to Susan and Wendy, her eyes flitting from one to the other. 'Are you coming out?' she asked.

They both lowered their heads. They'd already made their choice to stay with Janet but were nervous of Adele's reaction.

Before they got a chance to say anything, one of Anthony's friends pointed at Adele's chapped knees, 'Ooh, look at her scabby knees,' he shouted.

'Scabby knees, scabby knees, Adele's got scabby knees,' sang the boys. Janet joined in while Susan and Wendy laughed until, feeling hurt and upset, Adele ran from the Hampsons' home without saying another word. She passed Peter without stopping.

'Hang on, Adele. Wait for me,' he shouted before running after her.

Adele continued to run until she was several streets away, but she couldn't escape her inner turmoil. When her feet stopped pounding the pavements, she was still feeling upset and angry. She stared down at her blemished knees while troubling thoughts raced around inside her head. Why had her other friends sided with the Hampsons? Why had everyone turned against her? All she had done was try to protect her brother. Surely any of them would have done the same! Wouldn't they?

She watched in annoyance as Peter ran to catch up with her. This was all down to him but she didn't want to pick a fight with her brother. At the moment, he was all she had. Instead, once he had reached her, she cursed the Hampsons and all the others who had sided with them. Peter joined her, equally furious that all their friends had supported Anthony.

For several minutes they wandered aimlessly, unsure how to pass their time now they had no friends to hang around with. They looked a sorry sight; two forlorn youngsters, slumping their shoulders and dragging their feet. Their clothes were well-worn, and their dark hair luggy and unkempt. Adele's attractive face bore a scowl and she kicked sulkily at clumps of grass while her mischievous-looking brother paused at intervals to pick up stones to hurl.

They needed a diversion; something or someone to distract them from their boredom, anger and frustration. Ahead of them they saw another lonely figure: Shelley Tucker. Shelley was what was referred to as 'backward'. Although she attended the same school as Adele and Peter, she struggled, not only with her classwork but making friends too. Other children homed in on her weaknesses and either avoided her or picked on her. Normally Adele left her alone; but Adele was used to being one of the popular girls, surrounded by friends who looked up to her. Today was different.

Peter and Adele had found their diversion.

'Come on,' said Peter, growing excited. He was no longer dragging his feet but had become animated as he approached Shelley.

'Hey Shelley, d'you wanna play?' he shouted.

Shelley smiled in response, flattered at his approach.

Adele could have stopped him. Normally, she would have done. But not today. Today she was full of hurt and anger, and she needed to vent that anger on something or somebody. Unfortunately, poor Shelley had become the target.

She could almost read Peter's mind, trying to think of ways to use Shelley for his own amusement. He started by grasping the top of Shelley's arm tightly and dragging her.

'Ouch, that hurts,' said Shelley, her lips trembling as she tried to back away.

'It's a game,' said Peter. 'I'm the master, and you've got to do everything I tell you. OK?'

Shelley gazed at him, uncertain, then looked to Adele for reassurance. Adele nodded, curious to see what direction this game would take and relishing the feeling of power.

'Right,' said Peter, pausing while he decided what to do next. His indecisiveness intrigued Adele. 'Right, we're going ghost hunting. We're going to the haunted house.'

Adele guessed that he was probably referring to a house on a nearby street, which had stood empty for a while. The house, which was boarded up, had become increasingly run-down, and parents had warned their children to stay away from it. Janet said it was because, according to her mother, tramps went there at night to drink.

Instead of deterring the children, the stern warnings had piqued their curiosity and started the rumours that the house might be haunted. Lots of the local kids wanted to discover whether the rumours were true, but they were all too frightened to investigate.

As Peter led Shelley by the arm, Adele followed, keeping a step or two behind. They drew closer to the house, and Shelley stopped.

'I don't want to go,' she said. 'Adele, tell him!'

They both turned to Adele, Peter's face full of determination while Shelley was beginning to whimper.

'Don't be so soft!' said Peter. 'There's nothing there. Gary Healey's been inside and he didn't see anything.' The deliberate lie tripped off his tongue easily.

Adele knew she held the balance of power. 'Peter's right,' she said. 'We won't come to no harm, but we can tell all the other kids that we saw the ghost.'

'I don't want to see the ghost,' Shelley cried, the tears now streaming down her face.

'There isn't a ghost,' said Adele. 'We're just going to pretend there is.'

Once he had received Adele's approval, Peter continued to drag Shelley by the arm in the direction of the empty house while Adele reassured her that everything would be fine.

They arrived at the garden gate and Peter stopped to pick up a stick from the ground. 'This is my weapon to fight the ghost with,' he announced.

'I thought you said there weren't any ghosts,' cried Shelley.

'He's only pretending,' said Adele, while Peter carried on dragging Shelley inside the gate.

'No, no! I don't want to go in,' screamed Shelley. 'I'm scared of ghosts.'

She bent her knees so that her feet dragged behind her. Peter struggled to pull her into the garden so Adele rushed to his aid, grasping Shelley's other arm to prop her up.

Once they were inside the garden, Peter held the stick up. 'Right, we're here now. You're gonna climb through that window and tell us what you find.'

'No! Please, don't make me,' Shelley screamed, becoming hysterical.

'You're going or I'll jab your eyes out with this stick,' said Peter, thrusting the stick towards Shelley's tear-stained face.

Shelley spun her head away from him till she was facing Adele. Their eyes met. Shelley gazed beseechingly at her until Adele was forced to see the fear on the poor girl's face. She'd seen that look before. On her mother's face. Every time their father came home late from the pub. In that instant Adele was overcome by pity and self-loathing.

'No, Peter!' she ordered, letting go of Shelley's arm. 'Leave her alone.'

Peter looked at her, confused.

'She's frightened, leave her alone. If she tells anyone, we'll be in trouble.' Then, as if suddenly realising the implications of what they had been about to do, she turned to Shelley. 'We weren't gonna hurt you, Shelley, honest. We just wanted to have a look inside. We would have come in with you, so don't you go tellin' anyone we were pickin' on you.'

'Yeah, you better hadn't,' said Peter, raising his stick again, 'or I really will jab your eyes out.' He let go of Shelley's other arm and, without waiting to hear any more, the girl ran. 'Spoilsport!' Peter said to Adele as he watched Shelley race away.

'Oh, shut up,' said Adele. 'It was a stupid idea anyway. I'm going home.'

She walked away, not caring whether Peter was behind her or not. By this time, her anger of earlier had gone, replaced by shame at her bad behaviour, which had been so out of character. She couldn't understand why Peter wasn't ashamed too. It didn't seem to bother him, but maybe it was his way of hitting back at the world. Adele knew she would continue to feel guilty about frightening poor Shelley for several days afterwards.

After a few minutes Adele arrived home. Her mother was the only person indoors. Remembering how the children had teased her about her knees, Adele told her mother about them.

'My knees are sore, Mam.'

'Let's have a look.'

Adele sat down, lifting each of her legs in turn so her mother could examine the broken red skin on the inner side of each knee.

'Oh, they're chapped again. You get it whenever it's cold. A bit of ointment will soon sort it out. You're best putting it on before you go to bed.'

But when bedtime came, Shirley had forgotten all about Adele's chapped knees and she had to remind her. Shirley couldn't find any ointment in the cupboard where it was usually kept so Adele helped her to search the house. It was no use; there was no ointment to be found.

'Never mind,' said Shirley. 'I'll get some tomorrow. You'll be all right.'

But Adele knew that by tomorrow her mother would have forgotten about her knees; she'd have found something else to worry about. No, her mother wouldn't do anything to rid Adele of the shame and ridicule. She couldn't understand why, but her mother *never* seemed to do anything.

7

A visit from Grandma Joyce on Sunday morning was just the tonic Adele needed. Her father was in bed so they had been careful not to make too much noise. But when her grandma arrived, Adele couldn't resist rushing up to her, flinging her arms around her neck and letting out an excited squeal.

'Hiya Grandma,' she exclaimed while Peter vied for Joyce's attention.

'All right you two, settle down,' she said, adding, 'There's nowt in there for you,' when she spotted Peter's eye on her handbag. 'I haven't brought any sweets today.'

Peter shrugged and turned away. 'Are you coming out, Adele?' he asked.

But Adele didn't want to go out. 'Not yet, in a bit,' she said, and she continued to hover around her grandma, comforted by her presence.

With no one to go around with, Peter sloped off upstairs.

'Well I hope you're going to put some trousers on when you do go out,' said Joyce, eyeing Adele's short dress. 'It's bitter out there.'

'I haven't got any.'

'Course you have,' said Shirley. 'What about the blue ones?'

'They're too short,' she said, knowing she had told her mother already.

'Well what about the others, those with the stripes on them?'

'They're ripped... remember?'

'Well you must have some more.'

'I haven't.'

Joyce interrupted when she noticed Adele's sore legs, 'Bloody hell, Shirley. Look at the state of her legs; they're chapped to buggery! And it's no wonder if she's walking about in short skirts in this weather.'

'She's got trousers; she just can't be bothered looking for them,' Shirley answered defensively and too quickly. It was an obvious lie.

'Have you put ointment on them?' asked Joyce.

'No, my mam couldn't find it.'

Joyce tutted. 'You won't get any today either; the shops are shut.' She was pensive for a few moments before saying to Shirley, 'Right, send your Peter round to mine. He can bring the tube I've got. Those sores will have to be tended to as soon as possible. They look bloody painful. How could you let them get like that, Shirley?'

'I didn't know they were that bad till she told me last night, and I was going to get some ointment as soon as the shops were open.'

'Just get Peter!' Joyce demanded, irritated with her hopeless daughter.

As soon as Peter returned with the ointment, Joyce spread it liberally onto the sore patches on Adele's legs before handing the tube of ointment to her, 'Right Adele, that's yours now. Put it somewhere safe and I want you to rub it on again tonight, and every morning and night, until your legs are better. All right?'

'Yes, Grandma.'

'And if you must go out, you'll have to put your old trousers on for now. Fetch them here. Let's have a look at 'em.'

Adele found her ripped trousers and handed them to her grandma.

'Is that all that's wrong with them?' Joyce asked after examining the garment. Without waiting for a reply, she continued, 'Jesus Christ, Shirley! What the bloody hell's wrong with you? You could have had these repaired in no time! Fetch me a needle and cotton. That's if you can find any in this bloody tip.'

When Joyce had finished mending the trousers, she passed them to Adele. 'There. Good as new,' she said. 'They'll have to do for now if they're the only pair you've got, but I want you to put them on before you go outside.'

'Thanks, Grandma,' said Adele, pleased that no-one would be calling her scabby knees anymore.

When Tommy got out of bed in the early afternoon, Shirley was putting the finishing touches to the Sunday dinner, which her mother had helped her prepare that morning.

'What did *she* want?' he grumbled.

'Just visiting,' said Shirley.

'Well tell her to come a bit bleedin' later next time. I can do without her big gob waking me up!'

'She probably didn't think,' said Shirley.

'Course she did. She does it on bleedin' purpose to wind me up. I'm entitled to have a lie-in on a Sunday when I've worked hard all fuckin' week, you know! But you wouldn't know about that, would you, seeing as how you do bugger all.'

'I'll have a word with her,' said Shirley.

'Yeah, you better bleedin' had do.'

'She's brought something nice for us, though,' said Shirley, trying to calm him down. 'Home-made apple pie.'

Tommy grumbled in response, dragging out a kitchen chair. Adele tensed at the sound of the chair scraping across the floor and the loud thud as her father plonked himself down next to her.

'Come on then, get the dinner served up!' he ordered.

It was a traditional Sunday dinner. Despite having help from her mother with the roast, Shirley had prepared the vegetables herself. This was evident from the state of the unpeeled carrots, and the sprouts, which contained dark outer leaves, peppered with black spots.

The smell of overcooked sprouts had hit Adele as soon as she walked into the kitchen. She mentally prepared herself for the challenge ahead while trying not to heave.

'There you go,' said Shirley, putting their meals on the table, 'and there'll be no apple pie till you've eaten all that,' she added to the children while looking at Tommy for his approval.

'Yeah, get it eaten, and no buggerin' about,' he reiterated.

Adele battled her way through the meal. She used the succulent roast lamb and crispy roast potatoes as a foil to disguise the taste of the bitter outer leaves of the overcooked sprouts, and the occasional grittiness of the bland carrots. She carefully cut chunks of meat and roast potato, ensuring that she would have enough to offset all the remaining vegetables. Then she took each measured forkful; a mix of the foods she enjoyed and those she loathed. By doing so, the meal was just about palatable, but she noticed that Peter had already eaten his lamb and roasters and was now toying with the rest of his food, pushing it around his plate. Her father noticed too.

'Get it eaten!' he ordered, raising his knife and pointing it in Peter's direction.

Peter took a forkful of the sprouts then gagged as he forced them down his throat.

'It's not bleedin' poison, y'know. Now get it eaten, and stop pissin' about,' said Tommy.

'I don't like it.'

Tommy swiped Peter round the back of his head. 'I don't give a shit what you like. Do as you're bleedin' told, and stop givin' me your backchat!'

Peter continued to struggle through the meal and Adele could feel his discomfort as he forced each morsel into his mouth and swallowed. She tried not to watch.

Then her father got up, shoving his chair away from the table. He left his plate with his meal unfinished. Adele noticed the remnants of sprouts and carrots, and so did Peter who mimicked his father's actions, putting down his knife and fork on his uncleared plate.

'What the bleedin' hell do you think you're doing?' demanded Tommy.

'You've left yours, so I'm leavin' mine.'

Adele braced herself as she saw her father's face turn crimson. She silently willed her brother not to provoke him, but it was too late. The sharp blow from Tommy knocked Peter off his feet, sending him scudding across the kitchen floor and landing next to the oven.

'You cheeky little bastard! What I do is none of your

bleedin' business. Now get back to that table and get your bleedin' dinner eaten.'

Shirley stepped between Tommy and Peter, 'You go and watch the telly, love. I'll make sure he eats it,' she said to her husband.

'Get out of my way!' he ordered, pushing her aside.

Adele could sense his building fury as he stood over Peter. 'Right, are you gonna eat your dinner or do I have to make you?'

Peter cowered against the oven then gasped in shock as heat from the oven door stung him, penetrating his shabby clothing. He gripped his arm where it had made contact with the searing hot metal and squealed as the pain struck. Looking at his father with eyes full of agony and fear, he spun around on his bottom, using his feet to pedal across the kitchen floor towards the back door. But he didn't get far.

Tommy tugged furiously at the fastening on his sturdy leather belt, and Adele flinched at the sight of the metal buckle and eyelets as he removed it. He strode across the kitchen, passing Peter, then slammed the bolt shut on the back door.

'You're not bleedin' going anywhere! I'm giving you one last chance to eat your dinner or I'll make sure you do, and you won't sit down for a week,' he said, wrapping the thick leather belt around his right hand.

When Tommy had secured the belt, he checked that he had a good length remaining, running the belt and its metal eyelets through the fingers of his left hand. Peter gazed up at him, a look of terror on his face, but he still didn't go back to the table.

'Tommy, it's all right. I'll make sure he eats it,' pleaded Shirley.

'Just fuckin' keep out of this!' he yelled, stepping forward and bringing the belt crashing down onto Peter's legs. Peter let out an agonised yelp.

Adele almost choked, her shocked reaction making her inhale sharply. She tried to relax the clenched muscles in her throat while she coughed up her food. Tears of distress sprang to her eyes as her father held up the belt once more.

'No, no!' Peter screamed.

Tommy paused. 'Are you gonna eat it then?'

Adele held her breath, awaiting Peter's reply, while her mother remained silent and afraid.

'Well?' urged Tommy when Peter didn't respond.

After what seemed an age, Peter turned his head down to the ground and let out a muffled sound.

'I didn't hear you!' said Tommy.

His reply was so faint, it was almost imperceptible. 'No,' Peter whimpered. 'I don't like it.'

Before Tommy had a chance to strike again, Adele rushed to his side and pleaded with him while a mix of tears and mucus ran down her face, 'Please, Dad. Don't! I'll eat it if you want.'

Tommy's eyes locked on hers, forcing her knees to tremble as his cold, hard stare bore through her like sharpened steel. Adele was shaking uncontrollably as she awaited his reaction. But then, for a fleeting moment, she thought she saw a glimmer of something behind his eyes. Pity? Remorse? Love? She couldn't tell, but her father's raised arm dropped down to his side. He turned to Shirley while he threaded the belt through the loops on his jeans.

'You're a fuckin' useless mother,' he muttered, and she visibly winced. Then he stormed from the room, shouting, 'Fuck the lot of you!'

Adele stood, trembling, while Peter stayed on the floor, sobbing. Shirley collected the plates with shaking hands, still not speaking. The tension in the room was palpable until they heard the sound of the front door slamming.

Putting down the plates, Shirley said, 'Go and get rid of your leftovers before he comes back. Quick.'

The children did as they were told, rushing outside to the dustbin then back again. Adele was the first one back inside the kitchen, just in time to see her mother grasping shakily at a bottle of her pills before swallowing two tablets.

Having recovered her composure, she turned to Adele, 'Can you clear this lot up for me, love? I need to have a look at Peter's arm and legs.'

Without waiting for a reply, she led Peter through to the living room and left Adele clearing away the devastation that had been their Sunday dinner.

8

The following day Adele and Peter returned home from school to find their mother out. As their father was also out at work, they had the house to themselves.

'Have you seen this?' asked Peter, pulling down his trousers to reveal a large welt on his leg where the metal eyelets of his father's belt had struck him.

Adele flinched, recalling the horror of the previous evening. 'Does it hurt?' she asked.

'It's not that bad,' he boasted. 'My dad's not that tough, y'know.'

Ignoring his attempt at bravery, Adele replied, 'It would have been worse if I hadn't have stopped him.'

Peter bowed his head as he muttered, 'I know, tah.' Then, after a pause while he fastened his trousers, he raised his head again and drew his shoulders back. 'Just wait till I'm older,' he said. 'I'll teach him a lesson. He won't think he's so tough then!'

'You should just do as he says then he wouldn't get so mad,' Adele said, but before Peter had a chance to reply, Grandma Joyce burst through the door.

'Hiya, Grandma,' they both gushed, running to her and flinging their arms around her neck.

Peter eyed the carrier bag she was carrying.

'Eh cheeky, you can put your eyes back in their sockets. It's not for you,' she said. Peter's bottom lip jutted out until his grandma added, 'I have got something else you'll like, though.' She reached into her handbag and withdrew a bar of chocolate for each of them. 'You're not to eat it till after your tea so put it away in the kitchen cupboard.' They did as they were told while Joyce asked, 'Where's your mother anyway? I thought she'd have had the tea started by now.'

'Dunno,' said Adele.

'Right, well while we're waiting you can have a look at these,' said Joyce, handing Adele the carrier bag.

Adele could feel her excitement mounting as she put her hand inside the bag and rummaged through the wrapping paper. She could feel material underneath the paper and her anticipation grew as she withdrew first one, then another, pair of trousers, which looked brand new.

'Wow!' she exclaimed, holding each of them up to the light.

'Well don't just stand there looking gormless. Go and try them on and let me have a look at you in them.'

Adele rushed upstairs clutching both pairs of trousers. She quickly donned the first pair and went to her mother's wardrobe mirror to admire herself. They were the latest fashion with a wide flare that covered her shoes and a sharp crease down the front of each trouser leg. They were also a perfect fit, and Adele couldn't wait to show them off to her friends at school. She raced back down to the living room to show her grandma.

'Ooh, you do look a treat,' smiled Joyce, urging Adele to turn around so she could admire them from every angle.

'Smashing! They'll keep your legs nice and warm, won't they? Do you want to show me the other pair?'

When Adele had finished trying on the trousers, her grandmother examined her chapped legs. 'They're much better,' she said. 'Put the ointment on a few more times and they should be healed. And if you wear your trousers when you go outside, it shouldn't come back again.'

Grandma Joyce didn't ask to see the marks on Peter's legs; she didn't know about them. Adele decided it was best if she didn't find out; it would only cause more trouble. Noticing the hurt expression on Peter's face, Adele knew he had reached the same decision. When he gathered that his grandma had nothing else for him, Peter left the house telling Grandma Joyce that he would be back at teatime.

Adele's grandma didn't stay long and, after she had gone, Adele went out in search of Peter. She found him at the local playground across from the Red Rec. From a distance she could see that he was alone, but he was spinning around and seemed to be clutching something in his hands. Something furry. Was it a soft toy? She was bemused; he hadn't been carrying anything when he went out. What could it be? Where could he have got it from?

She sped up, curious to find out what he was holding. Peter completed several revolutions, his arms outstretched and holding onto the item with both hands. It was when she drew closer that she heard the agonised screeching and realised that it wasn't a soft toy. It was alive! A cat!

He was grasping a front paw in each of his hands as he spun the poor animal round, its body outstretched due to the centrifugal force. She gasped, not quite able to believe what she was seeing.

Shock and anger drove her even faster towards him. 'Stop it! Put it down,' she shouted.

But Peter was enjoying himself.

When her shouts and screams failed to stop him, she rushed up to Peter and grabbed him, forcing him to a standstill. The shock of the impact made him topple to the ground and Adele reached out to grasp the poor cat. But it was too fast. She felt its fur brush against her skin as it gave out one last frightened yelp, jumped to the ground and ran away.

'Who d'you think you're pushing?' Peter shouted as he lay on the ground.

'You're disgusting and cruel! No wonder no one wants to go around with you. You deserve everything you get!' she yelled before stomping away from him.

Peter was equally angry and, as soon as he recovered, he followed her out of the park, hurling abuse at her. She tried to ignore him, not wanting to end up in another fight. But he wouldn't stop. By the time they had reached their street, she'd had enough. Adele turned around and faced him.

Before she had chance to do anything more, Peter shoved her. 'Don't you push me!' he yelled.

Adele stumbled backwards but managed to retain her footing. Already angry at his treatment of the cat, and his subsequent words of abuse, she retaliated, landing a punch on his chin. Peter rushed forward pulling at her hair and kicking. Within seconds they were both immersed in a full-on fight and were trading kicks and punches.

In the heat of the fight she spotted her father rounding the corner into their street. He hadn't seen them yet. He had his head turned while he said goodbye to a friend who was leaving him to continue along the adjacent street.

'Stop! It's dad,' she said as panic gripped her.

They both knew they would be punished if he saw them fighting in the street. Peter pulled away and for several seconds they both remained still, trying to steady their breathing and regain their composure.

Although the sight of their father's arrival home wasn't always a welcome one, in this instance Adele was relieved to see him. She hated fighting with Peter. He was dogged and stubborn, and any fight with him was usually a lengthy one with neither of them willing to back down.

As their father passed by, they both said hello, and he nodded and mumbled back. Adele and Peter looked intensely at each other once he had gone and Adele knew that their joint concern over their father's arrival home had surpassed their own squabbles.

'We'd better get home or we'll be in trouble,' said Adele. 'It's gonna be bad enough when he finds out his tea isn't ready.'

9

It was a few weeks later. Recent events were behind them and Adele and Peter had made up. Mrs Hampson had also finally relented and allowed her children to hang around with Adele and Peter, and they were all friends once more.

Adele was sitting in the school classroom ready for the spelling test that Mr Parry had set. She was eager to start, knowing that she always excelled at spelling.

'Quiet now everyone, please,' said Mr Parry after he had given out paper and pens to his pupils. 'Right, let's begin.'

Adele sped through the test with ease. The last word of the test was a difficult one, but it didn't give Adele any problems. She quickly wrote it down then gazed around the classroom while she waited for the other pupils to finish.

Adele noticed the class bully, Jessie Lomas, who had slapped her pen down onto the desk in defeat. Adele could read the dissatisfaction on Jessie's face as she frowned and pursed her lips.

Jessie caught her eye and glared at her in annoyance so Adele diverted her attention. As she lowered her head to avoid

Jessie's glare, she noticed the state of her white cardigan. She'd put it on in a rush that morning, not stopping to check whether it was clean. In her house, looking for something decent to wear was a bit like rummaging through the items in a jumble sale. And now, as she gazed down at herself, she saw several stains on the cardigan. Adele felt her face flush with shame. She put the largest of the stained patches of cardigan to her mouth and, using her own saliva, she dampened the patch and sucked at it to draw the stain out. Then she rubbed it against a clean part of the cardigan to reduce the stain. It was no use. Rather than getting rid of the stain, she found that she was spreading it.

When Mr Parry announced that it was time to check their answers, she released the cardigan and faced the front of the classroom. His eyes were on her and she flushed again as she realised that he had been watching. He wasn't the only one; Jessie Lomas had also noticed.

All thoughts of her dirty cardigan were temporarily forgotten however, as Adele was thrilled to gain full marks in the test. She didn't see the jealous look on the face of Jessie Lomas who had struggled to get half the spellings correct.

It was while they were leaving the classroom that Jessie made her feelings known. 'Teacher's pet!' she hissed into Adele's ear as they queued at the door waiting for the bell to ring. 'You might be good at spelling but you're a little tramp. I saw you trying to clean your manky cardigan.'

Jessie was a large, coarse-looking and troublesome girl who many of the other kids feared. Her clothing was also well-worn and dirty but Adele failed to notice this as she was so overcome with her own feelings of shame. She couldn't wait to get away, but Jessie wasn't finished with her yet. As Adele rushed past her, heading towards the playground,

Jessie stuck out her foot and Adele tumbled into the corridor.

Adele's feelings of shame were soon replaced by fury when she felt the impact of the hard, concrete floor on her knees. She dashed to her feet rubbing at her injuries then straightened herself up and instinctively rushed towards Jessie.

'You tripped me up!' she shouted and was about to launch into Jessie when Mr Parry stepped between them.

'That's enough!' he shouted. 'Jessie, go to the head teacher's office and explain to her why you just tripped Adele up.'

Jessie was about to protest but Mr Parry cut her short. 'I saw exactly what you did, and I want no arguments.' Raising his hand and pointing for emphasis, he added in a raised voice, 'Go. Now!'

The way in which Jessie glared at Adele before she walked away told her that this wasn't over. Mr Parry smiled at Adele. 'Don't worry about Jessie,' he said. 'She'll calm down once she's had a good ticking off. I suggest you stay out of her way for now but if she gives you any more trouble, make sure you let me know.'

Adele smiled back and nodded her head. She took Mr Parry's advice, avoiding Jessie for the rest of the day, and she was glad when it was finally home time. After she had helped Mr Parry tidy some books away, Adele set off for home. She was heading up the street outside school when she spotted a crowd of schoolchildren in the distance. She hurried towards the crowd to find out what was going on.

As Adele drew nearer, many of the kids turned to look at her. She carried on walking, noticing their nudges and whispers. Her scalp prickled and her stomach tensed as a feeling of dread took hold of her. She felt her heart plummet and was tempted to bolt. But it was too late. Adele was already in the thick of the crowd.

'Here she is,' somebody announced and the crowd parted to form an open pathway which led straight to her adversary. Jessie stood waiting, surrounded by her group of friends. Unfortunately Adele's own friends took a different route home so she had to face Jessie alone.

A sneer formed on Jessie's face as she watched her approach. Adele hesitated, feeling a tightening in her throat. Her blood was pumping. She looked around for an escape route. But the crowd had closed in behind her. They were pushing her forward. Adele had no choice. She had to face Jessie.

'I'll teach you not to get me into trouble, you little creep!' said Jessie.

Before Adele had a chance to react, Jessie was upon her. She grabbed Adele's hair with both hands and tugged her head downwards. The sharp stinging of her scalp brought tears to Adele's eyes, but she wasn't going to give in without a fight. She swung her fists, trying to make contact with Jessie's face. But Jessie had the height advantage. Adele couldn't see or reach her target. Her head was pulled low, her eyes staring at the ground. She grabbed Jessie's hands to wrench them away but the taller girl gripped onto Adele's hair more tightly. The pain intensified and Adele flailed around helplessly. She tried to kick, but Jessie pulled her head down lower so Adele's knees were bent. She pulled her leg up awkwardly aiming at Jessie. It unbalanced her and she toppled to the ground.

The crowd were roaring and cheering for Jessie who they saw as the guaranteed victor. Jessie stood back, gloating, while Adele sprang back to her feet. She stared at Jessie with hatred in her eyes.

'Come on then,' taunted Jessie. 'Do you want some more?'

The smirk on Jessie's face infuriated Adele. But she also felt powerless and vulnerable. When she pushed her hair off her face, a clump came away in her hand and she choked back a sob. The crowd fell silent. Adele's heart thundered in her chest. Jessie stood awaiting her reaction, a grimace painted on her face. Adele was tempted to charge at Jessie. But it was pointless. She knew she couldn't win, and was swamped by frustration and fury. It was taking all her self-control not to cry. The crowd parted as she walked away, humiliated for the second time that day.

'Coward!' shouted Jessie while the crowd jeered and declared her the winner.

Once Adele was safely home, she rushed upstairs and flung herself onto her bed. There she cried out all her frustration and anger. She was alone until Peter returned home. Adele could hear him shout her name. She ignored him, hoping he would go away. She didn't want him to witness her humiliation. But she soon heard him mount the stairs.

Adele wiped her eyes and runny nose on her dirty cuffs, straightened her hair and sat up on the bed. Peter entered the room. He had already started speaking before he saw her.

'Is it true what they're saying, that Jessie Lomas beat you in a fight?'

The sight of Adele's blotchy face and red-rimmed eyes gave him his answer.

'I can't believe she beat you,' he said. 'I thought you could fight. Why didn't you thump her?'

'I tried to but I couldn't reach,' sobbed Adele. 'She had my hair. I couldn't get her off.'

'Bitch!' cursed Peter. 'You're not gonna let her get away with it, are you?'

Adele shrugged.

'Why don't we get her together?' he asked. 'Do you know where she lives?'

She nodded.

'Come on then. What are we waiting for?'

'Not tonight,' said Adele.

'Tomorrow then?'

'Maybe.'

Adele wasn't sure she wanted a repeat performance with Jessie. Part of her just wanted an end to it. But it wasn't over. She would have to face her classmates tomorrow, and Jessie's gloating. Besides, Adele was still angry and she needed to put Jessie in her place. Unsure what to do, she decided to see how she felt the following day.

Feeling foolish in front of her brother, Adele stifled her tears before agreeing to go out with him. She had some money her grandma had given her so she could treat herself. At least it would take her mind off the fight for now.

The doorbell rang as Adele entered the corner shop with Peter trailing behind, prompting several women to pause in their gossip while they looked in her direction.

'This is them,' said the ageing shopkeeper, Mrs Roper, nodding towards Adele.

Mrs Roper was a small woman with sunken cheeks and pointed, bird-like features who always wore her grey hair scraped back into a tight bun. Adele met her eyes, expecting her to elaborate. But no! It soon became obvious that Adele was the topic of conversation rather than a participant. The women surveyed her through narrowed eyes; their facial expressions a disconcerting mix of pity and scorn.

Adele approached the shop counter self-consciously, her embarrassment evident from the rosy glow of her cheeks. She was alone now. Peter had disappeared behind one of the display stands. She felt the weight of the women's stares and her words faltered.

'Well, spit it out!' demanded the shopkeeper. 'What is it you want?'

Her tone and body language screamed contempt and Adele's voice shook as she asked for a bag of crisps, taking care not to forget her manners. She didn't want to elicit further criticism.

'Thank you,' she said, taking her crisps and heading to the exit. Peter followed her and, as they walked through the door, the women resumed their chatter.

'Shame,' Adele heard one of them say. 'You wouldn't have thought she'd have such good manners coming from *that* family.'

Outside, Adele felt the impact of the cold air on her hot cheeks. She paused for a moment, digesting what had just happened and overcome by feelings of inadequacy. Adele felt guilty, but she wasn't sure why. She couldn't understand why most grown-ups saw her in such a negative light.

Was she really so bad? Maybe the women had seen her fighting with Jessie Lomas or had heard about the incident of a few weeks ago involving Janet and Anthony. She wasn't to know they were judging her and Peter because of their parents' behaviour.

'Come on, what you waiting for?' asked Peter, eager to get away. At Peter's insistence, they turned into a side entry. 'Come on, I don't want anyone to see,' he said.

'See what?' she asked.

With a beaming smile on his face he reached into his

pocket and pulled out some sweets. Adele's jaw dropped and she glared at him. She knew he hadn't paid for them.

'What the hell have you done?'

'What's the matter? It's only a few sweets.'

'You could have got us both in trouble. They'll think I've helped you.'

'Will they 'eck. Anyway, they won't know. They never find out, and you'd better not tell anyone.'

'You mean you've done it before?' Adele asked, astonished.

'Course, it's dead easy. Me and Anthony have done it a few times. One of us goes to the counter and buys something small. Then, while they're serving him, the other one gets the sweets.'

They walked on in silence. Adele finished her crisps and watched Peter munching on a white chocolate mouse. It looked so good.

'Want some?' he asked, holding it out to her.

Adele could smell the faint aroma of white chocolate. She wanted to resist. She really did. Eating the sweets would make her culpable, and what would people think of her then? She looked at the chocolate. So tempting. She loved white chocolate; it was her favourite. Should she? After all, people already treated her as though she was guilty of something, so what difference would it make?

'Come on,' said Peter. 'You can get your own back on that old crow for being nasty to you.'

That swung it. Yes, the shopkeeper had been nasty. And the others. Why should she be made to feel guilty? She grabbed at the mouse and nibbled a bit. The sweet chocolate melted in her mouth. She felt bad for eating it, but it tasted so good! Yes, being bad definitely tasted far better than being good.

10

'This is it,' said Adele when they arrived at the street where Jessie Lomas lived.

'Right, we'll wait till we see her on her own,' Peter instructed.

'But what will we do then?'

'I told you, we're gonna get her.'

'Yes, but what are we gonna do to her?'

'Scare her.'

'How? Jessie Lomas doesn't scare very easily.'

'She will. You'll see. We'll hit her if we have to. We've gotta make sure she stops pickin' on you, haven't we?'

Adele wished she felt as sure about this as Peter did. She hadn't wanted to do it but after two days of taunts she'd had enough. It was making her school life miserable. The repetitive chants of Yellow Belly, Cowardy Custard and Scaredy Cat were getting to her. Then there were the sly digs from Jessie as she passed by; usually a poke in the ribs or a sharp stamp on her foot. Adele had been powerless to do anything. Jessie had the upper hand and she knew it. If Adele retaliated or reported her, then Jessie would wait for her after school. And Adele didn't fancy being beaten up again. So this seemed like the only alternative.

But now she was gripped by nerves. Her stomach fluttered and she wiped her clammy hands on her trousers repeatedly. Peter, on the other hand, seemed exhilarated. His eyes sparkled with excitement. While they waited, he chatted about how they were going to sort Jessie out once and for all. He was full of nervous energy and couldn't stay still.

The minutes seemed to drag until finally they caught sight of Jessie with another, much older, girl.

'There she is,' Adele announced and she felt her heart beat speed up as she watched her adversary walking along the street.

Spotting the friend, Peter echoed Adele's own thoughts when he said, 'We can't get her yet. We'll have to wait till she's on her own.'

Jessie and her friend were heading in their direction so they moved further up the street and ducked behind a Ford Cortina, out of sight. They continued watching as the other girl branched off and returned to her own home.

Jessie was alone.

'Come on, let's get her,' said Peter.

Adele checked the street. Noting that there was no one else around, she followed Peter as he made his way towards Jessie. He waited till she was crossing the entrance to an alleyway. Then he pounced. Attacking her from behind, he pushed her against a backyard wall.

Jessie spun round, ready to lash out against her attacker. But Peter stood back. Then Jessie spotted Adele. A flash of recognition crossed her face as she looked from one to the other.

'Aah, brought your little brother, have you?' she laughed. 'Don't think I'm frightened of that little squirt,' she added, stepping towards Peter.

Adele felt a rush of fear surge through her body. Despite being outnumbered, Jessie still wasn't frightened, and that unsettled Adele.

'Come on then!' said Peter.

Jessie took another step. Then suddenly she stopped short at the sight of the flick knife in Peter's hand. He pressed a switch and the blade sprang out, missing Jessie by centimetres. Her hand shot to her mouth. She cowered against the backyard wall, stunned.

Adele was also shocked. This wasn't part of the plan. She breathed in sharply before spotting the horrified expression on Jessie's face. Adele quickly recovered, feigning acceptance of Peter's actions. Reassured by Jessie's fear. She hoped he wouldn't use the knife but she couldn't be sure. And it was obvious from the look on Jessie's face that she was even less certain.

'You've been picking on our Adele at school,' Peter said, waving the knife in front of Jessie's face.

Jessie shrank against the wall, hugging herself. Her lips trembled and her eyes darted about, searching for an escape route. Adele stepped forward to block her way. Jessie looked from one to the other of them, tears welling in her eyes.

Adele felt the pressure of expectation. Sensing that she had to capitalise on the situation, she aimed a sharp kick at Jessie's shin.

'Yeah, bitch!' said Adele, as Jessie howled in pain, the tears now spilling from her. 'Who's a Scaredy Cat now?'

Peter was still poised with the knife. 'Should I stick it in her, Adele?' he asked.

'Not yet.' Adele thought about how she could take advantage. 'If she promises to leave me alone and tells her friends to as well, then we'll leave her.'

'I'm sorry, Adele. I didn't mean it,' babbled Jessie. 'I'll leave you alone tomorrow. Honest.'

'And your friends?' asked Adele, grabbing a lock of Jessie's hair and twisting it tightly till Jessie squirmed.

'Yes.'

'And after tomorrow?' Adele twisted again as she waited for Jessie's answer, refusing to let up until she was sure Jessie was defeated.

'Yes. Every day.'

Satisfied with Jessie's reply, Adele let go of her hair.

'Right, she's got to promise before we leave her,' said Peter, holding the knife under Jessie's chin. His whole attitude was full of menace.

Jessie was now in floods of tears, her body shaking. 'Yes, I promise,' she said.

'OK. We'll leave her now,' said Adele, feeling a pang of remorse, which she kept hidden from Jessie while she turned to her and added, 'But if you ever pick on me again, we'll come back and get you.'

Adele was secretly relieved that it was all over, and determined to have a word with Peter about the knife. She couldn't believe he had gone to those lengths to scare Jessie. His behaviour was becoming more erratic. Although she was grateful to him for frightening Jessie off, Adele was nonetheless worried about his actions. But she couldn't tell anyone without betraying him. And that wouldn't be fair after he had helped her out.

When they reached home, Adele was pleased to find her grandma in the house. She was chatting to their mother when Adele and Peter rushed over to hug her.

'What have you two been up to?' her grandma asked. 'I've been waiting bloody ages to see you.'

'Nothing,' they both replied, and Adele could feel her cheeks burning with shame.

'Aye, and I'm the bleedin' Queen Mother. You look like you've been up to mischief to me.'

'No, we haven't, honest,' Peter quickly replied.

'We've just been at the park,' said Adele.

Joyce gave them a knowing look before referring to a carrier bag that she had left on the sideboard. 'There's some stuff in there for both of you.'

'Ooh, let's have a look,' said Peter.

'Hang on a minute, wait your sweat,' said Joyce. She grasped the bag and pulled out a package. 'This one's for you, Adele. The rest are for you, Peter,' she said, handing him the bag.

Peter quickly riffled through the bag, pulling out several items of clothing, 'Ew, clothes,' he grumbled.

'Don't be so bleedin' cheeky,' said Shirley. 'You should be grateful to your grandma for bringing them for you. What d'you say?'

'Thank you,' Peter muttered.

'Thank you, Grandma,' said Adele, clutching her package.

Seeing the number of items that Peter had taken out of the bag, Shirley said, 'Oh, Mam. You shouldn't have. That lot must have cost you a fortune, and you've only just bought our Adele some new trousers.'

'They didn't cost much,' said Joyce, tapping the side of her nose.

As Peter sloped off towards the stairs, Shirley dashed after him with the clothing, 'Not so fast,' she said. 'Take this lot with you and try them on. You can tell me which ones fit.'

When he was out of the room, Joyce whispered, 'Margaret Jones fetched them. She's got a grandson not much older. Don't worry; they've come from a good home. I've known Margaret for years. She's clean and so are the rest of her family. But don't let Peter know. He won't want to wear anything that's second-hand.' Then, switching her attention to Adele, she added, 'Aren't you gonna open yours then?'

'Yes,' said Adele who tore at the package excitedly.

She pulled out two cardigans, brand new, with the labels still on. Then she held them up, one by one, so she could examine them.

'Thank you very much, Grandma,' she said, a smile spreading across her face. Adele hadn't even mentioned to her that she needed new cardigans, and yet her grandma knew. Grandma Joyce always knew. She felt content knowing that, no matter how bad things got at home, Grandma Joyce could always make her feel better.

11

It was now the height of summer and Peter had found a new pastime swatting flies while their parents were out. Adele and Peter were in the living room at home. It was a particularly hot summer, and the smell emanating from the house was attracting the flies. Peter was frantically chasing around the room after them.

'You won't catch any, y'know. They're too fast,' said Adele.

'I will. I've done it before. The big ones are easiest; they're not as fast.'

'Why don't you go for one of the big ones then? Here's one now,' said Adele as a bluebottle buzzed past her ear. She watched it land on the wall. 'There it is. Get it, now!' she demanded.

Peter approached stealthily. He didn't give it a chance to get away. Before the bluebottle became aware of his presence, he whacked at it with some rolled-up newspaper then drew back. He examined the wall and was happy to see the dead bluebottle stuck to it by its glutinous insides.

'I got it!' he shouted. 'D'you wanna have a look?'

Adele didn't particularly want to see the squashed insect but she humoured him while he used another piece of newspaper to scoop it off the wall and place it on top of the rolled-up newspaper.

'Eh, look at this,' he said, approaching Adele with a look of glee on his face. 'It's got babies.'

He held it out in front of Adele's face. The blow from Peter had ruptured the insect's body revealing numerous tiny eggs. Adele sat up. She examined it from a safe distance, fascinated at first. But when Peter started to pull the eggs away from the dead body of the bluebottle using a spent match stick she felt repulsed. The creature was dead. They had killed it. And now Peter was jabbing at its offspring.

'Ew, don't! It's yucky,' said Adele, backing away now.

Despite her protests Peter carried on until he grew tired of it and flung the roll of newspaper on the floor with the dead insect still stuck to it.

'You can't leave it there,' said Adele. 'You need to get rid of it.'

'No chance!'

As Peter wasn't going to get rid of the fly, she decided to do it herself. She picked up the rolled newspaper tentatively and turned it over. The dead insect remained stuck there surrounded by its eggs. She recoiled as she held the news-paper at arm's length then dashed to the toilet to dispose of it.

Adele tore a strip of newspaper around the bluebottle and threw it down the toilet. She flushed the toilet, but it wouldn't go down. She winced as she watched the insect bobbing about on the water's surface then flushed again. After three attempts it finally sank.

She returned to the kitchen cringing as she imagined hundreds of tiny maggots climbing up her arms. The bluebottle was gone but she felt as though it was still there and a shiver ran up her spine.

Adele switched the tap on and reached for the soap and a scrubbing brush. After a few minutes of scrubbing at her hands, nails and arms, she still couldn't get rid of the creepy feeling and it was unsettling her. But she didn't know what had made her feel so bad. Was it repulsion at Peter's morbid fascination or guilt at the loss of life?

When Adele heard her mother arrive home with Grandma Joyce, she finished scrubbing at her hands and nails, dried her hands and rushed into the living room, greeting her grandma.

'She never seems that pleased to see me,' muttered her mother.

'Course I am, but we see you every day,' said Adele. Her response was automatic but, if she was honest with herself, her mother didn't rouse the same feelings in her as Grandma Joyce did. Although she didn't dislike her mother, her grandma was the true mother figure to Adele. She was strong, determined and resilient, and Adele could always turn to her for help or advice. But Adele didn't view her mother in the same light. She was just Mam; someone Adele was linked to by blood, but who was weak and apathetic and couldn't be relied on for anything.

Adele looked at Peter for backing but he was too busy hovering around Joyce to see if she had brought any treats for him.

Joyce was too concerned about the state of the place to take much notice of Peter. 'Bleeding hell, Shirley! The place is swarming. Haven't you got any fly spray?'

'I forgot to get it. I'll get some next time I'm out.'

'I've been trying to get rid of them,' Peter gushed.

'How?' asked his grandma.

'I've been whacking them with newspaper.'

A grin spread across Grandma Joyce's face. 'Eeh lad, you won't get rid of many like that,' she said, patting him on the head.

It was a few minutes later when another visitor arrived; Mrs Roper from the corner shop.

Adele overheard Peter's name being mentioned and Mrs Roper didn't sound too happy. Peter was a picture of guilt with his eyes darting around the room as his grandma tried to hold his gaze.

When Shirley shut the door and came back into the room, Grandma Joyce asked, 'What the bloody hell was all that about?'

'It's our Peter,' Shirley sighed.

Peter was heading for the front door but his grandma stopped him, 'You can bloody well stay where you are till your mother's finished talking,' she said.

Peter snuck back into the room, still avoiding eye contact with his grandma.

Shirley continued. 'He's been nicking sweets from her shop. She caught him at it and shouted him back, but he ran off.'

'I did not!' Peter protested. 'She's lying.'

'Well why the bloody hell would she come round here if you didn't do it?' asked Shirley.

'It wasn't me; it was that Anthony. I always get blamed for everything!'

'Oh, so you were there then?' asked Joyce.

Peter bowed his head, aware that he had slipped up.

'Well? Come on, we're waiting to hear it!' said Joyce.

'Anthony did it when I was with him.'

'Well why did she see you with the sweets then?' asked Shirley.

'He passed them to me on the way out. I didn't realise he'd nicked them. He was just trying to put the blame on me.'

'What a load of bloody nonsense!' said Joyce. 'The lad's younger than you, isn't he? Why would he be leading you astray? More like the other way round if you ask me.'

Shirley tried to defend her son. 'He might be telling the truth, Mam. That Anthony's no angel, y'know.'

'Right, well there's only one way to find out,' Joyce replied. 'Why don't you go round to that Anthony's house and ask?'

'No!' Peter protested.

'Sounds bloody guilty to me,' said Joyce. 'Was it you, Peter?'

Peter looked down at the ground and nodded his head.

'Oh, you little swine!' said Shirley. 'Wait till your father comes home and I tell him. He'll have your bloody guts for garters.'

'No, don't do that!' said Joyce. 'You know what Tommy's like. There's no point getting him riled, is there? I'll tell you what we'll do,' she added, pulling some money from her purse. 'Take this round to the shop, Adele,' she said, handing her a brand new shiny fifty pence piece, 'and tell her your grandma sent you to pay for the sweets Peter took.'

Adele wasn't pleased at being roped in because of Peter's misdemeanours but she knew better than to question her grandma's authority. 'Go on, love,' her grandma continued. 'I'd send Peter, but I can't bloody trust him to bring the change back.' She then turned to Peter, adding, 'And you! You can pay me the money back out of your spends. If it was up to me I'd make you stay in for a week as well, but that's for your mam to decide.'

Shirley looked despondent. 'No, I think that's punishment enough. But don't let me hear about you doing anything like that again, Peter. You're lucky Mrs Roper didn't get the police. She will do if she catches you again though.'

Her response was half-hearted as though she was struggling with the burden of it and only trying to appease her mother.

When the fuss had calmed down, Adele put on her shoes ready to go to the corner shop with her grandma's money. She dreaded the reception she would get, which would probably be worse than normal because of what Peter had done.

She felt trepidation as she pushed open the door to the corner shop. Mrs Roper's face was set in a steely gaze. As Adele nervously walked towards the counter she could feel the weight of Mrs Roper's harsh stare.

'My grandma sent this,' she murmured, holding out the money.

Mrs Roper snatched at the fifty pence piece, examining it carefully, as though she thought it was counterfeit. 'It'll have to do,' she said.

Adele waited.

'Well, off you go then,' said Mrs Roper.

'My grandma told me to fetch the change back.'

'She'll be lucky. He's probably been at it for months. I bet this won't cover a fraction of what he's had from this shop,' said Mrs Roper, looking at the money in disgust before continuing, 'You make sure your grandma knows that.' She waited until Adele was on her way out of the shop before she added, 'Tell your grandma I'm very grateful though. At least she's tried to make amends for her naughty grandchildren.'

Adele heaved a sigh of relief when she got outside the shop. But she was overcome with other feelings too. A feeling of fury mixed with shame. '*Naughty grandchildren*,' Mrs Roper had said, but Adele had done nothing wrong. Yet again she was being judged for the sins of others, and the feelings of bitterness gnawed away at her.

12

'Anthony, you need to run faster next time. We nearly got caught,' said Peter, pausing to catch his breath once they had rounded the corner.

They were playing knock-a-door-run, one of Peter's favourite games. Although Anthony wasn't as enthusiastic about the game, he had given in to pressure from Peter. Anthony was two years younger than Peter and desperate to impress him.

'Right, your turn this time,' said Peter. 'Do that one there with the brown door and don't forget to leg it as soon as you let go of the knocker.'

'But that's Mrs Thomson's house,' said Anthony. 'She'll go mad if she catches us.'

Peter knew whose house it was, which was why he had deliberately chosen it. He didn't like Mrs Thomson. She was one of the old women who stood gossiping in the corner shop with Mrs Roper. He hated the way she made him feel with her snide comments and sly looks.

'She won't catch you though, will she?' said Peter. 'As long as you're fast. Come on, it'll be a laugh.'

Anthony still didn't look convinced.

'What's the matter? Are you scared?' asked Peter.

'Am I 'eck. I'm not scared of that old bag.'

'Well come on then. What are you waiting for?'

Peter stood back while Anthony approached the house, the thrill of anticipation sending a buzz through Peter's body. He could see that Anthony was nervous and this added to his excitement.

'Come on, just do it,' he urged.

Anthony lifted the door knocker and banged it against the brass plate several times. As soon as Peter heard the loud thud of the brass knocker, he was off, running as fast as he could up the street. Anthony tried to keep up with his rapid pace but was trailing behind.

As Peter rounded the bend, he heard Mrs Thomson yelling after them.

'What d'you think you're playing at, you cheeky little sods? If I get my bloody hands on you, I'll swing for you!'

Anthony followed Peter into the side street and, once they were out of sight, they stopped running. While Peter took a few seconds to get his breath back, Anthony leaned forward, puffing and panting.

'God, I can't believe you're so out of breath,' said Peter. 'You're a rubbish runner.' Anthony looked up at him and Peter laughed, 'I told you it would be fun. She went mad, didn't she?'

'I knew she would. What if she tells my mam and dad?' asked Anthony, looking frightened.

'Nah, she won't. She doesn't even know it was us.'

'She didn't see you 'cos you were round the corner but she might have seen me.'

'Yeah, but she won't know it was you. She'd have shouted your name if she knew. She only saw you from the back.' He paused then, waiting for Anthony to regain his breath, before adding, 'Come on, let's go back.'

Anthony stared at him, open-mouthed.

'Come on. You're not scared, are you?'

'No!'

'Well, come on then,' said Peter, who had already set off eagerly in the direction of Mrs Thomson's house, with his face full of glee.

'It's your turn,' said Anthony as he followed behind.

They stopped a safe distance from Mrs Thomson's house and Peter spent a few seconds in thought. 'I tell you what we'll do,' he said. 'The old bag might be ready for us, so instead of knocking on the door we'll throw stones at it from here. She'll never be able to catch us then.'

Anthony looked sceptical but didn't say anything. Peter wasn't bothered what he thought. He was confident that Anthony would join in; he'd be too worried about being labelled a coward otherwise.

Peter chuckled in satisfaction as they hurled stones at Mrs Thomson's front door. They threw small stones at first, but when there was no response Peter decided to chance his luck and picked up a chunk of brick that was lying by the roadside.

'Stop a minute,' he ordered Anthony. 'Right, I'm gonna chuck this big ducker so get ready to run.'

Anthony's eyes opened wide as he took in the size of the lump of brick.

Peter hurled the brick, hearing a resounding crash as it impacted with Mrs Thomson's front door.

By the time Mrs Thomson came to the door to see what the disturbance was, both boys were out of sight. She waved her fist in annoyance, examining the damage to her front door. The brick had left a small dint and brought off some of the paint.

'Just you wait till I get my bloody hands on you!' she shouted. 'I'll find out who you are, don't you worry. And when I do, you'll be in big trouble.'

Hearing her harsh words, Peter was doubled up in the side street, fighting to contain his laughter. The fact that she didn't know their identities enhanced Peter's enjoyment.

'I think we should pack it in now,' said Anthony. 'I don't want her to catch us.'

Peter thought fleetingly about the consequences and an image of his angry father flashed through his mind. 'All right then,' he said. 'It was a good laugh though, wasn't it?'

Anthony just shrugged in response and they then made their way back to the street where Peter lived, passing Mrs Thomson's house on the way. Peter noticed the dint in Mrs Thomson's door and a smug grin spread across his face.

'See that?' he asked Anthony, but Anthony wasn't amused. Peter, on the other hand, felt immense gratification knowing that he had damaged the old bag's door and got away with it. He had just taken another step towards a life of crime and was soon to find out just how rewarding that life could be.

PART TWO
1979-1980

13

Peter, Alan and David were sitting inside a souped-up Ford Escort. They had parked next to a church and across the road from a four-bedroomed detached house in Bramhall. They'd deliberately selected this location in which to park. They were near enough to observe the houses but not near enough to attract complaints from residents objecting to them parking outside their homes. That would have made the car memorable and they didn't want that.

They had been watching this particular house for days, waiting for the right opportunity. The couple from this house had gone out in a taxi half an hour previously, and theirs was the only house on the row without a burglar alarm.

It was a quiet neighbourhood and one that was considered desirable, with private houses set back from the tree-lined roads. Rich bastards with money to spare as far as Peter was concerned.

While Peter and his friends waited, the only sound they could hear was the distant hum of traffic and the occasional faint bark of a dog coming from one of the houses.

'Come on, let's do it now,' Peter said. 'They've been gone fuckin' ages. They'll be out till late.'

He was buzzing with the thrill of anticipation. At sixteen years of age he had found his new high, and it was far more rewarding than toeing the line for grown-ups who didn't appreciate it anyway.

He looked to Alan Palmer for agreement, knowing that Alan was their unofficial leader. Although Alan wasn't as daring as the other two, he was sharper. He had a way of thinking things through to make sure everything went as smoothly as possible. Alan was also older than Peter and had acquired a car, which cemented his role as leader. He did have a tendency to flip, however, when things didn't go according to plan.

David, on the other hand, was the most impulsive of the three. He seemed to have little sense of danger and would do anything to display his bravado, but he wasn't too bright.

'OK,' said Alan. 'You go round the back first to check it out. Me and Dave will wait here. Give us the thumbs up when you're ready for us.'

Peter glanced out of the car window, making sure the coast was clear. His handsome face wore a satisfied smirk and he couldn't wait to get started. He then stepped out of the car and crossed the road, looking around him to make double sure that no one was around but they were all tucked up in their nice big houses.

As he pushed the gate back, it creaked and Peter tensed as he stepped onto the drive, checking once more to make sure it hadn't caught anyone's attention. He shivered as he pushed the gate to and lifted the latch, taking care to place it back into position as quietly as possible.

Peter tiptoed onto the drive and crept down the side of the house. A side gate barred him from the back and he tested the latch to see if it was locked. The gate wouldn't budge. It was obviously bolted from the other side. He would have to climb over.

Looking behind him once more, he wedged his left foot against one of the thick gateposts to gain purchase while he launched himself upwards and his hands reached for the top of the gate. His right foot followed, digging into the other gatepost a little further up until he was high enough to drag himself over. He dropped down onto the other side, the rubber soles of his trainers softening his landing.

Peter then crept round to the back of the house and checked the back door and windows. They were all locked but the back door had glass panels. He glanced through, a smug grin curling up the sides of his mouth when he noticed the householders had left the key in the lock on the other side of the door. The dickheads! This one would be a breeze.

Keeping an eye out for nosy neighbours, he sneaked back round the house and slid the bolt on the side gate then inched it open. He slipped through the small opening and continued round to the front of the house. Alan and David were watching from the car and he gave them the signal to join him before returning to the back of the house.

Once they were inside the house, Alan whispered, 'Let's check out the upstairs first.'

Peter led the way and they arrived at what was obviously the master bedroom. Peter stepped onto the plush mink-coloured carpet and glanced around the room. Two of the walls were lined with fitted wardrobes and cupboards, with a huge double bed nestled into a highly polished wood surround.

Opposite the bed were other matching units; a dressing table and a cabinet housing a TV and video recorder.

'Lucky bastards!' said David.

Ignoring him, Peter approached the TV and video recorder, and unplugged them from the wall sockets. He knew these items would fetch a lot of money, especially the video recorder, which was something he didn't come across very often. Only very well off people had video recorders.

David stepped up to the dressing table while Alan searched the cupboards and wardrobes, pulling out their contents as swiftly as possible as he tried to spot items of higher value.

Peter lifted the TV and carried it out of the room. 'Dave, can you manage that?' he asked, nodding his head towards the video recorder. Placing the TV on the landing, Peter scouted around the other bedrooms quickly before establishing there was nothing of value in any of them.

Next, they made their way downstairs. David was like a kid in a candy shop as he grabbed at anything of value, squealing with excitement.

'Turn it in, will you?' Alan demanded. 'We don't want anyone to hear us!' Then, thinking he had heard something, he held his hand to his ear and said, 'Shush a minute.'

They all stopped what they were doing and remained quiet while they listened out for any signs of danger. The boys soon identified the sound Alan had heard. It was a hamster racing around on its wheel. Apart from that all was silent. The inactivity made Peter aware of how hyped up he was. He could sense his heart thudding in his chest and feel the buzz of adrenalin pumping around his body urging him to carry on. He loved that feeling.

'OK, let's go before anyone catches us,' said Alan.

But Peter and David were enjoying themselves, rushing around the room now, smashing vases and ornaments for the sheer hell of it.

'We're not here to take the piss,' said Alan. 'We've got what we came for, let's just go.'

He and Peter picked up their loot, ready to leave the house. But David wasn't finished yet. 'Hang on,' he said. 'Watch this.'

Peter and Alan turned around, and Peter let out a roar of laughter as David unzipped his trousers and shot a stream of urine onto the carpet. An acrid stench filled the air and the luxury pile became sodden, the pool of urine giving off a frothy steam.

'*I'm* taking the piss,' he sniggered. 'Might as well have some fun while we're here. See how the snobby bastards like that!' He quickly zipped his trousers back up and the three youths dashed back to the car with their stash of electrical goods, jewellery and cash. Peter couldn't wipe the smirk off his face, thinking of the snobby homeowners' reactions when they arrived home to find their precious goods taken and their carpet wet and stinking of piss.

The house was silent; Adele was downstairs, her parents were both out and Peter was still in bed. She was making the most of the peace and quiet to catch up with her studies. The silence was broken when Adele heard the sound of footsteps on the stairs. She looked up from her exercise book, knowing that her peace was about to be shattered.

'Hiya, Peter. Where were you last night?' she asked when he walked into the room.

'Out with the lads, and I've told you, it's Pete not Peter.'

Adele tutted on hearing his familiar complaint. It was since he started hanging around with Alan Palmer and David Scott that he had insisted on being referred to as Pete. Apparently, 'Peter' wasn't cool enough for him now. Adele wasn't keen on the two boys. They were trouble with a capital T and, as far as she was concerned, they were leading Peter astray.

'I know you were out, but where were you?' she added.

'Just out. That's all you need to know.'

She stared hard at him and noticed his eyes flitting around the room. It was obvious to her that he had been up to no good.

'Well, whatever you've been up to, don't let my dad catch you. He'll go mad!'

Peter smirked. 'Don't worry, he won't find out anything.'

Adele sighed and returned to her studies. Things had changed between her and her brother in recent years. As a child he was forever getting into mischief but now his escapades had become more serious and Adele preferred not to get too involved. No matter how much she tried to warn him about getting into trouble, he didn't seem to take much notice.

Encouraged by Grandma Joyce, Adele focused on her studies instead and she was currently in the first year of her A levels. If she could get some good qualifications then she would get a university place away from the area and not have to put up with the behaviour of her father and brother any longer. She couldn't help but worry about Peter though. They had shared a bond since childhood, and that would not be broken just because they had each chosen a different path in life.

Adele didn't know the full extent of what Peter got up to

but she had her suspicions. Alan and David were older than Peter. They had bad reputations, and most of the local kids knew that they were thieves. Alan had even spent time in a detention centre when he was caught robbing a shop. Adele just hoped that Peter would eventually see sense and give them a wide berth.

She looked up and watched Peter go through to the kitchen, then she continued with her essay. Adele only had a chance to write a few more sentences before her parents walked in. They had returned from one of their rare outings together and were having a row when they walked into the house. Some things never changed.

'You do it every fuckin' time, don't you?' her father shouted.

'I've not done owt wrong,' muttered Shirley. 'I don't know what you're talking about.'

Adele gathered her books together. She needed to get her essay finished and handed in tomorrow, and there was no way she could do it with this racket going on.

'I'm going to the library,' she announced.

Her mother nodded her head briefly but her father didn't even notice she had spoken. He was already on his way into the kitchen. As Adele packed the last of her books into her school bag, she overheard him verbally attacking Peter. 'There you are. I want a bleedin' word with you! What fuckin' time did you come in last night?'

Without waiting to hear any more, Adele dashed out of the door and headed for the peace and quiet of the library.

Two hours later, after finishing her work, she set off for the ten-minute walk back home.

Adele had just left the main road and was walking along the pathway leading into her estate when she saw a group of young people ahead of her. She carried on walking, but as she drew nearer she noticed that Peter's friends, Alan Palmer and David Scott, were amongst the group, which consisted of a few boys and two girls.

When Adele drew even nearer she noticed that they were nudging each other, and looking in her direction. David Scott said something to the others, which she couldn't hear, and they all laughed. Adele sensed trouble and her stomach began to churn. She was tempted to turn back but this was the quickest way into the estate.

She continued to walk towards them. Her heart was pounding and her mouth felt dry. The laughter became louder and she could now hear what they were saying.

'Here she is, the stuck-up bitch!' announced David Scott.

The others jeered and laughed.

Adele could feel all eyes on her. It was an eerie sensation. A prickle ran down her spine and her hands became clammy as she prepared to pass through the group.

She was within a few metres of them now. They stood still, watching, their eyes boring into her. Then, once she had drawn level, they crowded around, jostling her and shouting abuse. *Swot! Bitch! Slag!*

Adele stiffened but continued walking while looking straight ahead with her chin raised. In spite of her fear, fury coursed through her. But she didn't respond to their taunts; that would only have made matters worse. Instead, she kept moving, her motions rigid but resolute. She swallowed down the angry retorts, which threatened to overwhelm her. Scum! How dare they?

Then she was through the crowd. But they were still within reach. She felt a cold chill pass through her. The sound of footsteps. A strange sensation of proximity. Then a savage blow to her back.

'Snobby cow!' shouted David Scott as the punch from his fist struck her.

Adele felt the fierce impact and her legs weakened. She fought to stay upright and hold back the tears that sprang to her eyes. Still she kept walking.

Adele heard David Scott rejoin the crowd, evidenced by his retreating footsteps then further jeers and laughter. She maintained the same pace. The sounds diminished. An excited murmur replaced by faint chatter. Then, nothing. She was safe, at last.

When Adele reached home, she was trembling but her eyes were dry. She raced upstairs to find Peter. He was lying on his bed reading a comic.

'What's wrong?' he asked when she appeared in the doorway.

'I've just been attacked by your mates.'

Peter sat up. 'What d'you mean?'

Adele explained what had happened.

'Don't be daft,' he said. 'They're just having a laugh.'

'David Scott thumped me in the back. It really bloody hurt!'

'That's just Dave clowning around. He's daft like that. Did you say anything to him?'

'No! I didn't know what they would do.'

'No wonder they think you're a snob! That's your trouble, Adele; you go around with your nose stuck up in the air. They're all right really. If you talked to them, you'd know that.'

Adele was livid. 'I'm not talking to them. They're scum!'

'What the bloody hell's going on up there!' shouted her dad on hearing her raised voice.

'Nothing!' shouted Peter. 'We were just having a laugh, that's all.'

Adele retreated to her room knowing that to involve her father would only invite a load more trouble. And she knew from painful experience that once her father got riled, anything could happen.

14

It was Sunday, which was usually cleaning day. Sometimes Grandma Joyce came round to help out, but she hadn't been round for a couple of weeks.

'Is Grandma coming today?' Adele asked her mother.

'No, she's not so good. I'm going to try and go round to see her when I've got a minute.'

Shirley's response was lacklustre and Adele realised there probably wasn't much chance of that.

Adele sighed. 'Do you want some help with the housework?' she asked.

'Oh please, love. I could do with some help today; I'm not so good myself. I tell you what, you start on the dusting and I'll go and get the hoover.'

Adele soon set to work on the shabby furniture, which was covered with a thick layer of dust. It had been several minutes and her mother still hadn't returned to the living room. Adele couldn't hear the sound of the hoover elsewhere either. She went into the kitchen to see whether her mother had taken it out of the pantry yet.

Seated on a kitchen chair was Shirley, who was putting some pills into her mouth and washing them down with a glass of water. The pill bottle stood on the kitchen table, its lid still off. Adele recognised the pills. They were diazepam, which her mother still took regularly.

'I'm not feeling very well, love,' said Shirley. 'I'm just having a little sit-down then I'll come and join you.'

'Have you not got the hoover out yet?' asked Adele, a look of scorn on her face.

'No, I was just going to get it when I started feeling unwell.'

It was clear that her mother wasn't going to do anything so Adele strode over to the pantry and dragged the hoover out. By the time she had finished hoovering the house her mother was still sitting at the table, although Adele noticed that she had managed to make a cup of tea for herself, which she was now drinking.

'Oh, you are a good girl,' said Shirley. 'I don't know what I'd do without you.'

Adele said nothing. Instead she looked around at the state of the kitchen. The bowl was full of dirty dishes, and the table was stained and littered with crumbs. Despite her desire to get on with her studies, she knew that unless she cleaned up the mess, it wouldn't get done.

She set to work but she was annoyed. How could her family live in such a pigsty? Adele felt irritated by her mother's slovenly ways and, despite her protestations of illness, Adele didn't feel much sympathy. She hated the way her mother shirked the housework. She also became annoyed at the way her mother took pity on herself and adopted a pathetic, timid tone of voice when it suited her.

At seventeen years of age, Adele had little understanding as to why her mother was the way she was. As far as Adele was concerned, if something needed doing, you just did it. But although she became irritated with her mother, she would then feel affection towards her and a tremendous guilt for being short-tempered. What if her mother couldn't help it? Maybe she really did find it difficult to carry out the most basic tasks. But then Adele would spot her mother idling over a cup of tea or chatting with the neighbours, and she'd become irritated once more. While she toiled, she worked herself up into a fury and when she had finished she decided to go out.

'I'm off out!' she shouted to her mother once she had put her shoes on. She slammed the door behind her without waiting for a reply. Then she walked off in the direction of Grandma Joyce's house.

Adele was curious. It wasn't like her grandma to leave it so long without calling round. She also missed her. No matter how fed up Adele was feeling, Grandma Joyce always managed to cheer her up. She often brought small gifts for Adele and Peter, but even when she didn't, her kind and supportive words gave Adele strength.

It wasn't long before Adele arrived at her grandma's home near Belle Vue. She knocked on the door and waited. And waited. Grandma Joyce didn't usually take so long to answer. Adele's curiosity turned to concern. But before anxiety could take hold, Grandma Joyce appeared at the door wearing her housecoat.

'Oh hello, love. I was just having a lie-down.'

Adele stepped inside and closed the door behind her.

'I'll put the kettle on,' said Grandma Joyce.

Adele watched her walk into the kitchen. Her movements seemed laboured but Adele didn't think much of it. Perhaps she was still tired because she had just got out of bed, although it was a bit late in the day for her grandma to be having a sleep. When Joyce came back into the room, Adele noticed her pallid complexion, her ruffled hair and the way her housecoat hung haphazardly.

'How are you?' asked Adele.

'Oh, not too bad. Just a bit of a bad stomach, that's all,' she said, rubbing her abdomen.

Despite Grandma Joyce's words of indifference, her face was strained.

'How long have you been like this?' Adele asked.

'Only a few days. Don't worry, love; it'll pass. It's something and nothing.'

A niggling thought went through Adele's mind; the contrast between her mother and grandmother. Her mother seemed to seek pity at every opportunity whereas her grandmother refused to let illness get the better of her.

'I'll see if that kettle's boiled,' said Joyce, rising from her chair.

'No. You sit down! I'll go and make the drinks. What do you want?'

'No, it's all right. I'm not ready for the knacker's yard yet. *You* sit down!'

Joyce's dominant tone forced Adele to remain seated. She watched her grandma walk across the room, noting how frail she seemed. She looked as though she had lost weight too.

'Are you sure you're OK, Grandma?' Adele asked when Joyce handed her a cup of tea and a plate of biscuits. 'Only, you don't look so good.'

'Eee, what do you expect at my age? It's all right for you youngsters; you're fit and strong. But when you get to my age it takes a bit longer to shake things off. Give it a few days, I'll be right as rain. You'll see.'

'Have you been to the doctors?'

'Have I buggery! They'll only tell me what I already know. There's nowt you can do for a stomach bug but let it run its course.'

She put up a convincing argument and, as a girl of seventeen, Adele didn't have a lot of experience with doctors so she accepted her grandmother's word for it.

'How's your mother, anyway?' asked Joyce. 'She was supposed to come round but I've seen nothing of her.'

'She told me she was going to try and come round too but she isn't very well.'

'The usual, is it?'

'I think so,' said Adele, although she wasn't sure what 'the usual' referred to.

Grandma Joyce rolled her eyes. 'Never mind, I'll be round as soon as I'm feeling up to it to see if she's all right.'

After a while Adele asked, 'Is there anything I can do for you while I'm here? Shopping or housework?'

A smirk spread over Grandma Joyce's face. 'Will you give over?' she said. 'I've told you, I'm fine. Now, stop worrying and enjoy your tea and biscuits.'

'I've finished,' said Adele, placing her empty cup on the coffee table. 'Those biscuits were lovely, thanks, Grandma. Have you not had anything to eat? Perhaps I could make you something while I'm here.'

Grandma Joyce rolled her eyes and shook her head, and Adele knew what was coming.

She quickly interrupted, 'It's OK. I know... you're fine.'

They looked at each other and laughed. Then Adele picked up her empty cup and plate, and took them through to the kitchen to wash. She noticed other cups in the kitchen which were stained with dried-on tea and Adele gave them a quick wash too. It wasn't like Grandma Joyce to leave dirty pots lying around.

'Right, I'm off,' said Adele when she returned to the living room.

Before leaving, Adele planted a kiss on her grandma's face. 'Take care, Grandma,' she said. 'I'll be round to see you again soon.'

Then she set off for home, trying hard not to worry about her grandmother.

15

Tommy was on his way to the office to collect his wages. He trudged across the tarmacked builder's yard in his muddy work boots heading for the Portakabin situated at the far end. He was looking forward to getting paid, especially as his money had run out the previous evening and he'd had to rely on his mates to sub him a few pints in the pub.

Tommy pushed open the office door so forcefully that it bounced back on its hinges. He then entered the Portakabin and nodded at his boss, Don, who was sitting behind a teak desk. Don shuffled uncomfortably in his seat as though something was amiss.

As Tommy approached the desk, Don ticked off his name in the ledger then searched through the collection of pay packets on the desktop.

'Here you go,' he said to Tommy, handing him the packet with his name on it. He waited until Tommy turned to go before adding, 'There's a deduction for being late back to the job last Wednesday afternoon.'

Tommy swung round, 'You what?' he demanded.

Don visibly tensed before responding, 'We've had a complaint from the customer. She said you were slightly tipsy as well.' He allowed a few seconds for his words to sink in before continuing, 'It's not good enough, Tommy. You can't be arriving back late to the job, half-cut.'

Tommy had been mulling the details over while two more workers had entered the office and were waiting to collect their wages. 'Last Wednesday?' he asked.

'That's right,' said Don. 'The customer said you were several minutes late, but it's not the first time, apparently, so we've deducted an afternoon's pay.'

'Hang on a minute!' said Tommy, becoming angry. 'Is that the Beeston Street job?'

'That's right,' said Don, swallowing back his rising fear.

'No fucking way!' Tommy shouted, stretching himself to his full height and pulling back his broad shoulders. 'That old cow's had it in for me from day one. The cheeky old witch! I was only a couple of minutes late. And I made the time up! And it's the first time I've been back late from my dinner on that job.'

'Sorry, Tommy, but I've got to take the customer's word for it. We can't risk losing valuable business.' Don's speech had become harried and, as he spoke, he tapped his fingers nervously on the desk.

'Well the customer's fuckin' wrong! So you can fuckin' well get that money back in my pay packet!' yelled Tommy, feeling affronted that his boss was siding with the customer.

'Now, now, Tommy. I can't do that. Rules are rules and I've got to set an example,' said Don, glancing around the office and drawing comfort from the arrival of more of his workers.

Tommy hammered his fist on the desk, causing the items on top to jump about as the teak desk panel buckled under the might of his considerable strength. 'I want my full fuckin' wages; I've earnt it! And I'm already short this week. Now are you gonna make up my pay or do I have to do summat about it?'

Seeing the number of men now standing around the office, Don became emboldened, 'I've told you, Tommy. I can't do that. And if you're not careful, you'll be on a disciplinary.'

'You what?' shouted an enraged Tommy as he leant over the desk and hauled Don from his chair by his shirt collars before headbutting him sharply in the face.

The men rushed forward and pulled Tommy back as he struggled to drag himself out of their clutches.

'Leave it, mate!' one of them urged. 'You'll end up in lumber.'

Tommy bounced back and, for a few moments, the men kept hold of him while he puffed heavily, his fierce gaze piercing through Don. His adversary slumped back into his chair while a stream of blood flowed from his busted nose, colouring his lips and teeth.

'Right, you're sacked!' shouted Don, wiping his bloody nose with the back of his hand.

Tommy heaved against the men, boiling over with anger and outrage at the total injustice of it all. He tried to get to Don once more, but the men kept a tight grip on him.

'Come on, Tommy. Let's get you out,' one of them cajoled. 'You don't wanna end up in trouble with the cops as well, do you, mate?'

As his workmate's words sank in, Tommy relaxed a little, enabling the men to edge him towards the office door. They gave him a few minutes to calm down, pointing out the perils of taking another swipe at Don. Eventually, Tommy was persuaded to leave the site, but not before he had shouted a barrage of threats at Don. He marched out of the yard, kicking angrily at some wooden pallets. By the time he reached the gate he had already decided to drown his sorrows in his local pub.

When Adele answered the front door she was surprised to see her father standing there, because he had a key. But then the smell of alcohol hit her and she was shocked as she took in the state of him. His hands were bloodstained, his hair messy and his clothes dishevelled. She pulled the door back and he staggered over the threshold, his right hand grasping repeatedly at an imaginary object in an effort to steady himself.

Adele backed up while he continued to stumble into the house. She turned to see her mother standing further along the hallway and gave her a concerned look. Shirley responded by frowning. As Tommy teetered along the hallway, he muttered incoherently to himself. At first Adele couldn't decipher any words but then he raised his head, gazing unsteadily at Shirley before slurring, 'Fuckin' bastard's sacked me!' His head then slumped back down and he let out a loud belch before wobbling into the living room.

He plonked himself into his armchair, his arm brushing against the cup resting on a side table. Tommy cursed the object and swiped it viciously to one side. The cup bounced onto the threadbare carpet, its handle fracturing on impact.

'You hear me?' he asked, lifting his head again. This time his bloodshot eyes couldn't focus on Shirley. Instead, they drifted around the room, his head lolling about in a slow-motion parody of a nodding dog.

Adele could feel her heart speed up, as she dreaded the impact of this turn of events. She was glad Peter was out as he always seemed to make their father even angrier.

'I'm sorry to hear that, love. What happened?' Shirley asked, trying desperately to pacify him.

'Don's a fuckin' bastard! That's what,' he muttered before hiccuping. He then tried clumsily to remove his boots, finally succeeding in taking off the first before launching it across the living room. Shirley rushed to his aid and removed the second one, placing it to one side.

'Can I get you anything, love?' she asked.

Tommy continued to hiccup, and took a few moments to reply. 'What? Nah... fuckin' hiccups!' he shouted as they interrupted his words.

'I'll get you some water,' Shirley offered but Adele flashed her a worried look. She didn't want to be left in the room alone with him.

'Will you get it, Adele, love?' she asked, picking up on Adele's unease.

Adele dashed to the kitchen, pulled a dirty glass from the overflowing bowl and did her best to remove the stains using the rancid dishcloth. Her hands trembled as she held the glass under the tap and filled it with water.

When Adele finally re-entered the living room, she was met by the sight of her father half-asleep in his chair, his loud hiccups peppered with occasional outbursts containing Don's name and a variety of expletives.

Shirley held her finger to her lips to warn Adele not to disturb him, and Adele placed the glass quietly on the mantelpiece. Shirley flashed a warning glance, directing her eyes upwards, indicating they should go to bed.

'Will he be all right?' Adele whispered when they were

back in the hallway, worried that he'd be annoyed if he woke up and found they'd gone.

'Aye, for now,' Shirley sighed. 'But I'm not looking forward to tomorrow. He'll have a head like Birkenhead.'

Adele nodded, stuck for something to say. She headed towards the stairs, knowing that tomorrow would just be the start of it. Adele recognised that, although they hadn't borne the brunt of his misfortune tonight, now that her father was out of work, the worst was yet to come.

16

The following day Adele went to visit her grandma. It was almost two weeks since her last visit, but Adele had been too busy with her studies to visit sooner. During that time, they hadn't seen anything of her grandma and Adele's mother hadn't made the effort to visit her either, claiming she didn't feel well enough. So, Adele felt it was up to her to make sure her grandma was all right. She'd see if there was anything Grandma Joyce needed while she was there.

'Hiya, love,' Joyce greeted when she answered the door but her greeting was lacklustre.

'Hiya, Grandma.'

'It's nice to see you,' said Grandma Joyce, shuffling across the room and wincing as she bent to get into her armchair.

Her grandma's words sounded more like an accusation to Adele and she felt guilty for taking so long to visit.

'Are you OK?' asked Adele. 'Is your tummy still bad?'

'I'm not too bad. It's just taking a bit of shifting, that's all... Anyway, I'm at the doctor's on Monday so you can stop worrying. He'll sort me out.'

Adele noticed that Grandma Joyce hadn't offered her a drink, which was unusual for her, and her unease grew. 'Do you want me to make the drinks, Grandma?' she asked.

'Aye, go on. There's a love,' her grandma replied.

When Adele was in the kitchen she noticed that not only were there dirty pots in the sink but the cupboards were almost empty too. She searched for milk and found that there was none apart from a half-empty bottle, which had gone off.

'Grandma, there's no milk,' she shouted through to the lounge. 'Do you want me to nip out for some?'

When her grandma didn't reply straightaway, Adele went through to the living room. She was disturbed to find that her grandma's head was lolling and her eyes were shut.

'Grandma!' Adele called. 'Are you all right?'

Joyce jolted awake. 'Yeah, course I am. What's wrong?'

Adele felt relief flood through her and remained speechless for a few moments.

'What is it?' Joyce asked again.

'There's no milk,' said Adele, once she had recovered from her shock.

Joyce sighed heavily, 'Pass me my purse. Can you get some from the corner shop, love?'

Adele took the money from her grandma and rushed out to the shop, coming back with the milk as well as a few other items. Then she made the tea and put a few biscuits on a plate. While she polished off three biscuits, Joyce nibbled at one.

'Do us a favour, love, and pass me those paracetamols off the mantelpiece,' said Joyce.

When she struggled to take the lid off the bottle of tablets, Adele did it for her and slipped two into Joyce's hand. Her grandma swallowed them down with her cup of tea.

'Are you sure you're all right, Grandma?' asked Adele.

Joyce tutted, 'Do I have to keep telling you? I've just got a few twinges in my tummy, that's all. Now stop worrying about me; I want to find out what's been going on at home. How's your mam? And what about Peter? Is he still up to mischief?'

Adele quickly told her about Tommy losing his job, taking care to omit details of her father's drunken state the previous evening. But she underestimated Joyce's intuition.

'I bet he's upset someone, hasn't he?'

'Not really, no,' said Adele, feeling herself blush as she recalled how her father had cursed Don.

'What did he say? Go on, tell me!'

'He did go a bit mad, and cursed a lot,' Adele admitted.

'I knew it. The bloody big lummox! He'll have upset someone, mark my words.' Joyce was becoming irate now, channelling her remaining vestiges of energy as she worked herself up.

'Maybe,' whispered Adele, her eyes downcast.

'Well, never mind,' said Joyce, on noticing the effect her words were having on Adele. 'We'll all just have to manage as best we can.'

Joyce rolled her eyes but didn't say anything further. She stayed quiet for a few moments while she recovered herself.

Eventually she spoke again, calmer this time. 'What about you, Adele? How are your studies going?'

'Not bad. I got really good marks in my last exams.'

'Good,' said Joyce. 'You carry on working hard and make a better life for yourself.' Then her head lolled once more and she nodded off to sleep.

Adele cleared the dishes, gave the place a tidy then slipped quietly away.

Before she headed for home, she called at the home of Joyce's neighbour, Mabel Boyson, to see if she could find out anything further about her grandma's state of health. Mabel knew Joyce had had a bad stomach but couldn't offer any more information. She was surprised when Adele told her how ill her grandma seemed, and promised to call in and see if she wanted anything.

'Thanks,' said Adele. 'I'll call round again as soon as I get a chance.'

Despite her good intentions, Adele didn't have many opportunities to visit her grandma over the next few weeks. She was far too busy and had lots of other things on her mind; when she wasn't studying she was cleaning the house, or helping to pacify her volatile father. However, when she did visit, her grandma didn't seem much different. She was still ill and told Adele that the doctor had referred her to the hospital to see a consultant.

Despite her grandma's reassuring manner, Adele couldn't help but worry. She wasn't used to seeing her so ill.

So she told her mother how ill her grandma had seemed and Shirley promised to go round. Adele checked to make sure she had done so and was relieved to find out she had made the effort. She couldn't tell her very much though, just that her grandma was still waiting to see the consultant. When her mother didn't seem overly concerned, Adele brushed her worries aside. Perhaps she had been overreacting after all.

Tommy wasn't enjoying being out of work. He spent much of the daytime hanging around the house, watching TV and ordering everyone about. When the opportunity arose, he headed for the pub but, now that he was on the dole, he couldn't afford to go as often. He sometimes found a way round this though by borrowing from family and friends.

There were constant rows between him and Shirley over money. He would demand extra money from the housekeeping to go to the pub then complain when Shirley provided cheap, badly cooked meals on her limited budget.

Adele had noticed a difference in her mother too. No longer able to go to the bingo, due to a shortage of money, Shirley was becoming bored and frustrated. This meant she was often retaliating when Tommy criticised her. However, a rise in his tone or an aggressive stance could still silence her, as could the sight of Tommy tumbling home worse for wear after a session down the pub.

When Adele came downstairs that lunchtime she could hear the drone of the television set. She peeped inside the living room and spotted her father sipping from a can of lager while his attention was fixed on the television screen. She walked through to the kitchen where Shirley was slouched at the kitchen table with a cup of tea in front of her. She was fidgeting nervously with an empty tablet bottle.

'Oh, Adele love, I'm glad you're here. I was just gonna shout up to you,' she said.

Adele could feel the onset of disappointment, knowing that she was about to be roped into yet another job, which would ruin her plans for the rest of the day.

'What d'you want?' she replied, her tone sharp.

'Aah, don't be like that, love. You wouldn't go and pick up my prescription for me, would you? Please? I've run out of my pills and I need them.'

'I'm a bit busy, Mam. Haven't you got time to go?'

'Please, love. I'm not so good,' she said, grabbing hold of Adele's hand. 'I can't be going out today. I get all panicky when I've not had my tablets.'

Adele sighed deeply. 'Go on then, give me the prescription.'

Shirley rose swiftly from her chair and went over to the kitchen cabinet where she found her prescription and handed it to Adele. 'Thanks, love. I really appreciate it,' she said, grabbing hold of Adele's hand.

Adele noticed the unshed tears in her mother's eyes and she quickly grabbed the prescription form and backed away, irritated. She was still too young to have much understanding of her mother's mental illness. Instead, she saw her as weak and pathetic.

She wasn't in the mood for yet another emotional scene so, before her mother could say anything more, Adele dashed from the house and made her way to the chemists. She might not have voiced her feelings to her mother but they didn't go away. Suppressed deep inside her were confusion, anger and a festering resentment at the life she was forced to live.

17

The abandoned factory had been beckoning to Peter for a while and, although Alan was against the idea of going there, Peter insisted. According to Alan there were more lucrative ways to make money, but Peter was more interested in the thrill of it. He was backed up by David who would do anything for a dare. Once they were there Alan wanted to break in and see if there was anything inside worth taking. But Peter had persuaded him to go up onto the rooftop so they could collect some lead and bag it up to sell.

As soon as Peter stepped over the ledge and stood on top of the roof, he felt a surge of adrenalin. He straightened up and looked around him, surveying the surrounding streets with amazement. They had taken on a new perspective from this position, and he stared in wonder at the twinkling lights that ran in sequence down the darkened streets, bathing the buildings with a luminous glow.

'Wow! This is fuckin' brilliant,' he said to his friends who had followed him onto the roof.

Peter walked across the rooftop, his arms outstretched, enjoying the sensation of the wind caressing his body and ruffling his hair. He felt powerful, almighty; his senses heightened by the thrill of the forbidden. It was a sharp contrast to how he felt at home where he was always on his guard because of his father's temper.

'Come on, let's get the lead,' said Alan. 'That's what we've come for.'

'What's the rush?' said David who was now copying Peter's actions. 'Nobody's gonna see us up here.'

'We'll get the lead first then you two can dick about as much as you like while I check if there's a way in. I wouldn't mind seeing if there's owt inside worth nicking.'

Alan took out a roll of plastic bin bags from the pocket of his parka and handed Peter and David one each. For a few minutes they remained on one side of the rooftop collecting the lead that was in abundance.

It wasn't long before David became bored and he put down his bag, stood up then ran along the rooftop, his arms outstretched once more. Peter laughed and, after several seconds, decided to join him. He strained in the dark to see where David had got to and spotted his outline further along the lengthy roof. Peter was running towards him when he heard the sound of smashing glass. Then David disappeared.

'What the fuck?' he said.

'Where's Dave?' asked Alan, straightening up.

'He was over there,' said Peter. 'Come on, we'd better see what's happened.'

'Hang on! Don't rush. There's skylights on this roof.'

Peter's excitement turned to fear as they walked across the rooftop, desperate to find out what had happened to their friend. Then they spotted something. About two thirds of the way along the roof, and in the approximate area where they had last seen David, they noticed a skylight that was broken.

Peter approached cautiously, aware of what must have happened but not wanting to acknowledge it. He crept to the edge of the skylight and peered inside the gloomy, deserted factory. In the dark it was just about possible to spot the still form of David sprawled out on the floor below.

'Fuck! He's had it,' he said.

'Hang on, let me have a look,' said Alan. He joined Peter at the edge of the skylight and gazed downwards. 'David! David, are you OK?' he shouted but there was no answer.

'Shit! What are we gonna do?' said Peter. 'He might have snuffed it.'

'Shut up. He might not. We'll have to check.'

Peter stared inquisitively at Alan. 'How we gonna do that? We'll never get down there. We haven't got any rope or anything.'

'We'll have to get in through a window, like I wanted to do in the first fuckin' place! It was you that told us to go onto the roof to get some lead.'

Peter kept silent. He knew Alan was right. They shouldn't have gone up onto the roof, then this wouldn't have happened. He followed Alan back across the rooftop until they found a drainpipe and made their way down the factory wall.

Alan led the way until they came nearer to the area where David had fallen. He smashed a pane of glass and Peter followed him as he climbed through the broken window and made his way inside the factory. They landed in a room on the outer periphery of the building.

Looking around the deserted room, Peter had an eerie sensation and he shivered involuntarily. In the gloom he could see used documents scattered across the floor; the only signs of former occupancy. The musty smell of abandonment met him.

Alan marched to the door and pulled it open, kicking the discarded paperwork aside. He had now sped up in his quest to locate David. When Alan stopped dead, Peter knew he had found him, and he could feel his heart beating erratically. He sidled up beside Alan, his breathing now ragged and his hands clenched tightly.

Peter watched Alan kneel down beside David and call his name. His voice echoed in the cavernous interior of the factory. There was blood. Loads of it! Most of it sprang from the back of David's head. And his limbs were twisted as though he'd broken several bones on impact with the ground. David didn't respond. He just lay there, motionless and damaged.

Peter gasped as Alan lifted one of David's hands and felt his wrist for a pulse.

'He's alive,' he said, and Peter let out a sigh of relief.

'How we gonna get him out?'

Alan didn't reply for several seconds. Instead he gazed around him. 'We're not,' he said. 'It's too risky. He's too badly injured.'

'But we can't leave him like that.'

'No, we won't. We'll make a run for it then call an ambulance.'

'But what if it doesn't get here?'

'It will. We can keep watch to make sure.'

Peter gazed at him, open-mouthed.

'It's the best way,' said Alan. 'We can't risk getting caught, and they'll know what to do with him.'

'But what if the police ask who he was with? He might tell them.'

'Don't worry; he won't.'

Peter couldn't think of a better option so they left the factory and found a phone box nearby. Then they had a tense wait, seeking cover behind a parked van while they watched first the ambulance, then the police, arrive. It seemed to take forever until the ambulance men finally lifted David from the building. Once they were satisfied that they had done all they could, Peter and Alan made their way home.

They'd had a fruitless night and the bags of lead lay abandoned on the rooftop. With all the worry about David, even Alan had forgotten to collect them.

Adele was in her room trying to study while her parents were having yet another of their endless rows. She tried to tune it out but it was impossible, and she felt her heartbeat speed up as her father's voice took on an increasingly aggressive tone.

She gazed at the bedside clock, toying with the idea of going to the library. Twenty to nine; it was too late. She was relieved in a way because her trips to the library were still filled with trepidation following the previous visit when David and his friends had attacked and intimidated her on her way home.

After several more minutes she gave up on study and attempted to read. Even that was difficult, especially when she heard a door slam and her father's voice at the bottom of the stairs complaining about Peter's whereabouts.

Then she heard him shout, 'That lad's bleedin' useless and you know it! And she's not much better. She should be out at fuckin' work, not scrounging off us to do bleedin' A levels. What's she need them for anyway?'

Adele didn't hear her mother's response. She tensed, expecting him to mount the stairs and confront her, but then it went silent. Still, it took a while before her erratic heartbeat returned to normal. As well as being fearful, she was angry. Why did he begrudge her an education? Her friends' parents didn't have a problem with them staying on at school.

Then a thought occurred to her, which brought a brief smile to her face; her father was still out of work and yet he was calling her a scrounger. The irony of the situation was completely lost on him.

After reading for over an hour she drifted off to sleep, but her sleep was fitful and she woke up with a start at ten past one in the morning following a bad dream. As she glanced at the clock she wondered whether Peter was home yet and decided to check his room. He wasn't there and the bed was cold.

She returned to bed, dreading the following day when her father was bound to tackle Peter about where he had been. Her father had been so moody since he had been out of work and the last thing she needed was for Peter to annoy him. She knew too well that with her father in his current frame of mind anything could happen.

18

The following day was Sunday and, as Adele had anticipated, her father interrogated Peter as soon as he was out of bed.

'What time did you get in last night?'

Peter shrugged his shoulders, 'Dunno, late.'

'I know it was late; I asked you what bleedin' time it was!'

'Not sure, about eleven, I think.'

Tommy took a swipe at Peter, knocking his head sideways. 'Oh no it fuckin' wasn't, you lying little get!' he said. 'I was awake at twelve and you weren't in then.'

On feeling his father's heavy hand, Peter jumped back and stood glaring at him but he didn't dare hit him back. 'About twelve then. I dunno!' he said. 'I didn't check the clock.'

'Well it's about bleedin' time you did! You know you're supposed to be in by eleven; you're only fuckin' sixteen,' he said, landing another blow to the side of Peter's head.

'Ouch,' yelled Peter. 'That hurt!'

'It was supposed to fuckin' hurt! I want you home by eleven in future or you'll get more than that. And you can stay in for the rest of today... What the fuck were you up to anyway?'

'Nowt. Just hangin' around with my mates.'

'I don't fuckin' believe you! Anyway, you can stay in tonight so I know where you are.' Tommy then looked at Peter suspiciously before walking away.

Adele was glad when it was over; at least her father hadn't found out the real time that Peter arrived home. She noticed that while her dad had been challenging Peter, she had been subconsciously holding her breath, hoping that Peter wouldn't try to retaliate. She tried to relax, allowing her tense muscles to ease.

Later that morning Adele chose a moment when her father wasn't around to ask Peter what time he had got in. He confirmed that it was sometime after two o'clock.

'Jesus, Peter! You're pushing your luck, aren't you? I won't ask what you were up to; I'd rather not know. But if he finds out, you'll be for it,' she said.

'He won't find out though, will he? Not unless somebody tells him,' he said, scornfully.

Adele was a bit put out that he should think she'd tell on him. 'You know I wouldn't do that, Peter,' she replied. 'Just be careful, that's all.'

It was sometime soon afterwards when the police arrived at the house. The family were all still at home.

'Does Peter Robinson live here?' asked the officer when Shirley answered the door.

'Yes, why? What's he done?'

'I think it would be best if we came inside to explain,' said the officer.

Shirley led them into the living room; two PCs, both male and aged somewhere in their thirties. Adele could see by the expression on her mother's face that she was about to go into panic mode. Her father, on the other hand, had adopted a stern expression as he surveyed the officers' arrival.

'Perhaps you'd like to switch off the TV while we discuss matters,' suggested the first officer.

Tommy stormed over to the TV screen, pressed the off button forcefully and slammed back down into his chair.

'Is Peter here?' asked the officer.

'Go and get him, Adele!' her father ordered.

Adele shouted up the stairs. Her heart was beating fitfully and there was a heavy sensation in the pit of her stomach. When Peter appeared at the top of the stairs, she gestured for him to come down. Before Peter could enter the living room she whispered into his ear to forewarn him about the police presence but he didn't seem too fazed.

The atmosphere inside the room was solemn and the formal scene looked out of place in Adele's home. She noticed that her mother was in tears already and was clutching a stained and soggy cotton handkerchief.

Peter sat down on the sofa. By this time he appeared contrite.

Before Adele could join him, her father said, 'There's no place for you here, Adele. Go up to your room till the police have gone!'

Adele did as she was told but she was annoyed. Why was her father taking his anger out on her? She realised that it was his way of maintaining a level of control and displaying his authority to the police officers.

While Adele was upstairs, she tried to listen to what was happening but it was no use, so she crept downstairs, hoping her father wouldn't hear her as she put her ear to the living room door and listened to what was being said.

'It's been confirmed that you were on the factory roof with

Alan Palmer and David Scott when David fell through the skylight,' said one of the officers.

'I wasn't,' said Peter.

'We've had it confirmed by David Scott who is currently in hospital suffering from injuries following his fall.'

Adele inhaled sharply. So that's what Peter had been up to last night! No wonder he had been looking so shifty.

'Don't tell bleedin' lies!' shouted her father. She assumed his comments were directed at Peter.

The officer chipped in. 'Peter Robinson, I'm afraid we'll have to take you to the station for further questioning.'

Then Adele heard movement and her heartbeat quickened. She dashed away from the door and up the stairs as quietly as she could. She was almost at the top when she heard someone opening the living room door. After a few seconds of steadying her breathing she turned and made her way back downstairs as though she had been in her room all along.

Peter was already in the hallway with the two policemen, and her parents were discussing who should accompany him to the police station.

'I'm not bleedin' going!' her father hissed, out of earshot of the officers. 'You brought him up so now you can go and fuckin' sort things out.'

Shirley stared back at him, aghast, and Adele noticed the tramlines running down her face, which were evidence of her earlier tears. Adele knew her mother wouldn't dare go against Tommy's decision.

Shirley wavered momentarily near the living room door before turning back and grabbing her bottle of pills. She then pushed them inside her handbag, put on her shoes and coat, and went to join her son who was now inside the police car.

As the car sped up the street, Adele could feel her heart thudding inside her chest in anticipation of her father's reaction. She stood in the hallway, waiting.

After a few moments he announced, 'I'm going for a fuckin' pint!' and pushed past Adele as he stomped out of the house.

It was a nervous time for Adele as she waited for her family to return home. She switched on the old black and white TV. The screen flickered, so she picked up the indoor aerial and moved it around the room until the picture steadied. Then she watched a film; a musical that didn't require much concentration and would help to take her mind off things.

Her father was the first to return. He was early; lunchtime opening hadn't quite finished. She guessed that his early return was either due to lack of money or because he wanted to be there when Peter got home. She hoped it wasn't the latter and a feeling of dread clutched her insides.

Unfortunately, he was in no better mood than when he had left. 'What's this load of shite you're watching?' he demanded.

It was obvious what the programme was so Adele ignored his remark. Instead she stood up. 'It's OK. I wasn't really watching it,' she said. 'You can switch it over if you like. I need to do some studying.'

As she walked out of the room, he muttered to himself, 'Dead right, I can fuckin' switch it over.' Then his voice rose as he shouted, 'I paid for the fuckin' thing! Course I can watch it.'

Adele hurried up the stairs, desperate to escape his anger. It was a while later when her mother and brother arrived home. Adele braced herself as she awaited her father's reaction.

'Here's the little bastard!' she heard him shout. This was followed by the sound of her mother screaming. Then her father continued to rant while Peter howled as though in pain.

Adele shot down the stairs and raced into the living room. The sight that met her was worse than anything she had ever witnessed. Her father was pummelling Peter with his fists while hurling insults and abuse at him. Meanwhile, her mother was crying and pleading with Tommy to ease up on Peter.

It was obvious to Adele that her mother's pleas were having no effect whatsoever. Momentarily stunned, Adele stared at the distressing scene with her mouth agape as blood pumped from Peter's nose. Then she came to her senses, taking a brave stance, in contrast to how she was feeling inside.

'Dad, stop it. For God's sake! You'll kill him,' she cried, noticing how bloody Peter's face was becoming.

Peter had raised his hands in a vain attempt to protect himself but the might of his father's fists broke through them.

'Come on, Mam! We've got to stop him,' she shouted.

Adele then ran towards her father, grabbing her mother and forcing her to join her. Between them they tried to shield Peter from him. But nothing could stop Tommy. His anger had become too intense. He took a swipe at Shirley, knocking her out of the way. Then he continued to throw punches. Most of them landed on Adele while her mother seemed to be avoiding them.

'Run, Peter, run!' Adele shouted.

Fortunately Peter took note of her words and escaped from the house just as a particularly vicious punch landed on the bridge of Adele's nose. The pain shot through her, sending her dizzy. She tumbled to the ground, unable to get up for a few seconds. Through bleary eyes she watched her father stagger out of the room in pursuit of Peter. She prayed he didn't catch him.

Several seconds later, Tommy was back. 'Little bastard's gone,' he said. 'Just wait till I get my fuckin' hands on him!'

Adele's heart was racing. As her father stepped towards her and her mother, she trembled with fear.

'Shouldn't have fuckin' stopped me,' he mumbled before sitting down and ordering Shirley to make him a cup of tea.

Shirley went willingly, leaving Adele alone with her father. Adele's face was sore. She could feel the bruises starting to form and her left eyelid was closing with the swelling. Tommy looked at her and for a brief time she thought she detected the faintest sign of remorse on his face.

'You shouldn't have got in the way,' he murmured before switching his focus to the television.

Adele got up slowly and went into the kitchen. The aftershock of her father's brutal attack took a hold of her and she broke down in tears, sobbing convulsively until her whole body was shaking.

'Oh, Adele love,' her mother said, putting her arm around her and shedding her own tears. 'You shouldn't get in his way when he's like that. Look at the state of your face.'

Shirley's words sickened Adele. Why hadn't she done something instead of standing by while her husband gave her son a savage beating? And why was she so accepting of his actions? It was wrong. What he did was wrong! And there was no way her mother should have condoned that kind of behaviour. What kind of mother was she? But Adele was too traumatised and angry to discuss things with her even though she was anxious to find out what had happened at the police station.

When Shirley left her alone while she went to take Tommy his cup of tea, Adele took several moments to compose herself before tending to her injuries. Then she slipped out of the back door in search of Peter. She needed to make sure he was OK, and she'd make sure she found out from him everything that had happened.

19

Adele spent almost an hour searching for her brother. The people she passed did a double take when they saw the state of her face. Some of them asked what had happened but she shrugged them off. It was more important that she found Peter. Nobody had seen him apart from one person who saw him from the back, running up their street, but he didn't know where he went or which way he turned when he reached the top.

She even tried some of his friends' houses but they hadn't seen him either. The only place she hadn't tried was her grandma's house. Grandma Joyce would instinctively know there was something amiss and, given her present state of health, Adele didn't want to worry her.

Thoughts of her sick grandma flashed through her mind. She was still waiting to see the consultant to find out what was causing her stomach problems. But Adele didn't have time to dwell too much; she had to find Peter.

Eventually Adele gave up searching and made her way home. As she was walking along she noticed one of the local boys, Gary Healey, approaching from the opposite direction. Gary was a year older than Adele. He had always been one of the cool kids and had a reputation as a tough guy. He was also good-looking but Adele had never shown any interest in him. She didn't see the point as he wouldn't be interested in her.

As he drew nearer she became aware of his keen gaze. Remembering the recent incident with David and his friends following her visit to the library, she grew uneasy. She played out various scenarios in her mind, planning how she would react if he became nasty.

'Jesus! You look as if you've gone a few rounds,' he said.

Adele subconsciously drew her hand up towards her face, 'I just had a bit of an accident, that's all,' she muttered.

He drew within a metre of her and stopped dead. Adele was scared. As she tried to step around him, she could feel the adrenalin pumping around her body. He mirrored her move, blocking her way. Adele looked at him, desperate to escape, her eyes pleading. He smiled as though taunting her. She looked around, ready to sidestep him and run.

But then he spoke again, and she noticed his concerned expression. 'Are you sure you're OK?' he asked. 'What happened to you?' When Adele didn't reply, he reached his hand up towards her face but she backed away. 'Sorry,' he said. 'There's a bit of blood coming from your nose. I was just trying to wipe it away.'

Adele reached her hand up to her face and ran it under her nostrils. She pulled her hand away, noticing the blood that was streaked across her fingers.

'Shouldn't you be getting that cleaned up?' he asked.

'I have already. I didn't realise it was still bleeding,' Adele said, her voice breaking on the word 'bleeding'.

'Come on, I'll walk you back to your house,' he said, putting an arm around her shoulder and turning her around.

She pulled away, shocked by the attention. 'It's OK, I'm fine,' she said.

'OK, as long as you're sure,' said Gary.

Their eyes met, then he seemed to hesitate as though he had something more to say but couldn't find the words.

She was just about to walk away when he said, 'I've been looking out for you. I've been meaning to ask...' He paused, as though searching for the right words, before continuing. Then his next words came out in a flurry. 'Do you wanna go out with me?'

Adele stared at him, incredulous.

'Sorry, I know it's bad timing,' he added, 'but it's the first time I've seen you for a while.'

Adele was so preoccupied with her current problems that she replied instantaneously, 'No, no I can't.'

'OK... You sure?' he asked.

'Yeah, I mean, no. No, I can't.'

Adele then rushed away before he had chance to say anything further. As she drew closer to home, all thoughts of her encounter with Gary Healey slipped from her mind. For the moment, she had more pressing matters to attend to.

When Adele arrived back home, she was relieved to hear that her father had gone out, but there was still no sign of Peter and she hoped he was all right. Adele noticed a bottle of witch hazel on the sideboard.

Following her eyes, Shirley commented, 'I got it from her next door. Your eye's come up something shocking. Let me dab a bit round it. Don't worry, I'll take care not to get it in your eye.'

Adele guessed that her mother must be feeling guilty because she had allowed Adele to bear the brunt of her father's wrath when she tried to defend Peter. But she let her feelings pass. What was the point? Her mother would never change.

'Let me just have a look at it first,' said Adele, stepping up to the mirror. 'Oh my God!' she said, on seeing her swollen eyelid and the bruising to her nose. She must have looked a sorry sight when she bumped into Gary Healey.

'Don't worry. We'll soon have it right,' said Shirley, mechanically, but Adele wasn't convinced.

While Shirley applied witch hazel, they talked about Peter's time at the police station.

'Oh, it was awful, Adele,' said Shirley. 'They made me feel like I was a bloody criminal myself. And my bleedin' hands were shaking something wicked.'

'What happened?' asked Adele, willing her mother to get to the point instead of harping on about her own feelings.

'What? Oh, Peter? They let him off with a caution. Apparently him and his mates were mucking about at that old abandoned factory and David Scott fell through the roof. Ended up in hospital. According to what he told the police, our Peter and Alan Palmer were up on the roof too and, when he fell, they did a runner and left him for dead.'

Adele looked at her mother with a doubtful expression on her face till Shirley continued the story.

'Peter says he's lying. They did see him fall but Peter and Alan were on the ground. They'd been shouting at him not to do it but he wouldn't listen. And the next thing they knew there was this bloody big crash and the sound of breaking glass. Then David was nowhere to be seen. So they rang an ambulance and waited till it got there before scarpering.'

'Hang on a minute,' said Adele. 'If they'd done nowt wrong, why did they scarper when the ambulance arrived?'

'They were frightened they'd get the blame. You know what it's like... give a dog a bad name and all that.'

Adele was amazed at her mother's gullibility but, again, she kept her thoughts to herself. She had no doubt, however, that Peter and Alan were probably up on the roof with David when he fell.

Shirley was putting the lid back on the bottle of witch hazel when they heard the front door being opened. They cast a look of curiosity at each other. It was Peter.

'It's all right, he's out,' said Adele when he walked in the room.

Peter heaved a sigh of relief but remained silent as though he was still stunned by the attack.

Adele cringed at the sight of Peter's face and her mother instinctively raised a hand to her mouth while her eyes filled with tears once more. His appearance was far worse than Adele's. Both of his eyes were almost shut and his face was a mass of bruises. The swelling was so severe that it distorted his features.

Noticing her mother was also lost for words, Adele said, 'You'd better sit down, Peter, while we put some of this witch hazel on your face.'

'I'll put the kettle on,' said Shirley, leaving Adele to care for her brother.

Adele started by filling a bowl with soapy water then soaking a flannel and using it to wipe away the dried blood that was now encrusted around Peter's mouth and chin, and smeared over his cheeks. While she bathed, he winced several times, his inflamed flesh sensitive to even the slightest touch. Then she gently patted his face dry with a towel and applied some witch hazel. She noticed that his arms were also dotted with bruises so she treated them too.

'I bet you two are hungry, aren't you?' asked Shirley.

Adele noticed the time. Ten past seven. It was getting late and they hadn't eaten for hours. Neither she nor her mother had had chance to prepare a meal so Shirley made some toast. They sat in silence for several minutes drinking tea and eating.

When they had finished, Shirley persuaded Peter to go to bed and rest because of his injuries. A look of fear flashed across Peter's face. None of them voiced their mutual worry; that Tommy might return and attack Peter once more. But Adele noticed how attentive her mother was being and she hoped that guilt would force her to step in if Tommy did return in another of his rages.

Eventually it was time for Adele to go to bed. Before reaching her own room, she passed Peter's. She paused and knocked on the door.

'Yes,' said Peter.

She turned the handle and entered his bedroom where she saw Peter lying wide awake on the bed.

'Are you all right?' she asked.

From his prone position Peter attempted an awkward shrug.

'You'll have to stop getting into trouble, Peter,' she whispered in as gentle a tone as she could muster.

'Fuck off!' he lisped through swollen lips. 'I don't need you having a go at me too.'

'I'm not! I'm just saying... you don't want to get on the wrong side of him.'

'Fuck off, Adele. I'm sick of your Miss Goody-Goody act. I've always been on the wrong fuckin' side of him. He's sick in the head. Don't you know that?'

Adele could see he was struggling to speak through his injuries so she didn't want to press him anymore. 'I'll leave you to rest,' she said, backing out of the room. 'Just be careful, Peter. That's all.'

Adele went to her own room and got ready for bed but she couldn't sleep. Thoughts of her father's vicious attack troubled her. Although she was used to seeing him hand out his punishments, this was the most violent one yet. There was no doubt in her mind that he was getting worse and she didn't know how she would cope with the situation.

Peter was also on her mind. She realised that a massive chasm was forming between them. She couldn't talk to him anymore and she was beginning to feel that the gulf between them was unbridgeable. But that didn't stop her from caring about what happened to him. He was her younger brother, after all, and they'd been through so much together.

Part of her felt guilty. She had always been their grandma's favourite. The support and encouragement from her grandma had stopped her from following the same path as Peter, who seemed to be rebelling against everything around him. Although Peter was sharp, he wasn't clever at school and maybe he thought that crime was the best way to get on in life. She only wished she could convince him otherwise.

Adele thought back with fondness to when they were younger and she yearned to have the old Peter back. She and Peter had always looked out for each other and she wondered whether they would ever be that close again. Now it was all so different. They had each chosen their own way of life and she would just have to accept that their different outlooks had driven them apart.

While she lay there she anticipated her father's drunken return home, and dreaded a repeat of the day's earlier events. But something inside told her that he had done enough damage for one day. She had noticed the remorseful expression on his face when he saw her injuries. Maybe even he had a conscience.

20

It was a few days later. Adele's warning words to Peter hadn't had any effect. He had his own thoughts on the subject. Who was she to tell him what to do, anyway? It was all right for her; she had always been the favourite. But he was the one who their dad always picked on. No matter what he did, his dad would always have it in for him, so why should he bother trying to please him?

He was currently engaged in a burglary with his friend Alan. They had picked a house in an affluent area, and waited until they knew the owners would be in bed asleep. Within minutes they were standing inside the lounge. Alan had already checked the location of the other rooms, noting that there was also a dining room at the front of the house with a kitchen beyond.

'Tell you what, to save time, you go and see if there's anything worth nicking in the other room while I get the TV and video,' Alan whispered to Peter.

Peter nodded then crept out of the living room, crossed

the front hall and eased open the door to the dining room. Spotting a mahogany cabinet at the far side of the room, he skulked over to it.

It had several cupboards, some of which were fitted with doors containing leaded glass panes. It was clear to see that there was nothing of value inside those. It was the cupboards without glass panes that Peter was interested in. He tried to open each of them in turn but, to his consternation, they were all locked.

Next, he tried the drawers. His luck was in. Neatly tucked into the corner of the top drawer was an ornate key. He picked it up and was just about to try one of the locked cupboards when he heard the faint sound of voices. He thought they were coming from upstairs, drifting down from the room above him. Was he imagining it?

He stopped what he was doing, and listened intently. Yes, he could definitely hear voices, and they were coming from inside the house. He managed to pick out the sound of two different voices; one female and the other male.

Realising he needed to warn Alan, Peter dropped the key and sped towards the door. But before he reached it, he heard heavy footsteps at the top of the stairs.

'What the hell's going on!' roared a man's voice as his speedy footsteps descended the stairs.

Peter could feel a cold shiver of fear running through him. He was too late to warn Alan, so he dashed behind the door, planning to pounce on the man as he pushed it open. Then he waited.

But the man didn't come inside the room. He took the other door instead; to the living room. As soon as Peter heard the man challenging Alan, he broke cover, dashed out of the dining room, across the hallway and towards the front door. A surge of adrenalin was driving him; his only thoughts were of escape.

A series of observations flitted through his mind. The shadow of a man through the open lounge door. His own harried breathing. His feet stumbling across the hall carpet. The front door still ajar where they had entered the property. His trembling limbs.

Peter grasped the front door, and tugged it open. Then he was on the driveway, sprinting towards the road, the sound of a woman's frantic screams echoing in his ears.

He reached the gate, gripping the metal rails for support as he turned onto the pavement. Almost slipping, but managing to steady himself. A quick glance upwards. The fleeting view of a terrorised woman at the window. Lights switching on in neighbouring houses. Running. Panting. Sweating. Desperate to escape.

Peter kept going, his feelings of panic urging him on. He didn't stop till he was well away from the house. And only then did he think about the plight of his friend who was still trapped inside.

It was the next day when the police arrived at their front door once again asking for Peter. Adele was relieved that their father wasn't home. But she was astounded to hear what the police had to say.

'Peter Robinson, we would like you to come down to the station for questioning in connection with the death of Mr Harry Burton,' said one of the officers.

Adele covered her mouth with her hand in shock while her mother remained slack-jawed and silent.

'He will need an adult to accompany him,' the officer said, looking at Shirley.

This prompted a reaction from Shirley who was so flabbergasted that she responded to the officer's previous statement. 'Who's Harry Burton?' she asked.

'We'll go through the details at the station,' said the officer. 'Would you like to get yourself ready to accompany us?'

Shirley nodded, still stunned, and mechanically carried out his instructions.

It was an anxious time for Adele while her mother and Peter were at the police station. As well as worry over what Peter had got himself involved with this time, she was fearful about having to tell her father when he arrived home.

Her mind was in turmoil; jumbled thoughts raced around inside her head. What if Peter had killed someone? Maybe he was just a witness and had evidence relating to a killing.

Eventually, when she had exhausted all possibilities, she decided to do something to occupy her mind until they returned home. She channelled all her nervous energy into cleaning and tidying the house. That seemed to calm her down until her father arrived home.

'Where the bloody hell is everyone?' was his first question. He was already in a bad mood.

Adele became flustered. Terrified of his reaction, she made an instantaneous decision. She wouldn't tell him. She couldn't. He'd never know. Not unless Peter was put inside. And by that time he'd be out of reach.

'I dunno,' she said. 'They didn't tell me where they were going.'

He grunted and sent Adele to make him a drink. She was glad to get away so he wouldn't notice the worry on her face. It suddenly occurred to her that he'd find out where they'd been as soon as Peter and her mother returned. Then she'd be in big trouble. She felt panicked. What could she do? She shouldn't have told him a lie.

Then it came to her. He needn't find out. She'd stop her mother and Peter from telling him. If she watched out for them coming down the street she could head them off and make sure they didn't tell him. Now she just needed to think of a cover story.

As soon as she had given Tommy his drink, she dashed upstairs and waited at the front bedroom window. There she had a good view of the street and would be able to see them on their way home.

It was only another ten minutes until she spotted her mother and Peter. Adele raced down the stairs and rushed from the house. She ran towards them.

'What's wrong?' asked Shirley when Adele reached her, breathless and flushed.

Adele put out her hand in a stop gesture. 'Wait,' she panted. When Adele had regained her breath, she said, 'My dad's not to know. I've told him I don't know where you are. We'll have to make something up.'

Shirley had a confused expression on her face and was about to respond when Adele continued, 'You know what happened last time Peter was arrested. We can't risk it happening again.'

'But he'll know,' said Peter. 'I've been charged so I've got to go to the magistrates' court tomorrow.'

Adele paled. 'What with?' she stuttered.

'Burglary.'

'What about the... the murder?'

'It was Alan,' said Peter, whose gaze then dropped to the ground.

'What happened?' she asked.

'We were caught. Well, Alan was. I was in the other room so I ran out.' Again his gaze shifted.

'But, why?' asked Adele.

'I dunno. I just saw the man going into the living room where Alan was. The police said he'd stabbed him.'

'Oh my God!' said Adele. 'What will happen?'

'He'll go down for it. He's admitted it, but he's saved my skin. The police would have had me for the murder too, but Alan told them I wasn't there when it happened, and the man's wife saw me running off.'

Although Adele breathed a sigh of relief, she couldn't help noticing that Peter's main concern was for his own welfare rather than for the poor woman who had lost her husband. But she let it pass for now. Despite being horrified that Peter had been connected with somebody's murder, she was more worried about how her father would react if he found out about Peter's crime. They needed to get back home before her father noticed she was missing.

'Let's think of an excuse for my dad,' she said. 'Hopefully he'll be out tomorrow so he won't know about you going to court.'

Her mother and brother agreed with her and they quickly strung together a cover story to explain their whereabouts.

Adele ended by saying, 'Let's see what happens tomorrow, then we can decide what to tell him. If you don't get sentenced then he won't be any the wiser.'

'But if I do…'

'Then you'll be out of his reach and we'll deal with him,' Adele cut in, looking at her mother for affirmation.

Shirley nodded.

'But he'll go mad!' said Peter.

'Not as mad as he would be with you if he could get his hands on you.'

'Thanks sis,' said Peter, barely audible, and Adele noticed how he lowered his head. It was as though he was ashamed at what he had done and the strain he was putting them under. He gulped then added, 'You're a lifesaver.'

Adele cringed at the irony of his words, thinking about the poor woman who had lost her husband at the hands of one of Peter's friends. As they continued to walk back to the house, Adele could feel a rising fear. She desperately hoped that none of them slipped up and gave the secret away because she was terrified of the consequences should her father ever find out.

21

It was some months later. Following his burglary charge, Peter had been ordered by the magistrate to attend juvenile court. The date for his court appearance loomed ahead of them and, as it drew closer, Adele's anxiety was intensifying. Not only was she concerned about Peter, but she also dreaded her father's reaction when he found out what had happened. He wouldn't be pleased that they had kept it from him all this time.

Adele was also thinking about her forthcoming date with Gary Healey. Since the first time he'd asked her out, he hadn't given up. At first she'd continued to turn him down. Aside from having enough to think about, she was nervous about going out with him. She didn't have any experience with boys and the thought of going out with one of the local heart-throbs terrified her. He was older than Adele too and was now working, which made him seem sophisticated to her.

But when he continued to ask, she'd finally conceded. *What harm could it do?* she thought, and it might even provide a satisfying diversion in the midst of all her troubles. She was due to see him this evening for her first date, and the mere thought of it made her pulse quicken.

Evening soon arrived and Adele could feel butterflies in her stomach as she thought about meeting Gary. She was filled with self-doubt. Did he really want to go out with her? What if he'd changed his mind? What if it was a trick? She had visions of arriving at the park to find Gary and his mates laughing at her gullibility.

Despite her doubts, she decided she would go and meet him. It was too good an opportunity to pass up. After putting on her trendiest outfit of a navy blue skirt with a split up the front and a cream blouse, she was currently in the living room applying make-up in front of the cracked wall mirror. Her father had gone out for the evening and Peter wasn't at home either but her mother was.

'What are you up to?' asked Shirley, turning round to face Adele.

'I'm going out, just to see some friends.'

'Oh,' sighed Shirley with little enthusiasm. Then, after a moment's pause, she added, 'Don't be too late. You know what he's like.' She then turned back around without waiting for a response from Adele.

Adele soon finished applying a little blusher, mascara and lipstick, which enhanced her attractive features. After running a brush through her long, dark hair, she left the house, her heart beating rapidly as she walked in the direction of the local children's playground.

When Adele arrived, she gazed through the park railings but couldn't see any sign of Gary at first. She checked her watch. It was 7.05 p.m., and they had arranged to meet at seven. Then she spotted a group of lads and girls entering the park from the opposite direction. Her heart rate speeded up. Was it him and his friends? She had expected him to be alone.

For several seconds she stayed rooted to the spot, wondering what to do. Was it too late to walk away? But what if he'd seen her? She could approach the group of youths but she felt too nervous and awkward. Then her mind was made up for her as she heard Gary shout across the park.

'Adele! Over here.'

Oh no! It was too late. She couldn't back out now; he knew she was here.

'OK,' she shouted back, swinging open the park gate and taking tentative steps in their direction.

As she approached the group, she could hear them chatting and laughing, and she wondered whether she was the butt of the joke. A feeling of dread took over her; she could feel her stomach churning and the dryness of her mouth. She continued to approach.

When Adele drew nearer, she recognised the faces of some of them. They were cool kids; all of them. What was she doing here?

Adele drew even nearer. The chattering had died down. All eyes were now on her. Studying her. She felt an odd sensation, as though her entire body was being held under a microscope, and she suppressed a shudder.

'Here she is,' said Gary once Adele was within a few metres of them. A big grin lit up his face and Adele flashed a nervous smile in return.

'Hiya,' she said, gazing around the group.

As Gary's friends returned her smile and introduced themselves, a feeling of relief surged through her. They actually wanted to be friends. Gazing around the group, it was obvious they were in couples; two girls and two lads.

Gary took hold of her hand and led her away from the group, towards the children's playground. 'See you lot later,' he said, and Adele thought she saw him wink at the others.

She turned to see the two other couples head towards a clump of bushes.

'Where are they going?' she asked.

'Behind the trees, where no one can see them,' he laughed.

On hearing his words, Adele suddenly felt exposed and vulnerable. What had she let herself in for? Anything could happen. But then she thought about the fact that the playground was out in the open, and she relaxed.

'Come on, let's sit down,' said Gary, releasing her hand and pointing to a battered wooden bench that had one of the slats missing.

As she sat down next to him, Adele could feel her nervousness increasing. He took hold of her hand again. Then they began to talk. She felt awkward and self-conscious at first, especially as Gary seemed so self-assured. But he also seemed a friendly, likeable lad, and she eventually relaxed.

'You look nice,' he said.

Adele blushed under his scrutiny. 'Thanks,' she said, glad she'd made the effort. 'So do you,' she added, noticing his fashionable, straight-legged jeans.

He turned away again, looking ahead of him and kicking the right toe of his boots against the gravel. Then Adele noticed a noise coming from the bushes. It sounded like a woman moaning, the noise guttural and intense. A look of alarm crossed her face as she thought about the two couples hidden there.

'Do you think she's all right?' she asked Gary, concerned.

He let out a loud, raucous laugh, and it took a while for him to calm down. When he spoke, there was still a note of merriment in his voice.

'You're really sweet, aren't you?' he asked.

Adele looked confused for a moment until she realised what was happening in the bushes and her face flushed with embarrassment.

Gary smiled. 'How are things at home?' he asked.

'What d'you mean?'

'That time when I saw you with your face bashed, you looked really upset.'

'Oh that. It was just an accident.'

'OK,' he grinned. 'I'll believe you, thousands wouldn't.'

They didn't speak for a while until Gary broke the silence.

'It's the same for me, y'know. My old man can be handy with his fists at times.'

'I don't know what you're talking about,' sniffed Adele. 'I told you, I had an accident.' Then she swiftly changed the subject. 'Anyway, what sort of a day have you had?'

'OK, y'know. Every day's pretty much the same in my job. What about you? Have you had a good day?'

'Not bad. I got really good marks for my English lit essay.'

'Oh, that's good,' said Gary.

'Yeah, I was pleased,' Adele smiled. 'It was on *King Lear*.'

'Oh yeah?' asked Gary, but it was obvious to Adele that he didn't have a clue who King Lear was, nor did he seem particularly interested.

Within a few minutes they had exhausted all conversation and Adele felt awkward once more. To fill the silent void, Gary slipped his arm around Adele and turned towards her. She knew what was coming and she twisted her head till she was facing him. Their lips met.

But all excitement evaporated when Adele experienced Gary's kisses. Yuck! She tried to feign enthusiasm as he slobbered over her, pushing his tongue down her throat. His mouth produced so much moisture that spit drooled down her chin. She pulled back, noticing that his breath also emitted a faintly unpleasant odour.

They sat in silence for endless minutes. For Adele, all sign of nerves had now vanished. She tried to appear enthusiastic as they shared stilted conversation, interspersed by soggy kisses. But the fact was she was bored. His kind of conversation just didn't interest her. Football. Friends he'd been to school with. His boring job!

She gazed around the playground, desperately searching for an interesting topic of conversation but they didn't seem to have that much in common.

Adele was relieved when one of the other couples emerged from the clump of bushes and came to join them around the bench. Then she noticed that the youth had a look of satisfaction painted on his face and the girl had the rosy glow of someone who had just experienced the excitement of open-air sex. She shuffled uncomfortably at first but nobody else seemed bothered.

They chatted for some time and, although the couple asked her questions about mutual topics, she didn't feel part of their group. Gary and the couple were relaxed with each other, sharing their own in-jokes and banter, and Adele felt like an outsider.

Eventually it became late enough for Adele to insist on going home so Gary walked her to her street. She wouldn't let him come too near to the house in case her father spotted them together. When it was time for Gary to say goodbye, Adele braced herself for more soggy kisses, willing it to be over.

'Can I see you again?' he asked when he had finished. 'I get paid next Friday. I can take you to the pub.'

This time Adele didn't hesitate with her response. Despite the disappointment of the date, she wanted to be one of the group. She'd earn respect amongst her peers and perhaps prevent any more taunts and bullying from Peter's group of friends. It would also provide an escape from all her troubles and might even bring her closer to Peter once he found out she went around with the cool kids.

'Yes,' she said. 'Course you can.'

22

A few nights later Adele rushed home from school so she could get ready for her second date with Gary. Although the first date hadn't gone well, she was excited at the prospect of being part of his group and felt sure that she'd eventually fit in. She was so intent on preparing for her date that she was only half listening to her mother's conversation.

'I've been to see your grandma today,' said Shirley.

'Oh yeah?'

'Yeah, she finally saw the consultant this week. It's only taken them bloody months to send for her. That Mabel from next door took her.'

'What did he say?' asked Adele, who had been on her way out of the room but stopped when her mother mentioned the consultant.

'Not much, just that he's sending her for tests. So now we've got to play the bloody waiting game again.'

Adele didn't respond straightaway so her mother continued.

'I'll be glad when they've sorted it out. She's no better, y'know.'

'Isn't she?' asked Adele, hovering close to the doorway. Concern over her grandma was battling with her wish to go and get ready for her date. She was already running late. 'I'll try to go and see her over the weekend,' she uttered before rushing from the room.

Adele meant what she said. She'd been intending to visit her grandma for the last couple of weeks but never seemed to find the time. When she wasn't studying she was doing the bulk of the housework and cooking. Her mother had become increasingly despondent since Grandma had taken ill, which meant that more of the responsibility fell to Adele. The last time Adele went to see her grandma, she didn't stop long as she was in a rush to get back to her studies but it was evident then that her grandma was becoming frailer even if she insisted that there was nothing for Adele to worry about.

Aside from concerns over her grandma, Adele was also worried about Peter whose court case was drawing nearer. She dreaded what might happen to him after that. And now she had to squeeze in time for Gary, which was important to her. She couldn't wait to see the looks on the faces of some of the local kids when they saw her with him.

Adele quickly got changed and put on some make-up, and she was soon ready to go and meet Gary. Her father and Peter were out so she muttered a quick goodbye to her mother before dashing from the house.

She met Gary outside the Dog and Bone pub. As soon as she arrived he took hold of her hand and guided her inside the pub.

'What do you want to drink?' he asked.

'Half a lager and lime,' said Adele, feeling all grown-up now she had a boyfriend taking her to the pub and buying her alcohol.

They sat down in a corner of the pub and chatted for a few minutes about what they had been up to since their previous date. Adele made sure she left out all the troubles at home and focused instead on events at school. Gary displayed the same low level of interest as she did to his conversation about his boring job.

Once the conversation had ebbed away, Gary slipped his arm around her and they sat in uncomfortable silence for several minutes. Adele then reached for her drink, loosening his hold on her. She took a large swig and settled back in the seat, noticing that Gary had once again slipped his arm around her.

In the silence that followed, Adele gazed around the pub. It was crowded with groups of people who were sitting or standing and chatting amicably. The sound of Abba blared out from the jukebox, and she noticed Gary tapping his free hand on the table in rhythm to the music.

She turned and looked at him, ready to pass comment about their surroundings, just for the sake of something to say. But before she could speak, Gary moved in for a kiss. She pulled her head quickly away, 'No, not here,' she said. 'There's too many people about.'

Gary grinned and took a swig of his pint. 'We'll go to another pub when you've finished your drink,' he said.

Adele took the hint and they walked from the pub hand in hand. As soon as they were outside Gary began kissing her. His kisses were forceful as well as sloppy and she found herself being nudged into the shadow of the pub building.

She responded to his kisses at first. At least it was one way of passing time on the date. But Gary took this as a sign of encouragement. Within no time his sloppy kisses were accompanied by clumsy fumbles. Adele stiffened and quickly removed his hand from her breast.

'What's wrong?' he asked. 'Don't you want to?'

'No, not yet. Not here.'

'OK,' he said. 'Come on, let's go.'

She felt as though Gary was intent on living up to his reputation, as she'd heard that he'd been with lots of girls. But she didn't want to rush into anything. Adele wanted more from the relationship. He may have been cool, good-looking and up for a laugh, but she was starting to feel that he had little else going for him.

He led her by the hand again in the direction of another pub, which was only a couple of hundred metres away. The rest of the evening followed a similar pattern although they became more talkative once they had a few more drinks. Adele was careful not to get too drunk though. She didn't want to get carried away. She had enough troubles in her life without being saddled with an unwanted pregnancy.

23

It was the day of Peter's court appearance. As Tommy was unaware of what was happening, it was up to Adele to support her mother. She doubted that her father would have gone anyway, if his reaction to Peter's previous arrest was anything to go by.

They'd been sitting in the public gallery for hours with a few breaks in between, and Adele was becoming stiff. She had been watching the jury for their reactions while the witnesses were examined. Things didn't seem to be going too badly until Mrs Burton, the wife of the man killed during the burglary, was called to the stand.

She was a middle-aged woman who bore the face of someone who had aged drastically during the preceding months. Her complexion was sallow and there were deep lines on her forehead and around her eyes, which were red-rimmed. Her hair was streaked with grey.

Mrs Burton stepped up to the stand looking timid and frail with her shoulders hunched. She avoided eye contact with everyone in the courtroom as though she was having difficulty facing this traumatic event. Adele was disturbed by the woman's pitiful appearance, which reinforced the enormity of what Peter had been involved in. She glanced across at the jury and could see by their facial expressions that Mrs Burton had gained their sympathy even before she spoke.

After she had sworn on oath, the prosecution barrister said, 'Mrs Burton, I can see that this is going to be difficult for you but could you please tell the jury what you recall about the events of Saturday night on the twenty-fourth of March 1979?'

Mrs Burton cleared her throat. Then she looked up at the prosecution barrister with sad eyes and began speaking, her voice shaky. 'We'd been in bed a while when I was woken up,' she began. 'I could hear noises downstairs.' She paused and swallowed, her eyes now flitting nervously from the prosecutor to Peter, then back again.

'It's all right, Mrs Burton. Take your time,' said the prosecution barrister in a soothing tone.

After a moment's pause, Mrs Burton continued. 'I woke Harry up,' she said, her voice shaking as she uttered her husband's name. 'He could hear the noises as well.'

'Can you describe those noises for us, Mrs Burton?'

'Yes, it was like someone was moving around downstairs and I thought I heard faint voices at first, but then the voices stopped. Then I could hear something coming from the dining room; footsteps again and other sounds, like rummaging.' She paused again before carrying on. 'Harry went downstairs… and I heard the sound of someone running towards the front of the house and voices; Harry's and someone else's. I ran to the bedroom window to try to alert the neighbours.' She stopped then, her voice breaking.

'It's OK, Mrs Burton. Take as long as you need,' reassured the prosecutor.

'Then I saw *him* running away,' she sobbed, pointing a trembling finger in Peter's direction.

Adele felt a sinking sensation as though her heart had plummeted. There were audible gasps from the jury and public gallery followed by muttering. The judge called for order so Mrs Burton could continue giving her evidence.

'Yes, it was definitely him,' she cried. 'He came out of our front door and ran up the path then out of the gate.'

There was more muttering from the public gallery and Adele noticed one or two members of the jury look at each other and nod their heads. As she listened to the evidence given by Mrs Burton, and watched the jury's reactions, she could feel her muscles tensing. She gazed across at her mother for the umpteenth time; her expression said it all. Shirley's brow was furrowed with deep lines etched into her skin; lines that Adele hadn't noticed prior to Peter's arrest. The look on Shirley's face was one of intense concentration, her features strained as a tear escaped from the corner of her eye.

Then it was time for the defence barrister to cross-examine Mrs Burton, but Adele felt that his cross-examination didn't really add anything. The jury seemed more interested in the state of Mrs Burton who battled through tears to answer the questions put to her by the defence.

Eventually it was time for the jury to retire to consider the evidence before they decided on the verdict.

'Come on, Mam. Let's go and get a cuppa,' said Adele but Shirley appeared reluctant. 'Come on,' Adele repeated. 'You won't miss anything. It'll take a while yet and they'll let us know when the jury's back in.'

But the atmosphere in the court restaurant was just as tense. Adele could sense her mother's anxiety as she picked at her food, her shoulders hunched. Adele didn't feel hungry either. Her stomach was unsettled, and it was an effort to digest the meal.

Shirley broke the silence that hung over them. 'I'm dreading the verdict,' she said.

'I know,' said Adele, covering her mother's hand with her own. 'Try not to worry. It might not be too bad.' But they were empty words; an automatic response. They both knew, deep down, that the outcome wouldn't be good. Not when Peter had already received a caution. And if he was put inside, how would they face her father?

They were called back into the courtroom sooner than anticipated.

'That was bloody quick,' said Shirley, a puzzled look on her face. 'It's not taken 'em long. I wonder if that means they've found him guilty.'

Adele shrugged but she knew that the evidence against Peter was overwhelming. They filed back into the courtroom and Adele could feel her muscles tense once more as they awaited the verdict.

When the guilty verdict came in, Adele heard her mother's pronounced intake of breath amidst the mutterings of the people around them. Then a strange feeling came over her; a light-headedness, as though the room had shifted. It took her a while to steady herself so she could focus on the judge who was about to pronounce the sentence.

His preamble went on and on, and Adele wished he would get to the point. She was still feeling disorientated. His words seemed to hover in the air. Sounds without meaning. But when he gave the sentence, she snapped to.

Six months' detention.

Adele and her mother exchanged anguished looks. Even though they had half expected a custodial sentence, it still didn't lessen the blow. 'Six months,' Shirley muttered as though she hadn't heard the judge correctly.

Adele caught sight of her brother being led away, a scowl on his face. She and her mother watched as he left the courtroom. But Peter didn't meet their eyes; instead he kept his gaze fixed straight ahead.

For several seconds they remained seated, neither of them knowing what to do or say. Then the people around them began to leave their chairs. The woman next to them stood up and tutted as she waited to pass them.

'Come on, Mam. We'd better go,' said Adele.

Adele left the courtroom in a daze, her mother following reluctantly behind. Shirley's tears were already beginning to flow but Adele couldn't say anything to comfort her. She was too busy dealing with her own sorrow at the news, and soon her own eyes had misted over. She let her tears flow, releasing the pent-up tension that had gripped her during the court proceedings.

As they walked from Deansgate, through the Royal Exchange with its exclusive shops, then turned into Market Street and onto Piccadilly to catch their bus home, neither of them spoke. By now the initial shock had worn off and they had both stopped crying.

Adele voiced what was on both of their minds. 'My dad will go mad when he finds out,' she said.

Shirley sniffed and pulled her shoulders back, a resolute expression painted on her face. 'Leave him to me,' she said, surprising Adele. 'I'll tell him when you're in bed. He doesn't have to know it was your idea to keep it from him.'

'You sure?' asked Adele who was flabbergasted by her mother's uncharacteristic show of strength. She wondered fleetingly whether her mother still felt guilty, recalling the hiding that Tommy had dished out last time Peter was in trouble.

When they arrived home, Tommy was out. Adele surmised, with dread, that he had gone to the pub. As she and her mother waited for him to come home there was an air of anxious expectation between them.

Adele noticed her mother looking at the clock repeatedly while pretending to watch the TV. Despite her act of nonchalance, Shirley couldn't hide her true feelings from her daughter. Adele knew the signs; her mother's muscles were strained, her movements jittery and her speech flurried.

Eventually Shirley sent Adele up to bed.

'Are you sure you'll be all right, Mam?' asked Adele.

'Yes, don't worry,' Shirley said, although her facial expression said something else. 'Besides,' she sniffed, 'there's no point in him having a go at both of us, is there? Just remember, if he asks you tomorrow, I told you to keep it a secret and it was my idea.'

'OK,' said Adele.

Before she left the room, she glanced at the clock herself: 10.40 p.m. It wouldn't be long now till he was home. She got into bed and waited. But she soon fell asleep; the strain of the day had taken its toll and left her exhausted.

Shirley was glad when Adele went to bed. It was difficult to hide her true feelings from her daughter. Despite reassuring her that everything would be all right, she was dreading Tommy's return.

She continued to watch the clock, her mind unable to settle on anything else, until she heard him stumbling through the front door. She braced herself as he walked down the hall and flung open the living room door.

'You still up?' he said, his eyes gazing unsteadily at her. He'd obviously had a bit to drink.

'Yeah, I need to have a word with you,' she began, her voice trembling.

Tommy sniffed then flung off his coat and sat down. 'What about?' he asked.

'Our Peter.'

'Oh, fuckin' hell! What's he been up to now?'

Shirley could see that he was already getting annoyed and she wished she had left it until tomorrow when he had sobered up. But then he might have been more annoyed that she had left it even longer. Besides, she'd already started telling him so now she'd have to finish.

As she briefly outlined what had happened, she could see Tommy becoming more irate. His hands were bunched into fists and his nostrils flared.

Before she could finish, he cut in. 'You mean to tell me all this has been going on behind my fuckin' back?' he demanded.

'I didn't want to upset you,' Shirley muttered.

'You what? Are you fuckin' serious, woman?' he shouted as he got up from his chair and stepped towards her.

Knowing what was to come, Shirley bowed her head and put her hands in front to protect herself. Tommy grabbed her by the tops of her arms and dragged her out of her seat.

'Don't you think I'm upset now, you stupid fuckin' bitch?' he spat, pulling Shirley's hands away from her face.

She felt a sharp blow as he slapped her hard across the cheek.

'Don't Tommy, please. I can explain,' she begged.

'I've fuckin' heard enough!' he yelled, thumping her hard in the face.

Shirley raised her hands once more and stepped out of his reach. 'I was only trying to help,' she cried. 'You already had enough on your plate with you being out of work.'

'What the fuck would you know about work? You good for nothing, lazy bitch!' he shouted, stepping towards her again and pushing her to the floor. 'Get out of my fuckin' sight,' he said as he kicked her in the stomach then crossed the room again and plonked himself back into his armchair.

'Go on, fuck off out of it before I really lose my temper!' he shouted.

Shirley crawled to the living room door. Relieved that it was over with for now, she pushed herself to her feet and crept upstairs to bed, her flesh already feeling tender and sore.

Adele's sleep was sporadic and strange thoughts raced around in her head. She pictured the faces of the judge and members of the jury. Then they would fade and be replaced by others; her school teacher speaking to her. '*I want that essay handed in in six months. Six months, Adele. You've got six months,*' he kept repeating. And her classmates sat around her and gasped.

Then a disturbance broke her sleep. In her semi-conscious state she heard the sound of raised voices. Her heart was racing. She sat bolt upright listening for other sounds. Her father yelling. Her mother pleading. Then nothing. Still semi-conscious, she drifted back off to sleep. Back to the nightmares. Prisons. People scowling at her. And her mother in tears.

When Adele got up the following morning she felt drained. After getting herself ready for school, she went into the kitchen where her mother was seated at the dining table with her back to her, nursing a cup of tea, her shoulders hunched. To Adele's relief her father had already left the house on his way to the employment offices. It was his signing on day.

Adele walked over to the kitchen cabinet and turned to look at her mother. She was about to ask how her father had taken the news of Peter's incarceration but something about her mother's body language stopped her. Shirley had her head sunk low facing the table and her hands grasping a mug so tightly that her fingers were white. Her hair was luggy as though she hadn't bothered brushing it that morning.

'Mam?' said Adele, approaching her mother, but Shirley didn't look up. 'Mam, are you OK?'

When Shirley slowly raised her head, displaying a black eye and moist cheeks, Adele instinctively raised her hand to her mouth in alarm, drawing in a sharp breath.

'It's OK, it's done now,' said Shirley as a swollen tear rolled down her face and tumbled off her chin.

'Oh, Mam,' said Adele, striding over to her mother. She felt awkward at first, unsure what to do, but when she saw the pain in her mother's eyes, she took her in her arms.

Her pity intensified her mother's distress and Adele felt her crumble beneath her. Then Shirley's shoulders juddered as sorrow overwhelmed her. For a few seconds Adele stood stroking her mother's back while Shirley sobbed uncontrollably.

Once her mother had regained control of her emotions, she muttered, 'It's OK, Adele. You go and get ready for school, love. I'll be all right.'

Adele rushed through her breakfast, finding it difficult to eat with her distressed mother sitting across from her. She was absorbed by guilt. Why had she left her mother to face her father's wrath alone? She should have stayed downstairs and supported her.

When Adele had finished her breakfast, she asked her mother once again if she was all right. Eventually, she reluctantly left her mother and set off for school, her mind in turmoil at the prospect of what lay ahead now that her brother was incarcerated and her dad knew they had kept it from him.

24

A week had passed since Peter's court appearance. The family were sitting in their living room and a heated discussion was taking place between Tommy and Shirley. Adele was becoming exasperated as she listened to her parents deliberating over whether to go and see Peter in the detention centre where he was being kept.

'Are you coming with me to see him?' Shirley asked her husband. 'Only, my mam's not up to it.'

'You must be fuckin' joking!' said Tommy. 'There's no way you'd catch me in a place like that with all the scum of the earth.'

'But he is your son, Tommy,' Shirley pleaded. 'He needs someone to visit him. Imagine how he'd feel if he was the only lad that didn't have any visitors.'

'He should have thought of that before he went pissing about robbing people's houses. It'd serve him fuckin' right if no one went. I'm not goin' and that's that! If you're daft enough to go then that's up to you but you can go on yer bleedin' own.'

He walked out of the room, signifying that it was the end of the conversation as far as he was concerned. Adele looked at her mother whose eyes were welling up with tears.

'What am I gonna do?' asked Shirley. 'I can't go all that way on my own.'

Adele knew her mother was trying to guilt-trip her. 'It's OK, I'll come,' she sighed.

'Oh thanks, love. I'll get in touch with them and make the arrangements,' said Shirley.

Adele didn't fancy the prospect of visiting Peter in a detention centre. After all, her dad did have a point about the sort of people that went to those places and she didn't like to feel that her family had sunk so low. But he was her brother and her feelings towards him were uppermost in her mind. Although Adele didn't like what he had done, she still felt loyal towards him and wanted to support him as best she could. She knew that her mentally fragile mother wouldn't cope with the trip alone, and Adele hated to think of Peter being stuck there on his own.

The day of the visit was bitterly cold. Adele wrapped up well in preparation for the two-hour journey to the far side of Yorkshire. They were catching a coach from Chorlton Street Bus Station in Manchester and their journey started with a bus trip into the city centre.

By the time they arrived at Piccadilly, Shirley was already in a state. 'I don't fancy this coach journey,' she said. 'It's a bloody long way and in weather like this too. I bet the roads will be icy especially up in them hills.'

'It'll be fine,' Adele reassured her. 'If the weather's too bad for the trip, they'll cancel the coach. Stop worrying, Mam.'

'Oh, I don't know,' said Shirley. 'Maybe it isn't such a good idea to go all that way after all. It's a pity my mam's not with us. She'd know what to do. But her stomach's got even worse during the last few weeks. I'll be glad when them bloody doctors sort it out and she's back to normal. It's been dragging on for months now.'

Adele felt a pang of guilt at the mention of her grandma. She still hadn't found time to visit her and she vowed to herself that she would soon. But at the moment her mind was on other things. Her mother's constant fretting was starting to get on her nerves especially as she wasn't looking forward to the trip herself. 'Will you give over, Mam?' she snapped. 'I'm not going back home now! We're already on the way. Imagine how Peter will feel if we don't visit him; he'll be gutted.'

'OK, I suppose you're right,' Shirley muttered.

For some time Shirley stayed quiet but Adele could see that she had turned her anxiety in on herself. She subconsciously frowned and pursed her lips as worrying thoughts raced through her mind.

When they arrived at Chorlton Street Station, they crowded onto the coach, along with the other passengers, and found a seat near the front.

The first half of the journey was fine, and Adele settled back into her seat, looking at the view through the window as they made their way out of the city. Eventually they hit the countryside and the coach began to crawl up endless hills. Then they reached a steep incline and the coach rounded several bends as it made its laborious climb. Some of the bends were hairpin and Adele found herself tensing as the coach struggled to navigate them, heaving its bulky metal frame to make the sharp turns.

They had just passed through one such bend and straightened out again. As the coach teetered on the edge of the hill, Adele looked out of the window. Big mistake! She inhaled sharply when she caught sight of the view. They were now high up on a hill with a steep drop down and only a slim metal bumper separating the coach from the edge. She could also see the remains of snowfall dotted about.

Adele turned away from the window and kept her eyes focused on the interior of the coach instead. She took a peek at her mother, curious to see how she was coping with the journey. Her knuckles were white and her face had turned pale.

'Not long now before we get to the other side of this hill,' said Adele, placing her hand over her mother's.

'Ooh, I hope so. This is bloody awful,' said Shirley, her lips trembling.

'Keep your eyes shut and try not to think about it,' Adele advised.

As they progressed on their journey, Adele noticed that few passengers remained on the coach and most of them were what she would have termed rough-looking. At long last the coach drew to a stop at a small village. Adele recognised the name of the town from the instructions they had been sent, and wondered where the villagers lived as there didn't seem to be any houses for miles around.

'We're here, Mam,' she said to her mother who seemed oblivious as to their whereabouts.

Adele was glad she'd taken charge of the instructions they had been given, which had directions on how to get there. They descended from the coach and Adele pulled the instructions out of her bag.

'Right, according to this map, we've got to take that path to the right,' she said to her mother.

Several of the other passengers were already walking up the path, which was on a steep incline. Adele assumed they were going to the same place and she and her mother followed them. They continued walking for about ten minutes, skirting around frozen puddles, and negotiating banks of snow and large tufts of hardy grass.

'Bloody hell!' said Shirley. 'It must have been snowing up here... Are you sure we're going the right way?'

'Yeah, there's no other path on this map. Besides,' Adele said, nodding at the people who were several metres ahead of them, 'they're still here, and they seem to know where they're going.'

It was a few minutes later when they noticed a large building in the distance.

'That must be it,' said Adele.

'Jesus! It looks a bloody long way,' her mother complained, stopping to get her breath back as her loud gasps formed small clouds in the chilly air.

'We'll soon be there,' Adele encouraged. 'Come on. Let's keep going. We've got most of the journey over with.'

A few minutes later they arrived at the building which was a modern, red-brick, featureless structure. It was surrounded by a high fence topped with barbed wire, which had been wound into impenetrable coils. Adele felt saddened as the reality of Peter's situation hit her.

They went through the main entrance, a dense metal door, and were searched as soon as they stepped inside. The guards then directed them along a corridor and told them to take the door on the bottom left. Adele led the way and pushed open the door to a large room. A sterile smell hit her straightaway; like disinfectant but more potent.

The room reminded Adele of the school hall set out for

exams, with rows of tables laid out before them, except that the tables were larger and the set-up was different. On one side of each table sat a boy and the visitors were seated on the other side. Most of the tables were fully occupied but at a few of them the boys sat alone awaiting their visitors.

Adele scanned the room, looking for Peter. She spotted him just as he noticed her and smiled.

As Adele and her mother walked over to Peter, she was astonished to see many familiar faces. They all lived only a few streets away from her and were mostly from the rougher families. She felt ashamed to be among them, and felt a brief stab of resentment towards Peter for bringing her to this. Adele hoped that this experience wouldn't drive an even bigger wedge between them.

Two of the women, who had never previously bothered with her, were eager to say hello. She cringed as she returned their enthusiastic greeting. It was as though she had now become an unwilling member of an elite but corrupt society. Or perhaps they were taking pleasure in her family's demise. She wondered fleetingly why she hadn't seen them on the coach. Perhaps they had taken an earlier one or they may have even driven here; in a stolen car most likely.

When they reached Peter's table, Adele was shocked by his appearance. In the space of only a couple of weeks he already had a haunted look about him. His complexion was pallid and there was fear in his eyes. She tried to mask her shock; it wouldn't help to mention it. Instead, they talked in general terms about what it was like inside.

'How are you finding it?' asked Shirley.

'All right, yeah.'

'Are the other lads all right with you?'

'Yeah, course. I already know some of 'em. Hey, you know that Vinnie off our estate?'

'Yeah,' said Adele, picturing a small, sly-looking boy who had always been hostile towards her.

'Well, you'll never guess what he's in for?' Peter asked, lowering his voice.

'Go on, tell us,' said Adele.

'He thumped a teacher,' he said. When Adele and her mother stared at him open-mouthed, he continued. 'I know, I was surprised. He's a good lad, always up for a laugh and that... but she was giving him a hard time.'

Adele was shocked by the act of thumping a teacher rather than by the person who had committed it, but she held her tongue. She was concerned though. Why did Peter think that these people were good when they clearly weren't?

For the remainder of their visit, Peter seemed to delight in telling them tales about the crimes some of the inmates had committed, who were the hard boys and who were the ones that weren't to be trusted. In spite of his haunted look, he seemed to be enjoying the camaraderie with the other boys. It was as though he felt he had arrived; he was now truly one of them. The idea sickened Adele. She couldn't understand why he thought it was OK to commit crime. But she didn't say anything. Time with him was at a premium and she didn't want to spend it arguing.

Adele noticed a putrid odour coming from the family sitting at the next table. Even the powerful sterile smell in the room didn't mask it. She was glad when Peter asked for chocolate from the vending machine, and a cup of tea, so she could escape the cloying smell for a short while.

When Adele returned from the vending machine, Peter chomped away at the chocolate, unperturbed by the vile stench around them. She guessed it was his first taste of chocolate since he had been sent down.

Adele was surprised by how quickly Peter seemed to have adapted to life on the inside. Apart from the horrible smell, he didn't seem fazed by the state of the people around him or the faults of his fellow inmates either. She had an unsettling feeling, though, that his overenthusiastic narrations were hiding a truth that he wasn't willing to share.

It was soon time to go. Despite her feelings about Peter being in this place and the sort of people he was mixing with, Adele was sad to say goodbye. It didn't feel right leaving him there. As a child she had always stood up for him but now she was powerless to help him out of the mess he had got himself into.

'Well, at least we know he's all right,' said Shirley, oblivious to Peter's troubled appearance as she dabbed at her tear-stained face.

Again Adele kept quiet. Why worry her mother unnecessarily? If Peter was having problems, there was nothing they could do about it.

Now that the visit was over Shirley seemed relieved and, on the way out, she struck up conversation with a woman she knew from their local area. A woman who had several unruly kids in tow. Adele didn't share her mother's delight on finding out that the woman was also getting the coach back to Manchester.

Great! thought Adele. *As if the journey here wasn't bad enough.*

They had just left Peter in that awful place. Who knew what kind of hell he was going through? And now her mother was treating it like a pleasure trip.

25

Once Peter had watched his mother and sister leave the room, his mask slipped. Now it was back to reality. No more putting on an act.

'Come on, Robinson. Your visitors have gone now. Get back to your cell!' ordered a burly guard.

Peter left the room reluctantly, his eyes downcast. Once they were out of view of the visitors, another set of guards took control. The next one to approach him wasn't quite as polite.

'You lad, stop dragging your feet. Get a bloody move on!' he shouted, cuffing Peter sharply round the back of the head.

Not wanting to upset one of the centre's meanest guards, Peter did as he was told. Slaps and jabs from some of the guards were a daily occurrence. But if you didn't toe the line things could get much worse. He'd heard about the beatings and seen evidence of it on the bruised and swollen faces of some of the other inmates. And even if you did toe the line, you sometimes couldn't escape some of the other forms of abuse that took place at the centre.

For Peter the other inmates weren't a problem. He had the advantage of already knowing many of them from his local area. They'd put him in the picture straightaway so he soon learnt the pecking order. And as long as you respected that, there wasn't a problem. Most of the lads here were OK. Sure, there were a couple of arseholes but he tried his best to avoid them.

Peter's problem lay with the guards. Apart from the physical abuse, there was verbal abuse too. Guards would constantly try to rile the inmates by putting them down. Peter had become used to being told, 'You're no fuckin' good; that's why you're here,' and being referred to as 'council estate scum'.

His friends had warned him from the outset not to divulge anything that happened on the inside. 'You're wasting your time,' they said. 'No one will believe a word you say, and they'll just make things harder for you.'

But for him, it wasn't just about the daily beatings and name-calling. No, his particular nightmare began after the lights went out. Officer Patterson had a penchant for young boys and he'd chosen Peter as his latest victim.

The first time it happened, Peter wasn't expecting it. Patterson called at his cell one night just as Peter was nodding off to sleep.

'Robinson, I want you for a special job,' said Patterson.

'At this time?' asked Peter.

'Less of your lip! Just do as you're told.'

Peter jumped out of bed and put his clothes on as quickly as he could while Patterson watched. He felt uneasy having to get changed in front of the guard. It was something he wasn't used to.

'Come on, hurry up! You don't need your shoes.'

Peter had thought that was a bit strange but he did as he was told.

'You're for it now,' his cellmate whispered, stifling a chuckle as Peter left the cell. He wondered what he'd done to get into trouble.

Peter had noticed Patterson that day. He was a big, lumbering guard with greasy hair and rotten teeth. At first Peter had felt unnerved at the way Patterson looked at him, but he'd later shrugged it off. Nobody had warned him about Patterson so he had no reason to suspect anything untoward.

The guard led him along the corridor, past rows of cells then down some stairs. Peter felt a chill as his bare feet made contact with the cold metal steps.

'Where are we going?' he asked.

'Never you mind! We're nearly there now,' said Patterson.

When they'd reached the end of another corridor, they arrived at a locked, steel door. Patterson pulled at the keys that were hanging from his belt. They jangled as he sorted through them. When he had found the right one, he turned the lock and led Peter into another corridor.

Immediately to the left of them was another locked door. Patterson soon found the key to this one and pushed Peter inside. It was a storeroom. There was nothing in there; just brooms, a bucket, some cleaning implements. And one chair.

Peter turned round. Patterson was locking the door again. He swung around, staring lasciviously at Peter. Realisation hit Peter like a thunderbolt. Patterson was a nonce!

He didn't wait to see what Patterson was going to do. No fuckin' way! Peter charged at him, throwing ineffectual punches. He tried to get to the bunch of keys so he could unlock the door and make his escape. But Patterson was too strong. Within seconds he had overpowered Peter and had him bent over the back of the chair with his trousers down.

It's often said that when you dread something, the anticipation is worse than the event. Peter wished that applied in this case. But nothing could have prepared him for what was about to happen. As Patterson penetrated him, Peter felt like a ball of flame was burning through his delicate insides. He couldn't even cry out with the extreme pain. Patterson had already thought of that. He'd gagged him.

As soon as Patterson had finished, he zipped up his trousers. 'Get yer clothes back on!' he ordered.

Peter grabbed at them and pulled them on quickly, tears of humiliation stinging his eyes as Patterson leered at his exposed body.

'Next time, don't try fuckin' fighting me!' said Patterson.

He led Peter back to his cell where his fellow inmate was still awake.

'Haha, are you Patterson's new bum boy?' he laughed.

Peter felt his humiliation intensify. He was too upset to even argue so he got quietly into bed. Not wanting to encourage more ridicule from his cellmate, Peter buried his face in his pillow to stifle his sobs. He continued sobbing until the early hours.

Joyce was having a bad day. Over the past few months the pains in her stomach had become progressively worse. She hadn't eaten anything since breakfast, which was half a piece of toast swallowed down with a cup of tea. She'd had two more cups of tea since then but each one had been a struggle to make. When she stood up, the pains seemed even more intense.

The doctor had given her stronger painkillers to keep her going while they waited for the outcome of the tests she'd had at the hospital. But even the strong painkillers didn't seem to be working anymore. She knew deep down that this was something serious. She had her suspicions but she daren't voice them to Shirley. Her daughter struggled to get through the day as it was. But Joyce was beyond helping her. Now all she wanted was for the pain to stop.

Joyce had just woken up from a nap in the chair and taken two more of her tablets. She needed to go to the loo but dreaded getting up knowing the pains would grip her as soon as she got out of her chair. So she gave it ten minutes for the painkillers to take effect. Then, deciding she couldn't wait any longer, she struggled to stand up.

As Joyce shuffled across the room, the pain became unbearable. She grasped her stomach and doubled over as intense wave after wave of red-hot torture pierced her insides. It wasn't easing and she needed the loo desperately. Joyce straightened up and took a deep breath, trying to stay in control.

By now her legs had become weak and she felt light-headed. As she tried to put a step forward, her legs gave way beneath her. Joyce tumbled to the floor. She knew she wouldn't make it to the bathroom and she couldn't wait any longer. So she relieved herself where she lay.

When the throbbing eased a little she tried to stand. But as she got to her knees a crippling pain seared through her and she passed out.

Joyce was out for a few minutes. When she came to, she noticed the dampness and the constant ache in her stomach. This time there was no point trying to get up. Instead, she dragged herself along the floor, taking a while to reach the wall separating her home from that of Mabel Boyson.

Joyce grabbed a book from the bottom shelf of the bookcase and used it to bang on the wall as hard as she could. 'Mabel!' she shouted, at the top of her voice. 'Help me!' Then another excruciating wave of pain came over her and Joyce passed out again.

26

'Do you want to go for something to eat in that pub?' Adele asked her mother, out of earshot of the woman with the unruly kids. She hoped that by going to the pub they could shake them off.

'Ooh yeah. That sounds like a good idea,' said Shirley. 'I could do with a bloody drink before we get on that coach again. My nerves are shot and I've got no more tablets with me.'

Adele was about to heave a sigh of relief when her mother called out to her new friend, 'Do you hear that, Bev? We're going for a drink and something to eat in that pub near the coach stop. Do you fancy it?'

'Sounds good to me,' said Bev whose children were growing excited at the prospect of eating out.

Sounds bad to me, thought Adele but she kept her thoughts to herself. Adele followed her mother and Bev into the pub and listened to their chatter.

'How's your Peter finding it?' asked Bev.

'All right, you know.'

'Our Mark says the food's better than school dinners.'

'Yeah, Peter likes it too. Maybe he's not so badly off in there.'

'Nah, Mark seems to cope all right,' said Bev. 'It's his second time.'

'Is it?' asked Shirley.

'Yeah.' Bev sniffed before continuing. 'I hoped he'd learnt his lesson last time, but still, it's one less mouth to feed, I suppose. Bloody awful trip though.'

'You can say that again.'

Adele couldn't believe what she was hearing. Bev's son was locked up for God knows what, and all she was bothered about was having one less mouth to feed. She was also annoyed at her mother who seemed to accept that this was Peter's lot in life. Why wasn't she more concerned about the path he was taking? Unwilling to listen to any more of their chatter, Adele left them at the bar and found a table.

While Adele was sitting at the table, she looked around her. There wasn't one friendly face in the place. The hostility was coming in droves as they stared down at their meals, tutted and whispered among themselves. The locals seemed to resent outsiders. But then Adele realised that it was probably because they'd come from the detention centre and she felt herself blush with shame.

Adele couldn't wait to get out of the place although she wasn't looking forward to the journey. Bev's kids had behaved badly enough in the pub so she dreaded to think what they would be like cooped up on a coach for almost two hours.

She was correct in her assumptions. The children sat behind her throughout the journey and entertained themselves by pulling Adele's hair and kicking her seat. Shirley and Bev, who were half-cut from their trip to the pub, ignored their antics despite Adele turning round several times and giving them a stern look.

By the time they arrived in Manchester, Adele was seething. As they got off the coach she ignored Bev who went off in another direction with her kids, saying she had some errands to do.

'That wasn't very nice, Adele,' said Shirley as they made their way to the bus stop in Piccadilly.

'Didn't you see what they were doing?' Adele demanded. 'They didn't stop kicking my seat and pulling my hair. And every time I turned round they just sat there laughing at me.'

'They're only kids,' said Shirley. 'They don't mean any harm.'

'I don't care. She should have stopped them!'

Shirley didn't reply. The alcohol was now wearing off and she didn't have any fight in her. They remained silent as they caught the bus home. By the time they had finished their bus journey, and made the short walk from the bus stop to the house, Adele had calmed down.

Shirley, on the other hand, appeared anxious now that she was sobering up. Adele noticed how her mother seemed to be in a rush to get home and she guessed it was because she wanted to take one of her tablets. They turned into their street and, as they approached home, they noticed a police car parked outside.

'Jesus!' said Shirley. 'What the bloody hell's Tommy been up to now? As if I haven't got enough worry with our Peter.'

Adele could feel her heart plummet. She hoped her father hadn't been fighting again. The day had been stressful enough as it was. They rushed to their house, anxious to find out what was happening. Adele hoped desperately that it wasn't bad news.

Shirley nodded towards the police car, 'Knock on the window and ask what they want while I get inside the house, Adele,' she said.

She did as her mother asked and the policeman rolled down the window. 'You must be Miss Robinson,' he said.

'Yes, I am.'

He nodded at Shirley's back, 'Is that your mother?'

'Yes.'

'Mind if we come inside? We need to have a word with your mother.'

'N-no,' said Adele, becoming anxious.

The two policemen followed Adele indoors. As she stepped into the living room, her mother quickly put the cap back on her bottle of pills and put it away. There was no sign of Adele's father and she dreaded what was coming next.

'They want a word with you, Mam,' said Adele, her heart pounding.

Shirley stared at the two policemen, an expression of horror on her face.

'Mind if we sit down?' asked the first policeman.

'No, go on,' said Shirley, pointing her hand towards the sofa.

'You may want to sit down too.'

Adele shared her mother's horror. Her pulse rate increased and she swallowed nervously. She sat on the arm of her mother's seat, anticipating that, whatever the news was, Shirley would need her support.

'Are you the daughter of Mrs Joyce Majors?' asked the officer.

No! Not Grandma, no. Please no! Adele's brain screamed, but she sat silently waiting for the words.

'I'm afraid...'

Before he could finish, Shirley let out a piercing shriek. 'No!' Then she began babbling, 'Not Mam. Oh my God! Please say she's all right.'

'Shhh,' said Adele, placing her hand on her mother's shoulder.

Even the policeman seemed to tense and his voice shook as he uttered the words, 'I, I'm afraid I have to report your mother's death. She died at home earlier today.'

Adele could feel her own tears flood her eyes but her first concern was for her mother. Shirley had buried her head in her lap, covering her eyes with her hands, which were trembling and causing her head to shudder from side to side. She let out an agonising yelp followed by uncontrolled sobbing. Adele patted her on the back as her own tears flowed. Through misty eyes she saw the two officers shuffle uneasily in their seats, their discomfort evident.

'Perhaps there's something we can do to help?' asked the second officer. 'A hot drink perhaps? Or is there a neighbour who could call round?'

Shirley was incapable of responding. Her loud sobbing continued. She was working herself up into a frenzy and Adele felt helpless. She didn't know what to do. At seventeen she felt lost; the burden of responsibility overwhelming her. She just wanted the police officers gone. It was a private moment. And they were strangers. She didn't want them to witness their heartbreak.

Adele nodded her head just to get rid of them and watched them slip out through the door. Within minutes a procession of neighbours crowded the house. Adele guessed they must have already been aware of imminent bad news when they saw the police car. And then they heard her mother's screams.

They rushed about the house, each trying to offer help and comfort in any way she could. Two of them were trying to calm Adele's mother down. Another had dashed through to the kitchen to put the kettle on. Their concerns were for their friend and neighbour.

Adele cried silent tears as she watched the scene unfold before her.

Nobody seemed to notice her tears, but she didn't want them to. She needed to be alone. She needed to release all the sorrow of the day. So she went to her room, flung herself on her bed and sobbed desperately for the woman who had meant everything to her.

It was Adele's first experience of losing someone close, and it would stay with her for the rest of her life.

27

It was a few weeks later. The neighbours had helped to organise the funeral. Shirley had been incapable of organising anything and Tommy didn't want to get involved so Adele let them get on with it. They seemed to know what to do whereas Adele didn't have a clue. Aside from that, she was still trying to come to terms with her own grief.

The house was quiet. Shirley had gone to visit one of the neighbours and Tommy was out. As Adele tried to focus on her homework the silence engulfed her and she found her mind wandering. Why did it have to happen to her grandma? She was only fifty-nine. It was too young! She should have had many more years with her. Instead she'd been snatched away. It wasn't fair!

Apart from being overwhelmed with sorrow, Adele felt guilt and regret. Was there more she could have done? Could she have visited her grandma more instead of being selfish and focusing on her own life? Her grandma had needed her. She could have found the time to visit more if she'd really tried.

Her eyes flooded with tears of despair. A teardrop slid off

her cheek and landed on her exercise book, smudging the sentence she had just written. But she didn't care; she just wanted her grandma back. To hell with school! To hell with everything!

Her grandma had always been there for her and now there was nobody to offer support. Peter was still inside and visits to him only made her feel worse. He was paler each time they went and Adele was convinced there was something he wasn't telling her. But she daren't ask. She didn't know if she could handle it at the moment.

She put her pen down and looked up from her exercise book, gazing around the shabby room. It was depressing! Stained carpet. Scratched, out-of-date furniture layered with dust. Broken ornaments covered in grime. Light bulbs dotted with fly faeces. And the stench! The all-pervading stench that was always there.

Since Grandma Joyce had passed away, her mother's illness had become even worse. Shirley was now taking so many tablets that she didn't rise from bed till lunchtime. And when she got out of bed she moved around slowly in a zombified, drugged-up state. Any energy she had was usually spent visiting the neighbours to enlist their support, as she didn't get any from their father.

The only housework or cooking that was done was carried out by Adele. But with the pressure of her studies, she struggled to keep up. It was all too much to handle. As the negative thoughts invaded her brain, she decided to call it a day. She couldn't do it anymore! She would drop out of school and sign on the dole.

Adele closed her eyes to block out her dismal surroundings. She sat back in the chair, resigning herself to her fate. The fight had left her.

Then a picture formed inside her mind. It was Grandma Joyce. Lifelike. Her feisty persona, unmistakable. Ready to speak; her face forming a scowl in that distinct way she had when she was about to give you a good telling-off. She looked the way she used to look before her illness got the better of her. Adele visualised her speaking.

'Now you listen to me, young lady! What's all this about you packing in your studies? Not bloody likely! Do you want to end up on the dole for the rest of your bloody life? Like all those silly little cows with a load of kids round their ankles and not a father in sight? You keep on working hard and make a better life for yourself. Do you hear me?'

Adele broke out of her reverie and continued to glance around the room, a small sad smile now forming on her face. Grandma Joyce was still here! In her mind. In her memories.

And no one could take that away.

This time, as Adele glanced around she felt invigorated and more positive. Was this how she wanted to spend the rest of her life? In this pit of despair? No! In that moment she realised that she owed it to herself, and to the memory of her grandma, to try her damnedest to do well at school. She dried her tears, went for a walk to clear her mind then returned to her studies.

It was still a struggle, but the memory of Grandma Joyce pushed her on. She would help her. Every time she felt low, all she needed to do was shut her eyes and picture her there.

She managed to get through some of her homework before her mother returned home and demanded her attention. Shirley was feeling low again. She needed to talk.

'The neighbours have been good, Adele. But nobody knows how it really feels. You're the only one who understands because we're going through it together,' she sniffed, dabbing her eyes with a tissue.

'I know, Mam,' she said, walking over to her mother and putting her arms around her.

Shirley's sobbing brought renewed tears to Adele's eyes and for a few minutes they stood there embracing each other and sharing their sorrow. Then Tommy returned home. Adele instinctively broke away from her mother and sat back down at the table where she had been writing in her exercise book. She lowered her head to hide her tears from her father but Shirley was beyond disguising her grief.

'Jesus Christ, not again!' he said. 'It's about bleedin' time you pulled yourself together, Shirley. It's been weeks now, and you're still scriking.'

Shirley dabbed at her eyes again and attempted to stifle her sobs.

'Anyway,' continued Tommy. 'I've got some good news that should cheer you up.'

He waited for a response but Shirley just stared at him vacantly.

'Did you hear me? I've got some good news... I've got a job, I start Monday.'

'Oh, that's good,' said Shirley but her voice lacked enthusiasm, which prompted an angry outburst from Tommy.

'Suit your fuckin' self!' he said. 'I thought you'd be over the fuckin' moon about it, not stood there with a miserable bleedin' face on yer.'

'I am,' said Shirley with a shaky voice. 'I'm really pleased for you, Tommy,' she added, her tone pleading.

'Well I'm off to fuckin' celebrate anyway. If you want to stay here scriking that's up to you.' He turned to walk back out of the door but left them with a few parting words, 'She was a moaning old bitch anyway.'

Adele was incensed. 'Did you hear what he just said about Grandma?' she asked.

'Don't let it bother you, Adele,' said Shirley. 'The two of them never saw eye to eye.'

'Don't make excuses for him, Mam! It's disgusting to speak like that about someone who's dead and can't defend themselves.' Her voice cracked as she spoke.

'I know, Adele,' Shirley sobbed.

'I'm going after him,' said Adele. 'He's not getting away with that!'

'No!' shouted Shirley, blocking Adele as she tried to get to the door. 'You can't. It'll only make matters worse if you antagonise him.'

'I don't care! I'm sick of him. I hate him! Why do you put up with it? Why don't you just leave him?' shouted Adele, backing into the room when she realised the futility of her actions.

Tommy's words had got to her and she was becoming more annoyed. As her heartbeat quickened and the blood pumped around her body, she could feel a mounting pressure inside her head. Her anger was all-consuming, an accumulation of all the sorrow of the last few weeks spurred on by a lifetime of stress and unhappiness. It was driving her, urging her to find the answers.

'I couldn't manage on my own, love,' said Shirley, half-heartedly. 'I've made my bed and now I just have to lie in it.'

Her apathy made Adele even angrier. 'But you don't!' she yelled. 'Why is he like that? Has he always been like that?'

'Pretty much, yeah.'

'Then why did you marry him?' she demanded.

Shirley looked away but Adele pressed on, turning her mother to face her. 'Why, Mam? Why would you marry someone like that?'

'I didn't have a choice,' Shirley muttered.

'What?' Adele stared back at her mother as the realisation slowly dawned on her. 'You mean... you had to get married?'

'Yes, love. I was expecting,' Shirley admitted, her face flushing with shame. 'Then, before I knew it, I was pregnant again with our Peter.' Adele was too flabbergasted to respond. 'I'm sorry, love,' said Shirley. 'That's how it was in them days. If you were expecting a baby you had to get married. And that was that.'

'And he didn't want to?'

'It was never really discussed. We knew what was expected of us, and the arrangements were made as soon as possible before I was showing.'

'No wonder he hates the sight of me and our Peter! He never wanted us, did he?'

'Come on, love. Don't go getting upset. What's done is done.'

'No, it isn't!' Adele screamed. 'It all makes sense now. He hates us! He never wanted us.'

Shirley reached out to touch Adele's arm but she pushed her hand away. 'Don't! Don't think you can get round me and make it right. You should never have married him!' She rushed from the room with tears streaming down her face. 'Leave me alone!' she shouted before slamming the door and dashing up to her bedroom. Anger still coursed through her body and she swiped her books off the shelf, throwing them at the wall as she sought an outlet for her aggression. It was some time later that she finally calmed down and started to face the brutal truth.

★

Adele was still in turmoil over her mother's revelation and found it even more difficult to relate to her father. Whenever he entered the room, she left. She didn't want to be near him let alone converse with him.

Sorrow over her grandmother was now suffused with feelings of rejection as well as worry about Peter. As she walked up the street painful thoughts crowded her mind once again. She found it hard to focus on her forthcoming arrangements to meet Gary and she found herself wandering aimlessly until she realised she had passed their meeting place.

Adele turned around and rushed to join him outside the park. She didn't really want to be there but he'd been pestering to see her again for weeks. And, with her grandma gone, she craved attention. She wanted to feel that somebody was interested in her. So, finally, she agreed to meet up, telling herself that her negative feelings towards him were because of her grief.

Maybe a date with Gary would cheer her up, she thought. But as soon as she saw him, she realised her mistake. She was too preoccupied to make the effort with small talk. And she soon became bored with him. His sloppy kisses repulsed her and his wandering hands irritated her.

As she slapped his hand away for the second time, Gary said, 'Aww come on, Adele. What's wrong with you? Why won't you let me?'

'Because I don't want to!' she snapped.

'But we've been seeing each other for a bit now. Why won't you let me? Are you frigid or summat?'

'No, I'm not. I just don't want to, so leave me alone and keep your bloody hands to yourself!' she cried.

'OK, snapper!' said Gary.

They sat on a park bench for several minutes, neither of them speaking, the atmosphere between them charged. Adele was tempted to walk away but she'd already upset him and didn't want to do more damage. She was used to seeing the bad side of an angry man and didn't know how Gary would react if she upset him further. He saved her the trouble when he stood up and announced, 'I'm going. You're a waste of time!'

Hurt that he was walking away from her instead, she reacted instinctively. 'Go on then, get lost!' she said. 'You're boring anyway.'

'I'm boring? Huh, what about you? All you ever do is study and talk about your dead gran. You need to get a life, Adele.'

'Don't you dare mention my grandma!' shouted Adele who was becoming irate.

'Fuck off!' he shouted back. 'My mates were right. You are a stuck-up little bitch who thinks she's too good for everyone. I don't know why I went out with you in the first place.'

By now he was several metres away and Adele was too upset to continue the argument. Instead she sat and cried as she watched him walk away. The break-up made her feel even more inadequate. And so rejected! She'd been dumped by her boyfriend. Her brother was drifting away. Their father had never wanted her or Peter. Their mother was too caught up in her own grief to notice her. And the one person who had really cared, her grandma, was gone forever.

Adele stayed in the park for several minutes sobbing to herself and wondering how she would cope with a life devoid of love.

28

Adele didn't stay angry with her mother for long. With her grandma gone and Peter locked away, it seemed like her mother was the only person she had left. Over the coming months she gradually came to terms with the decision her parents had made all those years ago. She still didn't like it but there wasn't much she could do.

And what alternative was there? If her mother had attempted to bring Adele up alone, with no money, would life have been even harder? And if her mother had made a different decision, Adele might not even be here.

Her anger towards her mother was replaced by pity; it must have been dreadful to have been stuck with a man who disrespected you and showed you nothing but contempt. To realise that this was how the rest of your life was going to be. At least Adele could dream of a way of escape, but her mother didn't even have that.

Where her father was concerned, Adele felt no pity. Despite her situation, Shirley still displayed some affection towards her children but with Tommy there was nothing. The notion that he had never wanted her and Peter festered in Adele's mind. Each time he displayed contempt and anger towards her and her mother, he drove an even bigger wedge between himself and his daughter. Adele hated him and couldn't wait to get away.

Despite all this, she found a way to cope. Adele's burden had been eased a little since her father had returned to work. Most evenings he went for a drink straight from work so he wasn't back until late. That made it easier for Adele to avoid him most of the time. But she could still hear the rows, which sometimes went on until the early hours and made it difficult for Adele to sleep.

The time for Adele's exams was fast approaching. She hadn't found it easy to continue her studies but she had persevered, fuelled by an inner strength. Whenever things got tough she closed her eyes and pictured her grandma. The memories gave her sustenance and enabled her to get through.

Adele was currently sitting in the sixth form unit after school. She paused in her writing and looked up at the calendar. It was only a little over two weeks until her first exam. But before that, in only a week's time, she had something else to face. Peter was due home.

She was looking forward to having her brother back but there was also a feeling of dread that sat at the pit of her stomach; a fear that things would escalate. Peter would perhaps get into more trouble, and there was bound to be more conflict between Peter and her father.

Adele also wondered how Peter's time inside would affect their relationship. Would he drift further away? She hoped not. Adele missed the closeness they had once shared and desperately hoped that he would return to her one day.

When Peter came home from the detention centre, she and her mother welcomed him heartily. They gave him something to eat and drink and Adele helped him put his clothes away in his room.

'Good to be home, sis,' he said.

Adele smiled on spotting a glimmer of his old self. 'It's nice to have you home,' she replied. 'I hope it wasn't too bad for you.'

'Nah,' he said. 'It was all right really.' Adele noticed his lip tremble slightly. Despite his bravado she could tell that things couldn't have been easy for him in the detention centre.

'I wish you hadn't been in there when Grandma died.'

'Me too,' he said. 'Can't wait to get in my own bed,' he added, changing the subject as he patted his bed.

They went back downstairs and joined their mother in the kitchen. For a while they chatted amicably, catching up with local gossip and finding out a little more about Peter's time inside. Adele was happy to have him back and for a short time all seemed fine. Then Tommy came home.

'What the fuck's he doing here?' he demanded.

Any hope that he had forgiven Peter's misdemeanours were destroyed by those few words. Their conversation ceased and they all stared silently at Tommy, waiting for the scene to unfold.

'You heard me. What's he doing here? You didn't fuckin' tell me he was due out!' he said to Shirley.

'I thought I had, sorry,' Shirley mumbled.

'It doesn't make any fuckin' difference anyway. I don't want him here!'

'Please, Tommy,' Shirley pleaded. 'He's got nowhere else to go.'

'I don't give a shit! I don't want the thieving little bastard here,' he said. Then he turned to Peter. 'You heard! You're nothing but a little shithouse and your mates are even worse. Murdering bastards! Go and live with them. That's all you're fit for.'

'I'm not going anywhere!' said Peter. 'I live here.'

Peter's words struck Adele. She was inwardly pleading with him to go silently. To save them from Tommy's wrath. But it was too late.

'You what?' shouted Tommy.

Without waiting for a reply, he strode across to Peter and struck him across the face. Peter tried to fight back but Tommy overpowered him, landing a few more punches on his face and torso. The smacking sound of Tommy's heavy punches impacting with Peter's flesh made Adele wince. A rumble of fear shot through her insides. Gripped by panic she hovered on the spot, wanting to help Peter but numbed with terror.

Adele looked across at her mother who remained motionless. Her eyes pleaded with Shirley to do something. But she did nothing. She was leaving it up to Adele again.

Before Adele could decide what to do, Tommy grabbed hold of Peter under his arms and shouted, 'You're fuckin' going and that's that!' He then hauled Peter out of the back door and slid the bolt.

Outside Adele could hear Peter hammering on the back door and begging to be let back in.

Tommy pointed at Shirley and Adele in turn, 'Don't you fuckin' dare let him back in!' he warned. 'And tell him, if he doesn't fuckin' shut it I'll go out there and give him the hiding of his fuckin' life!'

Shirley went to the back door and pleaded with Peter to go silently while Tommy ate his tea, banging his cutlery against the plate each time he took a forkful.

'What the fuck are you waiting for?' he asked Adele who was standing in the kitchen, unsure what to do next.

She ran up to her room, wary of inciting her father even more. Adele sat on her bed, wringing her sweaty hands and waiting for her heartbeat to return to normal. The sound of Peter pleading outside tore at her heart but she couldn't do anything to help.

When she could no longer hear Peter, she went to the window and saw him make his way down the back passageway. She waved, trying to draw his attention but he didn't see her.

Adele wanted to follow Peter but she was frightened of her father's reaction. So she stayed where she was and watched him walk away. He had been back in her life for little more than two hours. Adele felt that any hopes of repairing their damaged relationship were now shattered. He would never come back home. And how could she visit him? She didn't even know where he'd gone. She'd watched her father throw him out and done nothing to help.

While Peter had been at home, it seemed as though they had a chance of becoming close once more. But then her father had to go and spoil everything. She hoped Peter wouldn't feel betrayed by her. But what if he did? She worried that things between them might never be the same again.

29

It was two days since Peter's father had turned him away. He was homeless and hungry. But David had just taught him a new way to make money. It was quick and easy. And Peter was desperate. Although he had felt betrayed when David gave his and Alan's names to the police a few months previously, he had soon forgiven him. After all, David had come to his aid when he needed it.

They were currently hanging around in the gloom of late evening, looking out for a potential target. Then David spotted her; an elderly lady, weighed down by a heavy shopping bag full of her purchases from the off-licence.

The years hadn't been kind to Winnie whose face was deeply lined and whose wiry, grey hair was thinning. She had been trying to make her pension stretch; she didn't want to be forced to borrow from her friend, Gladys, again. But today was pension day and the lure of the alcohol had proved too much.

Winnie stepped out of the off-licence and pulled her shabby, stained mac tightly around her. She smiled a gap-toothed grin to a man as she passed him, her face a picture of glee as she thought about the comforts contained in her shopping bag. He returned a half-hearted smile, eager to escape the foul stench given off by her unwashed clothing and her tendency to leak urine; a result of years of child-bearing to children she rarely saw.

Peter and David were standing on the corner, just a few houses up from the off-licence. As Winnie approached, David nodded to Peter. He didn't need to say anything. They both knew she was what they were looking for.

Peter scanned the street. The man who had passed Winnie had sped off in his Vauxhall Cavalier and there was no longer anyone around. They feigned disinterest as Winnie passed by and took a cursory glance at them. She was too consumed by the prospect of an evening of sherry-induced solace to exercise caution.

David waited until she had walked a short distance then tailed her. Peter followed his lead. They crept silently, staying a few steps behind so she wouldn't spot anything untoward. When David saw a back entry some metres ahead of them, he nodded to Peter and they closed the gap between themselves and Winnie.

Winnie continued to walk, humming a cheerful tune to herself, oblivious to their presence. She was just about to pass the back entry when David sprang at her from behind, grabbing her by the shoulders and pushing her sideways into the entry.

Winnie put up a mighty struggle and clung to her shopping bag. Then Peter was upon her too, covering her mouth with his hand to stifle her screams and helping David to steer her towards the darkness of the back entry. Despite her determination, Winnie was no match for two strong, young men.

'Give us the fuckin' bag, grandma!' ordered David.

'No!' she yelled.

While Peter continued to push Winnie towards the back entry, David wrestled with her for the bag. But she wouldn't let go. Once they had her in the shadows of the back entry, David stepped up the pressure. He pulled the bag back and forth trying to loosen it from Winnie's grip. But still she held on to her precious load.

Spurred on by a rush of adrenalin, Peter joined in the fight. He pushed Winnie to the ground where the force of the impact made her release her grip on the shopping bag. Peter grabbed it quick while Winnie squealed in pain as her fragile old bones smashed against the cobbles.

'Silly old cow! Should have let go, you fuckin' old alky,' snarled David, giving her a sharp kick in her back.

Winnie yelled in pain but the two youths were devoid of sympathy. Their focus was on Winnie's shopping bag. They sped away with their prize while Winnie lay shocked and battered on the cold, hard cobbles, crying out for help.

When they had run a safe distance, they stopped at a school and made their way inside the grounds, which were unlit. They sorted through the contents of Winnie's bag. There were two bottles of cheap wine and one of sherry, which Peter passed to his friend. David took a few swigs from the bottle, laughing between sips.

'Come on, what else is there?' asked David impatiently.

Peter rewarded his curiosity by putting his hand back inside the bag and withdrawing a purse from the bottom. He quickly unfastened it to examine the contents.

'Wow!' said David. 'Who'd have thought a scruffy old alky like her would be carrying so much dosh?'

Little did they know that it was Winnie's pension. She was superstitious about leaving it in the house; too worried that burglars might break in and steal it. So she carried it around with her, foolishly assuming that it would be safe that way. Now that had gone, Winnie had nothing left to live on until her next pension day.

The boys weren't concerned about Winnie's circumstances. For Peter it was a matter of survival, and David didn't have a conscience. He would make money the easiest way possible despite the trauma to his victims. Peter sifted through the money, counted it, then divided it between himself and David.

'Nice little payout, Pete,' David said smugly. 'And she's even let us have some booze so we can celebrate,' he chuckled.

Peter grinned back at him and tucked his share of their spoils into his trouser pocket, satisfied that things weren't going too badly. Maybe he didn't need his father after all.

Adele had just finished a gruelling three-hour exam and was on the way home. She was heading towards the bus stop when she saw David Scott's younger sister, Lindsey, in the distance. Adele hurried to catch up with her despite her concerns that Lindsey might be as peevish as her brother, David. Adele hadn't seen anything of Peter since their father had thrown him out and she was worried about him. Perhaps Lindsey would know where he was.

'Lindsey, wait!' Adele shouted when she was within a few metres of her.

Lindsey turned around and surveyed Adele cautiously. 'What?' asked Lindsey when Adele drew level.

'I just wanted a word,' said Adele, pausing to catch her breath. 'I'm trying to find our Peter. I thought maybe your David would know where he is.'

'Yeah, course he does. He hangs out with him at that old squat where Peter's staying.'

Lindsey spoke as though Adele was aware of the squat but it was the first time she'd heard any mention of it.

'Where is it?' she asked.

'Why d'you want to know?' asked Lindsey, suspiciously.

'I just want to check he's all right,' said Adele. 'Maybe I could take him some food or something.'

Lindsey took some persuading but she eventually gave Adele the address. Adele scribbled it down on a piece of paper and put it inside her school bag. She intended to call round and see him as soon as she could.

When Adele arrived home she told her mother about Peter living in the squat. Her mother seemed concerned but she didn't ask where it was. Adele wondered if she really was bothered until a conversation between her parents later that evening made her think otherwise.

Adele was in the kitchen, clearing the dishes from that evening's meal, and her parents were in the living room. Her father's raised voice alerted her to their conversation and she crept up to the living room door so she could hear them more clearly.

'Bleedin' typical that is!' she heard her father say. 'So now I've got one in a fuckin' squat and the other still sponging off me. They're both fuckin' useless! All my mates' grown-up kids are out earning, but not them two. Oh, no. I've got a criminal for a son and a daughter who thinks she's bleedin' Lady Muck.'

Adele could feel a rage building up inside her but she tried to contain it. Her right hand gripped the door frame tightly as she waited to hear her mother's response.

'He needn't be, Tommy.' Shirley's voice was faint, pleading

with her irate husband. 'I'm sure he's learnt his lesson by now. Why don't you have him home on the condition...'

Shirley didn't get the opportunity to finish her sentence as Tommy cut in sharply, 'No fuckin' chance! I'm having no fuckin' criminal under my roof.'

'But he's your son, Tommy.'

'Not anymore, he isn't. He gave up that right when he had the fuckin' police round at my door. Now, shut it! He's not coming home and that's that.'

Adele could hear a noise that sounded like her father slapping the arm of the chair. Then, silence. She turned to walk away from the living room door and was startled when her father swung it open and stormed into the hall.

'What the fuck do you want?' he asked. 'Have you been earwigging?'

'No,' said Adele, wary in case he turned his fury on her. 'I was just coming to ask my mam something.' She stood there waiting for his response.

'Well, go on then,' he said. 'Don't just stand there looking gormless.'

She dashed into the living room, eager to be away from him, then sat next to her mother who was in tears again. For some time they remained silent until they heard the front door slam. Tommy was on his way to the pub.

'I heard what he said about me,' said Adele, still angry as she thought about his cruel words.

'Oh, don't let him bother you,' sobbed her mother. 'He's only letting off steam because of our Peter. Anyway, you'll be working soon.'

Adele shrugged. She was due to start work the week after her exams finished. She hadn't fulfilled her grandma's ambitions for her of going to university. With all the trauma of her grandma's death as well as her difficult home life, Adele had found it hard to study. She'd tried her best, focusing on positive memories of her grandma to drive her, but her heart wasn't in it, and she knew she wouldn't make the grades. She was halfway through her exams now and they weren't going as well as she'd hoped. With her chances of going to university already gone, Adele had found a job instead as an accounts assistant for a firm of solicitors.

She might not have succeeded in going to university but she was determined to do as well as possible in life. Not only would she do well, but she'd make her own way in the world. Her father's cruel words had stung and as she played them over in her mind she became determined that she would get away from home as soon as possible. She'd earn her own money and make sure she never had to ask him for anything in the future.

30

Adele looked up at the building and checked the address on the scrap of paper clasped in her hand. Yes, she had definitely got the right place. She looked up once more, disturbed by the sight in front of her.

It was an old house whose bricks were mossy and discoloured. Some of them were cracked or had holes in them and most of those on the corners of the building were chipped. The roof was in a similar state of disrepair with slates missing, exposing huge lengths of beam in parts.

The house was an end terrace. The rest of the houses on the row were similar in design but better maintained. Its windows were boarded and Adele tiptoed around the side of the building in search of a way in. She took care to avoid the animal faeces that littered the weed-strewn path.

At the back she found a gate and pushed it tentatively. It creaked on rusty hinges and gave way to a yard, which was in a similar state to the front of the house. With a pounding heart she stepped inside and negotiated her way around the abandoned bike frame, broken bits of wood and other unidentifiable items on her way to the back door. It was slightly ajar.

Not wishing to take any chances, Adele pushed the door gently and called Peter's name before stepping inside.

'In here!' he shouted.

She stepped inside an abandoned kitchen, the stench overpowering her straightaway. Mustiness and a pungent, offensive odour filled the dusty air. Adele heaved, her mouth filling with saliva. She swallowed down the urge to vomit and glanced around the room. It was dark and her eyes took a few seconds to adjust. She reached out to touch the wall and recoiled as her fingers grazed the slime that covered it in parts.

Several dated cupboards lined the walls, their battered doors either missing or hanging precariously. The room was full of rubble; plaster that had fallen down from the ceiling, and bits of brick. The walls appeared to be painted but the colour was nondescript and patchy in places where mildew clung to the ravaged plaster and exposed bricks. Everything had a dismal pallor; daubed in various shades of grey like an old black and white movie.

Adele moved on, treading carefully until she eventually entered another room where there was also little light. She assumed it was the lounge. Here the stench was stronger, suffused with urine, animal faeces and decay. Again she swallowed down the urge to vomit. She heard the wind whistling through the eaves and the constant drip of rainwater. The damp penetrated her bones and the stench clung to her clothing.

Adele's eyes flitted to the far side of the room where she could hear the sound of chattering and laughter. She stepped forward. There was Peter, amongst a group of boys of a similar age all sitting on rickety old chairs and crates, sipping from cans of beer.

This room was also full of rubble: chunks of cement and bricks, empty cans and bottles, some chip shop cartons and a discarded apple core. She eyed the worn-out mattress in the corner of the room, which was sunken in the middle and littered with several used condoms.

'Peter?' she asked as her eyes focused on her brother.

The boys stopped talking and stared in her direction.

'All right?' asked Peter casually, as though this way of living was normal.

'Yes; are you?' she said. Then, feeling discomfort in the presence of the other boys, she began to waffle. 'David's sister told me you were here. I've brought you some food in case you were hungry. Are you all right?'

One of the boys sprang out of his chair and grabbed the bag she was carrying. 'Give it here!' he said before rooting inside the bag and passing the food around the group.

Peter didn't respond.

David, on hearing his name mentioned, got out of his seat and stepped towards her. Adele hadn't noticed him at first and she could feel her back stiffen as he approached.

'Here!' he said, passing her a can of beer. 'You might as well have some.'

Not wishing to offend him, she took the proffered can and tugged at the ring pull. Despite the stench inside the room, she took a tentative sip. The beer felt acrid on her tongue. She gulped it down, washing away the taste of dust. Although she surmised that the offer of beer was a form of acceptance, she still felt wary of David.

'Come and sit down,' said Peter, pulling up a battered chair next to him.

As she stepped towards them, a mangy cat brushed past her legs, startling her. She let out a yell, which amused the boys. Adele felt embarrassed as well as uncomfortable. She sat down beside Peter and rubbed at her leg, which was itching from contact with the cat. She guessed that the animal was probably the source of some of the stench.

'Are you all right, Peter?' she asked again.

'Course I am. I'm with my mates, aren't I?'

She guessed that his bravado was intended to impress his friends rather than reassure her so she persevered. 'I've been worried about you. My dad still won't let you come back and I was worried how you'd manage.'

'Don't worry, I'll be fine. I don't need that stupid prick!'

Adele stayed silent. It was difficult to talk to him with his friends present. The conversation drifted, with a few of the boys complaining about their parents in support of Peter. Adele sat patiently, nervously gulping her beer. She got through the can quicker than she intended, her discomfort causing her to take large sips. David passed her another can.

'Eh, I didn't tell you about my dream last night,' Peter announced to the group. 'I had a stepdad in the dream and he was a right bastard.' This drew the attention of the other boys, and Peter continued. 'Yeah, he kept picking on me, so guess what I did?'

The others paused, waiting for him to deliver his punchline.

'I killed the bastard. Fuckin' slashed him to pieces. And it felt brilliant! A slash of the knife for every time he'd hit me. The blood was gushing out of him and he was fuckin' screaming for me to stop but I just kept letting him have it.'

'Stop it!' cried Adele, the vivid description sending a cold shiver throughout her body. 'That's horrible, Peter.'

'I can't help what I dream, can I? Anyway, he fuckin' deserved it, and it felt great.'

Some of the boys nodded and murmured their agreement. Adele wasn't sure whether Peter was referring to the stepfather in his dream or to their own father but either way it was disturbing. Would Peter really do something like that or was he just showing off in front of his friends?

After a lengthy pause, he added, 'I hate my dad, y'know, Adele.'

'I know,' she said. 'I know he's been bad to you, Peter, but that doesn't make something like that right.'

'For God's sake, get a grip, will you? It was only a dream! I didn't say I wanted to do it.'

Again, Adele stayed silent, her discomfort still evident. She waited until some minutes had passed then announced she was going. She hoped Peter would walk out with her; it might give her chance to talk to him alone. But he didn't. Instead, David offered to see her out.

Adele was surprised at David's change in attitude towards her. Gone was the hostility that she had experienced previously. It seemed to have been replaced with an urge to impress her for some reason. Perhaps Peter had had a word with him when he had thumped her a while ago, and he was now feeling remorseful. Or perhaps he had just grown up a bit.

She said goodbye to her brother and his friends. Peter's lack of emotion at her departure saddened her. Was he still displaying bravado or had they really drifted apart so much?

As she made her way out of the dilapidated living room, David followed her. His gait was unsteady due to the amount of beer he had drunk.

He waited until they had passed through the kitchen before

speaking. 'How about it, me and you, Adele?' He winked lecherously at her.

'What?' she asked, shocked.

'Y'know. We can go upstairs if you want.'

'You must be joking!' she cried. 'What do you think I am?'

'I thought you'd be up for it. After all, you went out with Gary Healey, didn't you?'

'So. That doesn't mean...'

'Aw, come off it. You must have shagged him. There's no way he'd have gone out with you otherwise.' He reached out and grabbed her arm.

'Get off!' she yelled. 'I haven't been with Gary. And what business is it of yours anyway?'

As she pushed David's hand away, Peter dashed into the kitchen.

'What's going on?' he asked.

'Nowt,' said David, stepping away from Adele and making his way back to his friends.

'You all right?' asked Peter.

'Yeah,' said Adele but she couldn't hide the fact she was shaken.

'What was he after?'

Adele blushed.

'I'll fuckin' kill him!' he said.

'It's OK. I think he got the message.'

There was an uncomfortable atmosphere between them until Adele broke the ensuing silence. 'Thanks anyway.'

'It's OK. You're my sister, aren't you? Come on, I'll walk with you to the street.'

He didn't say anything more but those few words had been enough.

31

After that, Adele tried to visit Peter whenever she could. She would take him bits of food to make sure he got something decent to eat. But whenever she visited she found it difficult to relax. David's presence unnerved her; he was so unpredictable.

The other boys could be quite raucous too, and she felt alarmed by their endless talk about the mischief they got up to and the crimes they committed. Sometimes it seemed as though they were competing to be the most outrageous. She was always ill at ease in their presence and had a sense of not belonging.

Adele wished that Peter could come back home but unfortunately her father wouldn't allow it. And as time passed, her visits became less and less frequent. Peter seemed indifferent towards her most of the time so she decided to spare herself the trouble of spending time in such an intimidating environment.

Instead, she focused on her own life. The week after her exams finished, she started work at a firm of solicitors called Scott and Palmer Ltd, in John Dalton Street. The work could be tedious at times but, for the main part, she enjoyed it. She got along well with her work colleagues and felt a sense of achievement now she was earning a wage.

The atmosphere at home didn't improve, though, and Adele decided she would move out at the earliest opportunity. Each payday she squirrelled away as much money as she could in order to raise the deposit for a flat, and kit it out with furniture and electrical goods.

Adele worried constantly about how her mother would survive once she was gone. But, like her mother had said, she had made her bed and now she had to lie in it. Adele, on the other hand, hadn't chosen Tommy for a father and she was determined to break away from him as soon as possible.

When she had been working a few weeks, the envelope containing her A level results arrived on the doormat. Adele nervously opened it while her mother looked on. She noticed her mother's sharp intake of breath as she took out the slip of paper and scanned it.

'Have you passed?' asked Shirley.

Adele stared at the piece of paper on which her results were printed; two Es and a D.

'Just about,' she replied, the disappointment evident in her voice.

'Well, that's good, isn't it?' her mother asked.

'Not really. My grades are rubbish.'

'But you've passed, love, and you've already got a good job so what are you worried about?'

Adele didn't bother explaining. Her mother wouldn't understand. Instead she put the piece of paper down and shrugged.

'Come on, cheer up,' said Shirley, hugging Adele then planting a kiss on her head. 'There's not many round here that can say they've got A levels, is there? I'm proud of you.'

'Thanks,' Adele muttered before going upstairs to her room.

Once she was alone, Adele shed a few tears. She was disappointed. Her grades wouldn't have been high enough to get into university anyway so perhaps she had done the right thing in getting a job. She'd just have to make the best of it, as her Grandma Joyce would have said. And she'd continue squirrelling away her money until she could afford her own place. She might not have succeeded in fulfilling her grandma's ambitions for her by going to university but she was going to escape her father somehow.

'Mum, there's something I need to tell you,' said Adele later that evening.

Shirley's eyes widened in apprehension. 'What is it, love? Is it about our Peter?'

'No, it's about me.'

'Oh. What's the matter?'

Adele noticed the look of alarm on her mother's face and knew this wasn't going to be easy. She decided to just get it over with.

'I've started saving up so I can move out. As soon as I've got enough, I'm going.'

'You're what?'

Adele could sense the first stirrings of panic in her mother. 'I'm moving out, Mam,' she said, lowering her voice.

'But why?'

'Need you ask, Mam?'

'But, Adele. You can't. How am I gonna cope?'

'You'll be OK, Mam. I'll come and visit whenever I can.'

Adele could see tears forming in her mother's eyes, and the guilt stabbed away at her.

Her mother sat down and lowered her head. 'That's knocked me for six, that has… bloody hell! I didn't expect that.'

Adele's feelings of guilt were battling with a burgeoning anger. She'd known her mother would make her feel guilty, and she resented it. Why should she feel guilty? Why should she be made to feel responsible for her mother? She was a grown woman when all was said and done!

She didn't respond to her mother's last comment, not trusting herself to remain in control. Instead she stood up and said, 'I'll put the kettle on.' She made her way to the kitchen and put a kettle full of water on the gas jet of the stove.

Once Adele had made a drink for them both, she spent a further few moments discussing her imminent departure with her mother.

'What's brought this on all of a sudden?' asked Shirley.

'It isn't sudden, Mam. I've been thinking about it since I started work. Anyway, it will be a while yet before I've saved up enough to kit the place out.'

'Do you have to go, love? Maybe he'll be better now our Peter's gone.'

'I want to go, Mam.'

'But why? You've always coped before.'

'That's just it, Mam. I coped because I had no choice. But now I'm working, I do have a choice. So, I'm going, and that's that.' Before Shirley had a chance to say anything more Adele announced that she was going out.

Adele needed to be alone. She needed to clear her head; she couldn't think straight with her mother present. Even if she disappeared upstairs, she wouldn't feel free. Her mother had gone into clingy mode and Adele had no doubt that she would be interrupting her constantly just to reassure herself that her daughter was still available to her; for the time being anyway.

Once Adele was alone, she felt liberated; free to make her own decision. And she resolved that her decision would remain no matter what her mother did or said. She would move out of her parents' home as soon as possible. She just hoped that her mother would be OK once she was gone.

32

Peter had been living in the squat for a few months now and found that he was quite enjoying it. No more hassle from his father. No more having to do as he was told. Instead he could do as he pleased; as long as he didn't get caught.

The need to commit crime in order to survive didn't bother Peter. It had become a way of life to him now and one that he quite enjoyed. It was the thrill of it. The rush of adrenalin when he knew he was doing wrong and that feeling of exhilaration when he'd managed to pull something off. He was giving a huge two fingers to society.

He had also become more hardened to his life of crime since he had spent time in the detention centre. His abuse at the hands of Patterson had changed him irrevocably. Deep inside he felt bitter about how he had been treated; firstly by his father and then by the staff in the detention centre. Why had Patterson singled him out? Was it because, like most of the other adults in Peter's life, he thought he was scum so he treated him accordingly?

Stuff all the adults who had wronged him and the people

who tried to keep him in check with their pathetic rules and regulations. Stuff the lot of them! What did he care?

Not long after Peter went to live in the squat, David left home to join him. Like Peter, he enjoyed the freedom. Another thing Peter enjoyed was the level of respect he got from the other lads. He'd been inside. He'd done daring things, bad things, and they admired him for it. With Alan still inside for killing a man, Peter became the unofficial leader of the group and it was a position he relished.

Tonight Peter and David were breaking into a shop. They intended to stock up with cash from the till, food, cigarettes and anything else they could lay their hands on. They'd waited till midnight, ensuring there was no one about and the owners' bedroom lights had been switched off for a while.

Once they had forced their way in, they crept about inside the shop. Peter felt a surge of energy as the adrenalin pumped around his body, sharpening his vision and hearing. David took out a crowbar. He used it to lever the till so they could grab any cash left on the premises. They were disappointed to find it empty. The owners must have gone to the bank that day.

Next, he and David packed the bags they had brought with anything edible to take back to the squat as well as plenty of cigarettes. They rushed around the shop as quietly as possible, grabbing anything they wouldn't have to cook.

Peter smiled at David when his bag was full, and David sniggered back at him. There was only one thing left to do now. Peter was looking forward to this third task most of all.

He nodded at David who set to work with the crowbar. Peter used a hammer he had brought. Within minutes they had knocked most of the goods off the shelves. They continued using their tools to wreak as much damage as they could, breaking the glass displays and splintering the shop's counter.

Then they heard the sound of footsteps above them and dashed outside with their bags full of goodies. They ran for several minutes, pausing to catch their breath once they were well away from the shop.

Peter felt triumphant as he pictured the reaction of the owners when they found their precious shop full of emptied packets, broken glass and damaged units. He and David had done what they set out to do, and the owners hadn't heard a thing until it was too late.

A smug grin of satisfaction lit up Peter's face. He had done it! He had finally got revenge on Mrs Roper, the shopkeeper who had scorned and belittled him and Adele throughout their childhood. That would teach her!

Adele had been saving for the last few months and the time for moving out was drawing closer. Since she first broached the subject with her mother, Adele had tried to discuss it with her several times. However, every attempt was met with a sombre response from her mother, who would usually mutter a few words then bow her head. They'd both agreed not to tell Tommy until Adele was gone, in case he caused a scene. Adele had already found a flat and paid the deposit and the first month's rent. For the past two weeks she had been kitting it out ready for her intended moving-in date. That day had now arrived. And it was time to broach the subject once more with her mother.

'Mam, you know what day it is today, don't you?' she asked.

Shirley didn't reply so Adele raised her voice, 'Mam?'

Shirley sniffed and hesitated before replying. 'You're going through with it then?'

'Yes, I told you I would.'

'Well, that's that then, I suppose. Don't worry about me, I'll be all right.' Shirley ended this last sentence with another sniff then drew a handkerchief from her sleeve and dabbed at imaginary tears.

'It won't work, Mam!'

'What?'

'You know what!' said Adele, becoming irritated. 'You're trying to guilt-trip me.'

'No, I'm not. I'm upset, Adele. I can't help it. How would you feel if you'd already lost one of your children and then the other decided to leave you?'

'For God's sake!' Adele snapped. 'You haven't lost Peter. You can go and see him any time you like. I can give you the address.'

'I can't be going round to a place like that. I don't know who I'm going to bump into. Anything could happen.'

'Well I've been there plenty of times and I was OK. You don't really think Peter would let anything happen to you, do you?'

Shirley didn't reply. She had exhausted this particular topic so after a few moments she returned to complaints about Adele leaving. 'It's gonna be a struggle y'know but, if you're dead set on leaving, I don't suppose there's anything I can say that's gonna change your mind.' Her voice was lacklustre and Adele could tell it was her way of trying to guilt-trip her again. But she wasn't going to let her get round her like that.

'No, you're right, Mam, there isn't,' she snapped. 'So stop bloody harping on about it. You're a grown woman, for God's sake! Why should I stay here and look after you? Can't you see? He's driven Peter away and now he's driving me away. If you're daft enough to stay with him, that's up to you, but don't expect me to do the same!'

As soon as she'd finished, Adele stormed from the room, slamming the door behind her. Eventually she calmed down. Then the guilt set in. She pictured her mother sitting weeping downstairs, her face blotchy and tear-stained, and knew she had gone too far.

But she wasn't as patient with her mother as she used to be. Since Adele had lost her grandma and found out about the circumstances surrounding her birth, she had contained a smouldering anger, which sometimes rose to the surface.

For almost an hour Adele wrestled with her conscience. On the one hand she told herself that her mother was a grown woman who shouldn't be so reliant on her but, on the other hand, she worried about how her mother would cope once she had gone.

For as far back as Adele could remember, Shirley had always been vulnerable. She wondered whether it was part of her make-up or just the effects of being married to her father for so long. Adele couldn't remember a time when her mother hadn't relied on tranquilisers to get her through the day, but since Grandma Joyce had died, she'd become even worse.

Adele waivered in her decision. Perhaps she should stay a bit longer just to see her mother over the worst. But what if she never got better? Maybe her mother would never improve while she had somebody else to shoulder the burden.

The thoughts swirled around in her mind, giving her a headache. But she was getting no further forward; just going over the same ground again and again. Eventually, when she had exhausted all possibilities, Adele reached a decision. She went back downstairs to tell her mother.

Just as Adele had surmised, her mother was sat at the kitchen table with a cup of tea, a blotchy face and a sodden handkerchief. As Adele approached, full of remorse, her mother looked up at her with an air of expectancy.

'I'm sorry for losing it and upsetting you,' Adele said.

She completed the last few steps to her mother and they embraced. Shirley clung to her for precious seconds until Adele loosened her grip.

'Are you going?' Shirley asked, her lips quivering.

'Yes, Mam. I'm sorry but I haven't changed my mind. And I need to go before he gets home.'

'Oh,' said Shirley, her eyes misting over.

'I'm sorry,' said Adele. 'But I'll come and see you as often as I can. You're welcome to come round and see me too. You've got the address. And I'll give you the phone number as soon as I'm connected.'

'All right,' said Shirley, despondently.

'Well, I suppose that's that, then,' Adele added, turning to walk out of the room.

She had almost reached the door when her mother called her back.

'Adele,' she said, choking back her tears. 'I just want to say that, well, I understand.'

Adele walked away, the emotion of the moment finally getting to her. But she refused to cry. She'd put up with her father all these years and now it was time she had her freedom. She deserved it.

33

'What d'you mean she's fuckin' gone?' asked Tommy, the veins in his neck protruding as his anger escalated.

'She's found a flat,' said Shirley who had been dreading telling him.

'Oh yeah? Like that is it? She's all right to sponge off me while she's still at school but the minute she gets a job, she pisses off and finds her own place!'

'I don't think she meant it like that, Tommy.'

'Well how the fuck did she mean it? Are we not good enough for her now she's got a job at a fuckin' solicitors?'

'No, it's not that, Tommy,' Shirley cajoled. 'I think she just wants a bit of independence.'

'Independence, my arse! She's too bleedin' young to be leaving home. Didn't you tell her that?'

'I tried to persuade her to stay, Tommy, honestly I did. But she was having none of it.'

'I bet you bleedin' did, you dozy cow. You're fuckin' useless!'

Shirley didn't reply. She didn't want to inflame the situation any further. Instead she watched Tommy as he tucked into his evening meal.

'This dinner's fuckin' cold!' he complained.

'It's been out for two hours. I'd have warmed it up for you if you'd asked.'

'Stuff it!' shouted Tommy, hurling the plate full of food against the wall. 'I'm not eating this shit!'

Again Shirley stayed silent, not sure how to react for fear of inciting him even more.

Tommy spent a few moments pacing the room before announcing, 'Right, you'd better tell me where she's living. I'll go round there and see if I can knock some sense into the silly little cow!'

'I don't know,' said Shirley.

'Don't tell me fuckin' lies. You know! And how long have you known she was moving out?'

'Only a few days. I was going to tell you but there never seemed to be the right time.'

'Don't tell fuckin' lies!' Tommy shouted again, emphasising his point this time by giving Shirley a smack across the face with the back of his hand. 'Tell me where she fuckin' lives!'

'I can't.'

'I said tell me!' shouted Tommy. He gripped hold of the top of Shirley's dress, his fists pressing into her throat. Then he dragged her out of the chair and slammed her up against the wall. His fists pressed against her windpipe and Shirley struggled to breathe. She could smell the beer as he exhaled sharply and yelled again, 'You better fuckin' tell me if you know what's good for you.'

Shirley couldn't speak. Her throat was constricted. Instead she shook her head from side to side while her eyes bulged in her head.

'I said tell me!' Tommy yelled again, releasing his hold then tightening it again as he bashed her head into the wall.

The colour drained from Shirley's face and she let out a strangled yelp. Tommy released his hold and let her drop to the ground. She could see the shock on his face as though he was afraid he'd overdone it this time.

He looked down at her, poised to strike again but also checking for signs of life. She stirred and groaned before realising that was a mistake. As rage consumed him, Tommy kicked at Shirley's legs and back until his anger was spent. Then he stopped, breathing heavily and surveying the damage. This time she kept still, relief flooding through her as she watched him walk away.

Adele was shocked at the sight of her mother. She had called around early on a Saturday morning when she knew her father would still be in bed. Straightaway she noticed the red mark on one side of her face and the bruises on her neck.

'What's happened to you?' she asked although she already knew the answer.

'You don't wanna know,' said Shirley, downcast.

'Has he been at you again?'

Shirley's lack of response confirmed Adele's suspicions and, as she noticed her mother limping, she suspected that the worst of her injuries were hidden. She was wearing trousers, something she rarely did.

'What's wrong with your leg?' asked Adele.

'What?'

'You're limping, Mam.'

'Oh, it's nothing. Just a bit of arthritis.'

'Are you sure?'

Shirley remained silent again and Adele followed her through to the living room where they both sat down.

'Tell me, Mam!' Adele demanded.

'Shhh,' said Shirley, pointing her eyes upwards to indicate that Tommy was upstairs in bed. Then she whispered, 'Don't let him hear you.'

Adele stared back at her mother, waiting for an explanation. Eventually Shirley gave in to her demands. 'I suppose it's best you know,' she said, sighing. 'He's not happy about you going.'

'I knew it!' Adele interrupted angrily, feeling guilty that Tommy had taken things out on her mother.

'Shhh,' Shirley implored again before continuing. 'The way he sees it is that you leeched off him while you were at school and then buggered off once you could afford it.'

'That's rubbish!' stormed Adele, lowering her voice when her mother put her finger to her lips. 'I left because of him; because I can't stand the way he treats us all. Just look at what he's done to you. It isn't right, Mam.'

'I know, love, but he's done his worst. He's calmed down now he's over the initial shock.'

Adele wasn't naïve enough to believe that Tommy was hurt because of any feelings he had for her. The most likely reason for his anger would be because he'd miss the money that she paid for her keep. Then there was the contribution she made to the housework. Not for the first time, Adele was tempted to offer her mother a place at her flat. But she resisted. It was time to be selfish now. She'd spent her life in sufferance because of her mother's past mistakes; so had Peter. And she'd had enough. Although Adele cared about her, she knew that she would drag her down. Besides, she reasoned to herself, there just wasn't room. It was only a one-bedroomed flat.

After a few moments' thought, Adele asked, 'Did you tell him where I'm living?'

Shirley flashed a half-hearted grin. 'No,' she said. 'Why d'you think he went to town on me?'

Adele inhaled sharply, raising her hand to cover her mouth at the shock of her mother's words. 'Oh, Mam. I'm sorry,' she said.

Shirley just shrugged.

'How bad is it?' Adele asked.

Shirley lifted her top, revealing a mass of bruises on her back, and Adele fought back the tears.

'Are your legs the same?'

Her mother nodded.

'Oh, Mam,' Adele said, her voice shaking. 'You don't have to put up with this. You could report him to the police?'

'No. It would only make matters worse,' her mother replied despondently.

Adele rose from her chair, 'I'm going to have a word with him. This isn't on!' she said, nodding her head angrily towards her mother's bruises.

Shirley was upon her before she reached the door, grabbing at her arm to pull her back. 'Please don't, Adele. It'll only make things worse.'

Adele stopped and stood in silence for a few seconds before walking back to her seat. 'What will you do?' she asked.

'Don't worry about me, Adele. I'll be OK. He'll be all right now he's over the shock of it. He's already sorry for what he's done. In fact, he brought me a takeaway home last night; chicken curry and rice, my favourite. It shows he's thinking of me, doesn't it?'

Adele looked at her mother with a confused expression on her face. She couldn't understand her at times. Her husband had given her a severe beating and yet she was grateful for the smallest sign of reconciliation.

Adele was tempted again to put her mother up at her place. But what was the point? She knew only too well what would happen. He'd find out where they were then come round to fetch her mother back. He'd turn nasty and violent and, if that didn't work, he'd beg and plead and promise to treat her better. And her mother would go. Adele might be able to save her from him for a short while but she couldn't save her from herself. Meanwhile, Adele would have all the stress and hassle of putting up with both of them.

Her mother had made her decision. That was clear. She might complain about Tommy but, despite all his shortcomings, she loved him. It was an odd kind of love and one that Adele would never comprehend. Shirley knew him and all his faults and yet she accepted the way things were.

At a loss as to how she could help her, Adele eventually let her switch topics while they drank tea.

When it was time to go, she hugged her mother and gazed at her with a strange kind of admiration. Despite Shirley's weaknesses, she had stood up to Tommy and refused to tell him where her daughter lived. Adele felt thankful for that at least. She also felt confident that Shirley wouldn't let him know, no matter what it took to keep her address secret. Perhaps her mother didn't need her quite as much as she had thought.

PART THREE
1983-1984

34

Adele arrived home feeling exhilarated after attending her kickboxing class. She had been practising kickboxing for some time now and she loved it. No matter what stresses she'd had to deal with during the day, they all melted away once she started fighting. Often she would feel tired and reluctant to go to the class but she'd push herself knowing that the session would re-energise her, and help her push away any troubled thoughts.

Life was good for her at the moment but the past always caught up. Her early life experiences had left her with an endless cycle of negative thoughts and a profound mistrust of men. Because of her damaged childhood she often felt insecure and jealous.

At twenty-one, Adele had already had a couple of brief relationships but they ended the same way. She became clingy, jealous and bad-tempered, which drove her partners away.

So, she'd begun kickboxing classes. She'd read somewhere that it was a good way to channel aggression, and it had proved true. Although she still lost her temper at times, her rages were less frequent. Adele couldn't do much about her jealousy though. She tried to contain it but there were times when that proved difficult.

Still, things were going well in her current relationship. She'd been seeing John for over a year and they were now living together in a lovely two-bedroomed house. She'd met him while she was out in the city centre one night after work, and they'd clicked straightaway. Adele had put her trust fully into the relationship, something she usually found difficult to do. But with John everything felt right and he'd never given her any reason to doubt or mistrust him. And he was a looker. He had just the sort of features she liked, and a good physique.

As Adele steered her car into the drive she felt a surge of excitement. John always had this effect on her. She walked into the living room to find him ready to greet her.

'Hi, love. How did it go?' he asked, walking over.

Adele felt a tingle as he gave her a quick kiss then grazed her throat with his lips. He raised his head and gazed into her eyes.

'Fine,' she said, smiling.

John took hold of her shoulders and gave her another kiss, this time more passionate, and she felt herself responding. His kisses grew in intensity and he moved his hands down to her waist, caressing her curves. Then he pulled her tightly towards him. When she felt him becoming aroused she pulled away.

'Don't,' she said. 'I'm all sweaty. I need to take a shower.'

Instead of being put off, John took this as a sign of encouragement. 'Come on then,' he said. 'I'll join you.'

They giggled like school children as they took the stairs two at a time. Once they reached the bathroom John undressed her. He removed her clothing slowly, kissing her sensuously on the lips as the garments dropped to the floor one by one.

When only her underwear remained, John broke away from his kisses. His eyes met hers, studying her reaction as he peeled off her bra and stroked her breasts, his hands brushing them lightly until her nipples were erect. As he took one nipple between his fingers, his mouth closed around the other one. Adele let out a squeal of delight.

John's hand travelled down to her briefs, his fingers slipping inside the fabric and exploring her. She was moist. Adele began to pant as his fingers entered her. She drew away and stepped into the shower while John threw off his own clothes.

'I'm still sweaty,' she said.

'Let's get you clean then,' he said, tantalisingly pouring shower cream into his hands.

He rubbed his hands together then slithered them over her naked breasts and worked the shower cream into suds. Within seconds her whole body was covered in creamy suds as he caressed every bit of her. Then his hands clenched her buttocks and lifted her. Adele's legs closed around his back as he entered her.

She didn't feel the cold tiles on her back, just the intensity of pure joy as he thrust inside her, sending her into spasms of delight. She watched his muscles tense and relax with each thrust and saw the release in his facial expression as he came inside her.

When it was over, her eyes locked with his and a smile graced her lips. He let her down gently. Then she was giggling again as she flicked suds at him; their sexual gratification morphing into playfulness.

Later that evening, John became more serious. 'There's something I need to talk to you about,' he said.

Adele's mood changed straightaway when she saw the serious look on his face. 'What is it?' she asked, her tone more grave than she had intended.

He shifted his position from where he was sitting next to her on the sofa and moved closer, taking her hands in his. 'I've been offered a promotion,' he said.

'That's good, isn't it?' she asked, almost relieved but somehow knowing there was more to come.

'Y-yes, it is. It's a great opportunity with a massive pay rise as well.'

'Sounds great. Tell me more.'

John took a deep breath, his shoulders heaving. 'It's in London. B-but it needn't be a problem…'

'You're going to leave me,' Adele cut in.

'No, not at all! In fact, I'd like you to come with me. It'll be a brilliant opportunity for both of us,' he gushed. 'You'll easily get a bookkeeping job down there and you'll probably be on more money too.'

Adele snatched her hands away. 'No, I can't go. My life is here; my family's here. My mother needs me.'

'But, you'll still be able to visit. Besides, you hardly ever see your brother, and your mother should be capable of looking after herself,' John said.

Adele realised that he had no real understanding of her situation. How could she leave her mother? She would go to pieces if Adele wasn't around; she had been bad enough when Grandma Joyce died.

'It's not the same,' she replied, walking over to the

mantelpiece and rearranging her coveted porcelain ornaments for the second time that day. 'My mam needs me! Please say you won't go, John.'

'But I want the job, Adele, and I don't see any reason why you shouldn't come with me.'

The conversation soon escalated into a row with neither of them able to see the other's point of view. Eventually they gave up arguing and an impenetrable barrier of silence fell between them until Adele went up to their bedroom. She picked up her silver-plated brush set, drawing comfort from the feel of it in her hands, turning it over and admiring the embossed flowers that surrounded it. She ran the brush briskly through her hair then sat down to read a book once she was feeling a little calmer.

The following day they made up and John didn't mention the promotion. But Adele knew it wasn't forgotten. He was just biding his time to keep the peace.

35

By the time he had reached the age of twenty, Peter, and his friend David, had progressed from mugging unsuspecting victims. Having summoned up the gall to carry out such attacks, Peter had realised that there were richer pickings available. Instead of randomly attacking anyone who looked vulnerable, he made sure that their victims were carrying plenty of cash: shopkeepers. They were his new targets and he and David were just about to hit one. Their attacks had become more organised too. They'd been watching this particular shop for some time and knew when the owner went to the bank.

'There he is now,' said Peter, pulling a mask over his face to disguise himself.

'Fuck! He's got someone with him,' said David as they watched the owner locking up the shop.

'It's OK; it's only his wife. You sort her out while I grab the cash.'

David nodded his agreement.

'Quick!' said Peter. 'Hurry up before they get in the car.'

He and David sped from behind the car where they were hiding and rushed straight into the shopkeeper and his wife. While David kept a tight grip on the wife, covering her mouth to stifle her screams, Peter grabbed at the bag of takings. He had relied on the element of surprise to knock the shopkeeper off balance so he could grab the takings before the shopkeeper had chance to recover himself. But he had underestimated him.

The shopkeeper was a bulky man and although he was middle-aged, he was still willing to put up a fight. As Peter clutched at the bag, his adversary wrestled him for it. Peter tightened his hold but the man still wouldn't let go, so Peter aimed a sharp blow to the man's face. His fist connected, stunning the man momentarily, but he soon recovered. The shopkeeper was a powerful man as well as a feisty one. He swiftly countered Peter's punch while holding tightly onto the bag with his other hand. The blow stung and the impact of his heavy fist unnerved Peter. This guy was strong!

Peter looked across at David who had his right hand covering the woman's mouth while his left arm came across the front of her body, pinning down both of her arms. David released his right hand, ready to grab the bag, but the woman began screaming. Peter felt the first signs of panic. He was tempted to run but they had been planning this snatch for too long. And they wanted the money.

Peter continued to wrestle with the shopkeeper, his eyes focused on the cash. David and the woman were in his peripheral vision. 'Shut the bitch up!' he shouted.

As Peter fought blow by blow with the shopkeeper, the woman suddenly stopped screaming, grabbing the attention of both Peter and the man. Peter saw the flash of steel through the corner of his eye. He looked across to see David holding a knife to the woman's throat. The woman's jaw hung loose, her eyes wide with fear.

'Give him the fuckin' bag or I'll slit her throat!' said David.

Peter knew he meant it; he had already drawn blood. The woman began to whimper, her eyes pleading with her husband to let them have the bag. He didn't hesitate. It was obvious from David's stance and tone of voice that he would carry out his threat.

As the shopkeeper let go of the money, Peter tightened his grip on the bag and moved away. 'Come on, let's go,' he said to David who released the woman and backed away from the shopkeeper, waving the knife in front of him to show them he still meant business. Once they were a few metres away from the couple Peter and David sped down the road.

'Right, let's count it,' said Peter once they were safely inside his flat.

Peter and David no longer lived in the squat. Peter was now renting a two-bedroomed flat near the centre of Manchester. Using money from his various illegal activities, he had kitted it out with all the latest electrical equipment and some top of the range furniture. He wasn't a petty crook anymore; he had become a career criminal and it was paying off.

During the last couple of years, Peter had spent more time inside. His last stint had been in an adults' prison and he had made a number of useful contacts during his sentence. Unlike many prisoners who attempted to go straight once they had served their time, Peter had no intention of doing so. Criminality was all he had ever known. Through living in the squat from the age of sixteen, he had learnt to survive the best way possible. And the easiest option for him had always been on the wrong side of the law. But it was no longer just a means of scraping by.

As Peter's crimes escalated, they were becoming more lucrative. And he enjoyed it. The lure of new money-making schemes. The adrenalin rush and excitement of evading capture. The thrill of counting his spoils. He loved it all. Peter also liked the respect he had gained within the criminal fraternity. He was earning a reputation. And he was going places.

'There's a new Chinese restaurant opened in town,' said Shirley.

Tommy didn't reply and Adele noticed him grunt as he chewed his roast chicken. Adele's mother had invited her and John for Sunday dinner and her father was home in time to eat it fresh for once. Although Adele didn't like taking John to her parents' home while her father was there, it was kind of her mother to offer, and she didn't want to let her down. Adele was painfully aware of her mother's futile attempts to imitate normal family life in front of John.

'Do you fancy going next Saturday?' Shirley continued.

'Dunno. Depends if we can afford it,' said Tommy.

He stabbed angrily at a roast potato, irritated at Shirley's constant chatter. She missed the signs, but Adele didn't, and she cringed, hoping he wouldn't cause a scene in front of John who had never seen Tommy lose it. She dreaded how John would react to one of her father's displays of temper. John's home life had been very different to hers and she didn't want him to judge her because of her father.

'We're doing OK nowadays, aren't we?' Shirley asked, in reference to their finances.

He ignored her, focusing instead on his meal.

'I believe the Peking duck's lovely,' she continued.

'What?' Tommy asked, oblivious to her last comment.

'The Peking duck at that new Chinese restaurant.' Then, turning to Adele she tutted and raised her eyebrows, feigning exasperation at her husband's disinterest, and said, 'What's he like?' Then she continued to address Tommy, 'Lucky Star it's called. The Hampsons have been. She was going on about it in the corner shop.'

'For fuck's sake! Can't I eat my fuckin' dinner in peace without listening to you rabbiting on?' stormed Tommy, slamming his knife against the plate.

Adele noticed the shocked expression on John's face, and she flushed with shame at her father's behaviour. But she kept quiet, nervous of inciting her father even more.

They continued to eat in silence, and Shirley didn't mention the new Chinese restaurant again. Adele was tense; her muscles were strained and she could feel her heartbeat speeding up. She glanced across at John and smiled at him nervously but he didn't return her smile. Instead he looked down at his plate and prodded at his vegetables.

Adele sped through the meal, sensing John's disapproval and anxious to be away. When she had finished eating she lined up her cutlery on her plate and looked up at her mother.

'I'll take that,' said Shirley, carrying Adele's empty plate over to the sink.

It wasn't like her mother to clear up the dirty pots straightaway and, despite her embarrassment at her father's behaviour, Adele was touched that at least her mother was making the effort. She smiled at her then turned her attention to John once more. He had only eaten half the meal and she willed him to finish quickly so they could make their excuses and go.

'Here, you can take this one as well,' said her father, letting go of his cutlery and giving a satisfied smirk as it clattered onto his plate.

Shirley sped over to the table and took Tommy's empty plate away.

'What's for afters?' Tommy demanded.

Adele made a show of looking at her watch. 'Not for us, thanks. We need to dash. Sorry, Mam, but I'd forgotten we need to call in at John's parents on the way back.' She looked at John, her eyes pleading, hoping he would back her cover story.

'Oh yes, I'd forgotten about that,' he responded, placing his knife and fork down onto his plate, which was still half full.

Her father sniffed before looking accusingly at John. 'You not gonna finish that then?' he asked.

'So sorry, but time's getting on and I'm afraid we really must be gone,' said John. Then, looking over at Shirley, he added, 'Thank you for a lovely meal though, Mrs Robinson. I'm only sorry we can't stop longer. Maybe another time.' He rose from his seat and put out his hand to Tommy. When Tommy ignored his gesture, John crossed the room and shook Shirley's hand instead. 'Thanks again for inviting us, Mrs Robinson,' he said, giving Tommy a sly glance as he walked away.

'Yes, thanks Mam,' said Adele.

Ignoring her father, she also left the table and gave her mother a hug before they left the house. Shirley followed them to the door.

'I'm only sorry you couldn't stay longer,' she said.

'Me too,' said Adele. 'Hopefully next time,' she added, quickly putting on her jacket.

John was already outside the house.

'Sorry about that,' she said to him once she was by his side. 'My dad can be a bit ignorant at times.'

'I noticed,' said John.

Adele's mouth dropped as his words cut through her.

'Not to worry,' he quickly added. 'It's not your fault.'

He placed a perfunctory kiss on her cheek but Adele wasn't convinced by his sudden bonhomie. She knew that, yet again, she was being judged by her parents' behaviour. Although she didn't live at home anymore, unfortunately for Adele, her parents still influenced her life. It was impossible for her to escape their grip.

36

Adele was lying in the bath. She was supposed to be relaxing but as soon as she was alone, with nothing else to occupy her mind, she began to think. Yes, she had a happy life with John but nothing could eradicate the painful recollections of her past. As she lay there, the memories surfaced. The violence at home. The taunts from other kids. And the scornful way she was treated by adults.

She missed her brother who she rarely saw nowadays. Their lives were too different, making it difficult to relate to each other anymore. But they were still linked together by the past.

There had been a time when Peter had been the closest person to her, and sometimes she yearned for that bond again. She knew Peter had moved on from the squat and now had his own flat. What she didn't know was how he found the money to pay for the rent and bills. But she had her suspicions, especially since he'd already been in prison, and she guessed that none of his earnings would be legal.

Although Adele had a loving boyfriend and good friends, nobody could replace her brother. There was something about suffering hardship together that brought you closer. A shared knowledge. An unwritten understanding. Years of looking out for each other, which somehow helped to ease the emotional burden. The absence of her brother had left a void in her life and it was one that nobody else could fill.

When her mind refused to switch off, she stepped out of the bath and pulled the plug. She didn't want to dwell; it wasn't good to dwell. Adele wrapped the towel around herself and made sure she put the lids back on the bottles of luxury bathroom toiletries which neatly lined the bath.

'That was quick,' said John when Adele joined him downstairs.

'I thought I'd join you to watch some TV,' she said, snuggling up to him on the sofa.

'OK, we've just got time for a chat before the film starts,' said John.

There was something about the way John said the word 'chat'; it sounded ominous. Adele stared at him, her face full of concern, but didn't say anything while she waited for him to speak.

'That promotion I told you about,' he began. Adele could feel the dread in the pit of her stomach as she listened to his words. 'They want a decision; they're giving me till Friday.'

'And?' she asked.

John took hold of the tops of her arms as he continued to speak, but Adele was stiff and unresponsive.

'I want to take it, Adele,' he said. 'It's a brilliant opportunity. We could be really happy there. I've been doing some research on the area and it sounds great,' he gushed.

'I don't want to go, John,' she said, exasperated. 'You know that; I've already told you! So what will you do if I don't come with you?'

John released his hold on her arms, creating a physical distance between them. 'I'm sorry Adele, but I'm taking it. Please say you'll come with me. It won't be the same if you don't.'

'For God's sake, John! There are more important things than money. Don't you think our relationship is more important than a flaming promotion?'

'It doesn't need to be the end of our relationship. Please, Adele, say you'll come with me!'

'No!' she yelled. 'I've told you, I'm not coming. I can't!'

John also started to become irate. 'You could come if you wanted to. The fact is, you don't want to come, do you?'

'I've told you, I can't!' she stormed, the rage building within her.

'Why? Because of your family. A brother you hardly ever see, a father you hate and a neurotic mother who puts on you.'

'Don't you dare!' she warned. 'My mother needs me. She can't help the way she is. And I do see Peter.' Even to her, the words sounded unconvincing.

'When do you see him?' John hit back. 'Hardly ever. He's a bloody criminal, Adele! You need to give him a wide berth. And as for your mother…'

John didn't get a chance to finish his last sentence. Consumed by temper, Adele reacted without thinking. She smacked him hard across the face, leaving him stunned. John automatically drew up his hand to cover his cheek, which was hot and stinging from the angry blow.

Adele stared, open-mouthed, shocked at her own actions. But it was done. She couldn't take it back. She waited for

John's words of retaliation. But he didn't speak; he just looked at her contemptuously then got up from the sofa and walked away.

That cut into her more than any words could have done. 'I'm sorry, John,' she said, speeding after him as he left the room. 'I'm really sorry!' she shouted up the stairs as she felt the sting of tears in her eyes. 'I shouldn't have done that.'

She caught up with him and placed a conciliatory hand on his arm.

John spun around, 'Take your hand off me!' he demanded.

Adele could see that an angry red welt was forming on John's cheek, and the guilt tore away at her.

'Leave me alone,' he said. 'I want nothing to do with you.'

'Please, John! I didn't mean it. I was just angry when you had a go at my family.'

'I don't give a shit about your family! Now go away and leave me alone,' he shouted. 'I want nothing more to do with you.'

She pursued him as he sped into the bedroom and took a suitcase from the top of the wardrobe, flinging clothing haphazardly inside it. Despite her pleas, John continued to fill the case. She was desperate; she didn't want to lose him. Reacting to her own despair, she grabbed at his arm to hold him back.

'Take your fuckin' hands off me!' he yelled. 'I've told you, I want nothing further to do with you.' She backed off but John wasn't finished. 'Y'know, I've put up with a lot from you and your family, Adele. Having to visit them when your father hardly speaks two words to me, and trying to make conversation with your docile mother. And as for your brother! I can't tell you what a relief it is to not be associated with the sister of a criminal anymore.'

Adele didn't retaliate. She was feeling too remorseful for what she had done to John's face, and looking at it was making her feel even worse. So, instead, she left him to pack, and returned to the living room. There she sat and cried desperate tears for what she'd lost.

She heard the door slam as John left. Now she had yet another failed relationship behind her. And she was alone once more.

37

Peter looked through the spyhole in his front door before opening it. He was always careful who he let inside. With some of the activities he was involved in, it paid to be cautious. He saw a familiar face staring impatiently at the door waiting for him to answer. It was his contact, Spikey, and he was carrying a package.

Peter opened the door and indicated for Spikey to come inside. Without preamble, Peter nodded at the parcel Spikey was carrying. 'You got 'em then?' he asked.

'Yeah, same price as we agreed,' said Spikey, holding out the parcel and waiting for the money.

'Hang on. I need to check 'em first,' said Peter.

Spikey followed Peter through to the living room. He sat down and waited, his restless twitch bearing evidence to his habitual use of cocaine.

Peter tore open the box and pulled away the strips of paper that covered its contents. When he had ripped away the last of the paper, he whistled. 'These are beauties,' he said.

'Told you they would be,' said Spikey as Peter took out the first of the guns and played around with it in his hands, feeling its weight and sizing it up. He pulled back the trigger and pointed, causing an upsurge in Spikey's twitching.

'I take it they're not loaded?' Peter asked.

'I don't think so,' said Spikey. 'But don't be taking any fuckin' chances!'

Peter chuckled and pulled out the other gun revealing the bullets which were laid out in a compartment underneath. 'Nice one. Looks like you got hold of plenty of ammo as well.'

'Don't be fuckin' loading 'em here,' said Spikey.

'Don't worry. As long as you say they're in full working order, I'll take your word for it. Besides, don't wanna draw any attention to us, do I?'

When Peter had spent some time toying with the guns, he reached inside his pocket for the cash and handed it over to Spikey. He noticed Spikey's shaking hand as he grabbed at it. Without waiting for Peter to lead him to the door, he left the flat. Peter followed him anyway just to make sure he'd shut the door after him. He sniggered as he peeped through the spyhole and watched Spikey rush off into the distance.

He'd known the guns would be kosher but he couldn't resist making Spikey sweat a bit before he handed over the cash. It amused him to see Spikey twitch, and it paid to make sure he stayed in line. Peter liked to let people know who was in charge.

Once Spikey had gone, Peter concealed the guns where nobody would find them and went into the living room to make a call.

'Hi Dave,' he said when David answered the phone. 'They're here, and they're good uns too. When you free?'

He listened to David before responding, 'OK, sounds good. Meet me here and we'll make the arrangements.'

When Peter put down the phone, a smile lit up his face. He'd been thinking about acquiring some guns for a while. A knife wasn't enough anymore and he'd had his fill of have-a-go heroes thinking they could take him on. One guy had even kicked the knife out of his hand, leaving him with no choice but to abandon the job. These guns would change everything. Nobody pissed you about when you had a gun. And, apart from letting the targets know who was boss, word would soon get out around the criminal fraternity. Peter Robinson was moving up a league. He and David now had guns, and they weren't afraid to use them.

Adele was regretting her decision to have Sunday dinner with her mother again, but she'd been at a loose end. She was already feeling down since her split with John a few days previously, but the atmosphere inside her mother's home only made matters worse. The stale aroma hit her as soon as she walked in. She followed her mother into the kitchen where she was busy sorting the washing.

Adele felt a pang of irritation as she looked at the washing stacked around the room. It was everywhere. Piles on chairs, some on the sideboard and dirty washing in two heaps on the floor. She was disconcerted to see that her mother hadn't started the dinner yet and instinctively knew what was required of her.

'Come on, let's get these sorted,' she said, lifting a pile of dry, clean washing off the chair nearest to her. 'Then I'll help you start the dinner.'

'It's OK, love,' said Shirley. 'I'll sort these; I know where

I'm up to with them. But you wouldn't be a love and start the veg for me, would you?'

Adele sighed heavily and moved over to the sink where she filled the bowl with water and threw the vegetables into it ready to wash and cut them.

'You don't seem so bright,' said Shirley after several seconds.

Adele sighed again, 'I've split up with John,' she said.

'Oh you haven't, love? What happened?'

'He's left me to go and work in London.' She didn't mention how she'd lashed out at him. Her mother didn't need to know that.

'Didn't he ask you to go with him?' her mother asked.

'Yeah, but I couldn't go, and he wouldn't stay here. So that's that.'

'Oh, I am sorry, love. I'll make you a cuppa when I've finished sorting these,' said Shirley. She didn't ask why Adele couldn't go to London. It was as though she already knew the answer.

Adele grunted in response and continued preparing the veg. She could feel herself becoming annoyed at her mother's lack of apparent interest. The offer of a cup of tea had irritated her even more. As if that could put everything right. What she really needed was reassurance; someone to tell her everything would be OK. But she knew she wouldn't get that from her mother.

Normally Adele would have made some excuse and left. But her mother had invited her for dinner and she hadn't even started making it yet. Adele bit back her irritation; there was no point taking things out on her mother.

While they worked, Adele listened to her mother's dull chatter. She couldn't have been less interested in the lives of

Shirley's neighbours and their relatives. Adele wasn't attached to any of them. But she nodded and made affirmative sounds in response to her mother's gossip while her mind drifted. She became lost in thoughts of her broken relationship with John.

'It's such a shame; she was only fifty-four,' Shirley continued. 'I don't know what her poor son's going to do. Do you think I should go and offer to help him?'

'Hmm,' Adele replied when her mother paused.

'What should I offer to do?' she asked.

When there was a pause in conversation, Adele looked at her mother's expectant face. 'Eh?' she asked.

'Oh, Adele. You haven't been listening to a word I've said, have you?'

Adele's eyelids flickered. 'Sorry, Mam,' she said. 'I've got a lot on my mind.'

'Aw come on, love,' said Shirley, hugging her awkwardly from behind. 'I'll make you that cup of tea and we'll have a sit-down. Don't worry about the veg; we can finish it later.'

But Adele didn't want to prolong her stay. 'It's OK, Mam. I've nearly finished. Just give me a few more minutes then the dinner can be cooking while we're having a drink. What time's my dad home?' she asked.

'Oh, you know him. He'll be home when he's home. It's OK; I can warm his dinner up for him.'

But Shirley didn't need to warm Tommy's tea. He walked in the house just as they were serving it onto plates then joined them at the table.

Adele had to listen to her mother's gossip all over again while she filled Tommy in on the latest happenings. He didn't even grace her with a nod or a mutter. He just continued eating.

The only time he responded to Shirley's gossip was when she added her latest instalment. 'Our Adele's finished with John,' she announced in a matter-of-fact way.

Tommy paused and looked across the table at Adele. She glanced away, not wishing to share her bad news with him.

He sniffed, raising his right nostril till his mouth formed a sneer. 'Ah well, you're better off shut of him,' he said. 'He was a bit of a snob if you ask me.'

'I didn't ask you!' Adele snapped. She could see her mother tense as she awaited Tommy's reaction.

'All right!' he hit back. 'Calm yourself down. There's no need to take it out on us, for Christ's sake! I was only saying.'

'Well, I don't need your opinions,' said Adele.

'What the bloody hell does it matter? You're not with him now anyway.'

Shirley quickly cut in before the row escalated. 'I don't think your dad means any harm, Adele love.'

Adele looked at her mother's pleading eyes and restrained herself. Now that she no longer lived under her parents' roof, Adele didn't fear her father as much. But her concern was for her mother. She knew that if she let the row escalate, her mother would bear the brunt of it once she had gone.

They ate the rest of the meal in silence; the tension in the air was almost palpable. Adele was glad when the meal was over so she could make her excuses and go. Back to her lonely home. She only hoped her father wouldn't take his bad mood out on her mother once she had gone.

38

By the time she arrived inside her own house, Adele was feeling even more down than before she had set off for her mother's. The silence felt oppressive. It was accompanied by an absence of feeling, which was emphasised by the sound of her footsteps echoing in the tiled hallway. There was no John to embrace her or make her pulse quicken. No messy male clutter to niggle her as she walked through the lounge. No coffee aroma to greet her. Instead there was nothing, and the rooms felt bare.

She looked around at the pristine furniture, ornaments and furnishings. They were nothing without the warmth of her lover. She'd give anything to see John's mess scattered around the place now. He had been so right for her, and she couldn't help but feel bitterness towards her family. If only she didn't feel responsible for them then she would have gladly gone to London with him. That was where she belonged, with John; not here by herself. But she couldn't change anything. She knew how much her mother needed her and, even though it grated on her, she felt responsible for her.

She felt OK while she was at work. Adele poured herself into the job, working much harder than usual, so that she could take her mind off things. She also had her bookkeeping exams to study for, which gave her something to focus on. But it was in the late evenings when she was at home that she felt the worst; there were just too many reminders of her absent ex-boyfriend.

Adele settled onto her cosy couch to watch some TV but nothing held her interest. She felt lonely. In the fridge a bottle of wine beckoned to her. She tried to resist but eventually gave in. It was the fourth time she'd drunk alone this week. As she sipped the glass of chilled white wine, she promised herself that she wouldn't let this become a habit. Thoughts of her father's bad relationship with alcohol were all too clear in her mind.

After two glasses she was becoming mellow and able to focus more on the television but as she neared the bottom of the bottle her sombre mood returned. She switched the TV off and played some ballads instead; sad songs which conveyed how she was feeling. She cried at the poignant words then muttered drunkenly in agreement with the sentiments.

When her tears had dried, she decided she needed someone to talk to. Someone who would empathise with her situation. Someone who understood her. And someone whose focus could help ease the pain. She ran through a list of people in her alcohol-fuddled brain. Who could she talk to?

Then it came to her. She lifted the telephone receiver and made the call, her greeting exaggerated and overenthusiastic due to her intoxication, 'Hiya Bro, long time, no see. How are you?'

★

Peter had just come back from a job, and was hyped up. He was counting out cash into two bundles; one for him and one for David. The ringing of the phone made him jump, his senses still finely tuned. He thought about ignoring the call while he continued to count but its ringing was insistent so he took a quick note of where he was up to and rushed to answer it.

The sound of his sister slurring down the phone caught him off guard. He hadn't heard from her for so long. She had always been the sensible one and the fact that she was ringing him drunk late at night must mean there was something wrong.

'Hiya, Adele. What's up?'

'Nothing, jussst thought I'd catch up with my little brother,' she slurred. 'How are you anyway?'

'I'm all right. What about you?'

It was obvious to Peter that the pretence of just ringing him for a chat was difficult to keep up in her drunken state so she got straight to the point. 'Bastard's dumped me.'

'What, that John d'you mean?'

'Yeah, pissssed off to London and left me here on my own.'

'Right. Well... he was a bit of a dick anyway to be honest.'

'Oh thanksss for telling me now. I've only been living with the dick for the lassst year.'

'Sorry, sis. I just meant he's a bit stuck-up, isn't he?'

'No, he isn't. He's all right once you get to know him,' she responded, defensively.

'So why didn't you go with him if you're that bothered?'

'Oh, yeah. And leave my mam on her own with *him*?'

When she mentioned her parents he was more responsive. Peter knew too well what things were like between his mam and dad, and he felt a sudden pang of guilt knowing that he had left Adele to do the lion's share when it came to helping their mother. He'd had the perfect excuse to opt out; his father hated having him around. That meant Peter had to choose a time when his father wasn't there and one which rarely seemed to fit in with his life.

'Can't you still see him; maybe arrange to go down there at weekends?' he asked She was obviously very stuck on the guy.

'He won't ssspeak to me.'

'Why not?'

'We rowed about him going.'

'Well make it up with him.'

'Dunno, maybe I could.'

After Adele and Peter had chatted for a while, they agreed to get together soon. When he had put the phone down Peter spent a few moments reflecting. He had mixed feelings about getting back in touch with his sister.

On the one hand, he was pleased as well as flattered that she had turned to him when she was feeling a bit down. But, on the other hand, he had concerns. He was involved in some heavy stuff now and the last thing he needed was his sister finding out and giving him grief. She was far too strait-laced to know what he got up to or what weapons he carried. So, while he was happy to meet up with her, he decided to keep quiet about some of his activities.

He strode over to where the guns were kept and examined them once more. *Yes,* he thought, fingering the smooth metal of one of the gun's barrels. *She must never find out about these beauties.*

39

The next day Adele thought about her conversation with Peter. He was right; she should try to make up with John. She missed him so much and knew that it would make her feel better if they could at least stay friends.

She picked up the phone with shaking hands and dialled the number of his firm in London. While she waited for the receptionist to put her through she could feel the throbbing of her heartbeat. She cleared her throat, ready to speak to him.

When she heard his voice her heart fluttered. 'Hello. John Mullen speaking.'

He sounded so self-assured.

'John, it's me,' she said, feeling her voice tremble.

'Oh!'

'John, please don't put the phone down. I need to speak to you.'

'I'm at work,' he whispered. 'It's a bit awkward,' but she could sense a softening in his tone of voice. Perhaps he had missed her too.

'I know, I'm sorry,' she said. 'It was the only way I could get hold of you. I'm sorry for what I did, John. I was upset. I know that's no excuse. It was wrong of me and I'm really sorry.'

He paused before responding. 'OK, well it's good to hear that anyway.'

He was right. It was awkward. He sounded detached and she felt as though he was holding back, conscious of eavesdroppers.

'I just want to stay friends, John. Maybe we could chat once in a while. I don't want to lose contact with you. We were too close for that.'

'All right. That sounds good,' he said, his voice formal.

'Is it difficult to speak?' she asked.

'Yeah, it is. But I can give you another number.'

'Wait. I'll grab a pen.' She rushed around trying to find a pen and paper, then quickly scribbled down his number, clutching the pen in her sweaty hands. 'OK, I'll speak to you soon,' she said.

Once he had bidden her goodbye, she put the phone down and smiled to herself, the relief flooding through her. Perhaps she hadn't lost him altogether after all.

Eric walked into the bank on King Street with his colleague, Steve. Eric was a big man at six foot three and sixteen and a half stone, and he stood tall and proud in his navy blue trousers and navy, ribbed sweater with the name of his firm embroidered over the left side of his chest. He enjoyed the respect that his security uniform gave him. Most people stared at his bulky frame and stepped to one side to let him pass as he and his colleague marched through the banking hall.

Eric and Steve were speedy and business-like and didn't stop long to chat to the banking staff; not when there was a huge amount of cash to be collected. It was important to get it loaded into the security van as soon as possible.

They collected the cash. Then they were on their way back outside, Eric holding the cash close to his body while Steve went in front, careful to keep only a step ahead of Eric. That was the way they worked, so that Steve would be ready to help Eric if anyone made a grab for the cash. They made their way to their company van, which was parked as near to the bank entrance as they could get on a busy afternoon.

Outside they walked the few metres to the van, keeping up a brisk pace. Steve went round to the front, ready to get into the driver's seat and start the engine, while Eric went to place the money into the back. All this was done automatically without exchanging words; they both knew the drill.

Eric had just opened the back doors of the van ready to store the cash, along with the others he had collected earlier that day, when two men appeared. They seemed to have come out of nowhere. But Eric was ready for them and within a split second he had sized them up and fancied his chances. They weren't the biggest men in the world but he could tell they meant business as they'd taken the trouble to disguise their faces by wearing balaclavas.

Eric was no fool; with his height and frame he knew he could take them on. He surmised that there were probably others at the front of the van but he was confident that Steve could take care of them.

One of the men made a grab for the cash but Eric kept a tight grip on it with both hands, his elbows turned out to the sides. He pivoted backwards, placing his right foot behind the left at a forty-five-degree angle then swung forward rapidly, raising his elbow, which connected with the man's face as he spun round.

The man rocked back on his heels with the force of the blow, clutching his bloody nose with both hands. The second man advanced towards Eric, but before he had chance to reach for the cash, Eric threw it into the back of the van. Then he stepped forward, blocking the man's way to the money. Eric swiftly cupped both his hands together, lifted them high and brought them down hard on the back of the man's neck. The man crumbled to the ground.

While his attackers were still stunned, Eric drew his keys out ready to lock the van's doors. His subconscious mind registered a scuffle at the front of the van, but he was too occupied to focus on it.

He was just about to put the key in the lock when the first man stuck a gun to his head. But Eric didn't scare easily. Acting on impulse, he swiped the gun away and it tumbled to the floor. While the man bent to retrieve his gun, Eric raised his fist in a swift uppercut to the man's face, sending him sprawling to the ground.

When the second man came back at him, Eric didn't see him approach. He just felt a presence followed by a sharp blow to the side of his head. Then everything went black.

Eric was only out for a few minutes. But when he opened his eyes a large crowd had gathered around him. As his fuzzy brain recalled what had happened, his first impulse was to check the van. He looked up. It was almost empty. The men had cleared as many boxes as they could in the limited amount of time they had. And they were gone.

Raising his hand to the throbbing pain at the side of his head, Eric gazed around him. Disorientated, he was deciding his next move when he heard the sound of a woman's voice break out from the crowd.

'He's coming to,' she said. 'Are you all right, love?'

Eric stared into the crowd, tracing the sound of the woman's voice, but before he could respond, a man also spoke out, his words devastating Eric. 'Thank God this one's still alive, at least,' he said.

The Ford Sierra drew to a stop on a track road in a desolated area of the Pennines. A few metres away, secreted under some trees and bushes, was another car, a blue Volvo, which had been driven there earlier that day. The five men got out of the Ford Sierra and one of them popped the boot open. They then transferred the cash from the Sierra to the Volvo, emptying it out of the banks' sealed plastic bags and putting it into their own bags instead. The men threw the empty plastic bags into the Ford Sierra to be disposed of later.

'Right, are we ready?' asked Sam, once they had finished loading the cash.

'Dave, have you got the petrol?' asked Peter, whose face was still smeared with blood from his fight with the security guard. David walked back from the Volvo with a petrol can in his hand.

'Mickey, have you checked there's nothing in there?' asked Peter.

'Yeah, but I'll give it a last look,' said Mickey, opening the front door of the Sierra and scouring the area around the seats, dashboard and footwell before moving onto the back of the car.

He was looking for anything that might incriminate them; something that might survive a fire, such as a fallen piece of jewellery. Once Peter was satisfied that Mickey had given the Sierra a good going-over, he nodded at David who emptied the contents of the petrol can liberally onto the car, making sure that he covered the interior upholstery as well as the body.

When the can was almost empty, David trailed the petrol away from the Sierra to a distance of several metres. Then he threw the empty can back to where the vehicle was parked.

'Right, stand back,' said Peter.

The men moved away, leaving the next task to Peter. He'd opted to finish it himself, and was looking forward to this part of the job. He joined his friends several metres away.

'You go back a bit further,' Peter instructed David. 'You might have traces of petrol on your clothes. We don't want you going up like a fuckin' inferno, do we?'

Once David was safely away, Peter lit a match and threw it at the petrol trail. He missed. Two more attempts and the match hit. The impact was instantaneous. Peter watched in awe as the angry flames danced along the ground then enveloped the Sierra. A ball of fire was soon shooting up from the car, which was now barely visible beneath it.

'Wow!' said David. 'Fuckin' brilliant.'

Feeling the intense heat from the burning vehicle, the men moved further back and Peter gave David a self-satisfied smirk. For several minutes they watched the destructive flames ravage the Sierra and its contents.

'Job done I think, lads,' said Peter, grinning. 'Let's get back.'

They crowded into the Volvo and began talking. On the journey up to the Pennines they had stayed silent. Peter wouldn't allow any discussion about the job until it was over.

They had needed to focus until they were away from the bank and had destroyed the Sierra. Now the analysis would begin.

'What the fuck happened, Dave?' Peter asked. 'I told you not to fuckin' shoot anyone unless we had to. The guns are supposed to scare 'em, that's all.'

'No choice, Pete. The bastard had his keys in the ignition and was trying to start the engine. I couldn't let him get away before we got the cash.'

Peter looked across at Sam who had partnered David. Sam quickly corroborated what David had said.

'Trouble is the fuckin' cops will be all over it now.' Peter sighed. 'A bank robbery's one thing, but they don't like fuckin' fatalities.'

'No choice, Pete. Like I said,' said David.

'All right, let's leave it,' said Peter but he wasn't happy. For several seconds he remained silent with a scowl on his face.

Mickey spoke next, breaking the tension inside the car. 'Fuckin' game for it, that security guard, wasn't he?' he commented. 'My fuckin' neck's still throbbing where he hit me.'

'Yeah,' Peter replied. 'I can't believe he knocked the fuckin' gun out of my hand. I'll have to watch out for that in future. It's a good job you had that fuckin' baseball bat hidden inside your jacket, Mickey. Nice one that. The bastard was out for the count.'

They continued discussing the job for several minutes and the atmosphere gradually eased between them. It wasn't long before they were back in Manchester.

The armed robberies were a new addition to Peter's criminal activities and they were proving worthwhile. The only snag was that it was high risk, which today's events had shown. But today had been an exception; usually things went much more smoothly.

Since Peter and David had acquired the guns, people had begun to show them more respect, as Peter had anticipated. It hadn't taken long until they found men willing to work with them so they'd formed a five-man team.

Knowing that the security guards worked in pairs, Peter allocated two men to each of the security guards while the fifth member of his gang stayed in the getaway car, ready to start the engine as soon as needed. His teamwork was paying off. As the gang leader, he took the biggest share of the cash. Not only was he building up a tidy stack of money but his reputation in the criminal world was also gaining momentum. People feared him, and Peter relished the feeling of power he held over them.

40

Adele walked into the Boardroom bar in the city centre. The place was full of trendy twenty-somethings and she made her way through several groups of people who chatted loudly while the sound of Spandau Ballet played in the background.

She had made an effort, as she always did, and was wearing a navy blue wrap dress, which accentuated her curves while also disguising the few extra pounds she had gained since her break-up with John. In her hand she clutched a black, patent leather handbag, which matched her stiletto heels. She stopped and glanced around the room, trying to find her brother.

There he was, sitting at a large round table surrounded by his friends, with two young, attractive women fawning over him. She recognised a few of the faces from her past and cringed at recollections of the torment she had suffered at their hands. She paused momentarily, deciding whether to join Peter or whether to turn around and walk out the door. But before she reached a decision her brother spotted her.

'Adele, over here,' he shouted.

She approached the table and noticed that the two women seemed to be competing for Peter's attention. When Peter introduced Adele to everyone the two women barely acknowledged her.

But David reacted, standing up and pulling out his chair with a flourish. 'Please be seated, Your Ladyship,' he teased and the group sniggered.

'What do you want to drink, Adele?' asked Peter, ignoring David's comment.

'Oh, thanks,' she said, flattered by his generosity.

Peter took a note of what Adele and his friends wanted to drink then he headed off to the bar. Adele sat on the chair David had provided while he dragged another chair up to the table and squeezed in next to her.

'Well, how've you been?' David asked, draping his arm over the back of her chair, his insincere smile revealing a broken and stained front tooth.

They made small talk for a few minutes. David was very interested in her job, especially when she told him about her recent promotion following completion of her bookkeeping exams. But she couldn't help feeling that his interest was disingenuous, as though it was leading up to something. Her intuition was right; the tone of the conversation soon changed.

'What brings you here, anyway?' David asked. 'We've not seen you for ages. I bet you think you're too good for us now you're a supervisor,' he sneered.

'Not really. I wouldn't be here if I did, would I?'

David sniffed and picked up his pint. Adele sat uncomfortably for a few moments waiting for Peter to come back from the bar. When he did, he was carrying several drinks on a tray, which he handed around to his friends.

It was obvious to Adele that they all looked up to Peter. She could tell by the way they reacted enthusiastically to his banter and attempts at humour. Then the conversation turned to recent activities.

'How'd that last job go?' one of the men asked Peter.

She could see Peter shake his head before replying, 'OK, you know. The usual.'

'Haha,' David interrupted. 'Best not let big sis know what you get up to, Pete. She'll have the law on us.'

'Shut up, Dave,' snapped Peter. 'It's all kosher.'

'Haha, yeah. Course it is,' David laughed.

The men then seemed to speak in a code that Adele didn't understand. There were references to jobs, targets and readies. It was obvious they were talking about something underhand but Adele was unable to comprehend the details. She shuffled uncomfortably in her seat, feeling entirely out of place. Because of her discomfort she found herself downing her drink faster than usual. It was soon finished, so she went to the bar to buy another drink for herself and Peter.

When Adele joined the crowd around the table again, their enthusiastic chatter dulled and the volume dropped. It was as though there was a swift change in topic as soon as she was within earshot.

'I tell you what,' said David, 'if you ever need a solicitor for your "kosher" business, Pete, maybe big sis can sort you out.' Then, turning to Adele, he added, 'Bet you know some big-shot solicitors where you work, don't you? Maybe they could help us out if we ever get in a bit of bother.'

'Not really,' said Adele. 'The accounts department is in a separate office. Anyway, it's not that kind of solicitors. They deal in conveyancing mainly.'

'Oooh, get you,' taunted David.

Adele had had enough. 'What is your fuckin' problem?' she snapped. 'Just because I work for a living, it doesn't make me a snob! You wanna fuckin' try it sometime instead of being a complete waster.' She scowled at David who jumped back in his chair. His movement was dramatic and exaggerated; another taunt.

'She bites,' he sniggered and the group joined in his laughter.

Adele stood up, scraping her chair across the floor. 'Fuck off, tosser!' she shouted before pouring her drink all over David's head and storming out of the bar to the sound of jeers and laughter.

Shirley sat sobbing in her living room. She knew she was becoming maudlin but she couldn't help it. She missed her kids and her mother even though she had been gone for a few years now. She stared up at the mantelpiece, admiring the porcelain figurine, which looked so out of place in her living room. It had been her mother's until she died, and Shirley treasured it. In fact, the figurine was one of the few ornaments she bothered dusting. That and the large brass cat, which decorated the hearth, were the only ornaments that Shirley lavished with any attention. She'd inherited both of them from her mother. Every time she stared at the figurine she was comforted. It seemed to reflect her mother's personality, standing proudly amidst the clutter.

When Tommy came home, Shirley sensed that he was in a mood straightaway. It was in his stance, the look on his face and the stomping of his feet. He was also drunk. Shirley quickly dried her eyes, hoping he hadn't noticed. But he had.

'What the fuck's wrong with you?' he demanded.

'Nothing, just having a moment. That's all.'

'No wonder you don't get any fuckin' housework done when you're sat scriking all the time. Your mam's been gone years, for fuck's sake! It's about time you pulled yourself together.'

Normally Shirley would keep her mouth shut but the mention of her mother annoyed her. 'You don't know what it's like!' she complained. 'It's never happened to you and, even if it did, you probably wouldn't bother.'

'What the fuck's that supposed to mean,' he asked, lumbering over towards her.

His rigid posture and glaring eyes were enough to quash Shirley, who began to backtrack. 'Nothing. I just mean that you're not that close to your mam and dad.'

'None of your bleedin' business,' he said, walking over to the fireplace.

He was carrying a lit cigarette, which had burnt down so far that the lit end was almost touching his fingers. He hovered against the mantelpiece, searching for the ashtray, which was concealed beneath the clutter. Shirley was up out of her chair anticipating his next move. She was ready to shift some of the mess so that the ashtray was visible. But she was too late.

'Fuckin' shite!' yelled Tommy, swiping at the items that crowded the mantelpiece.

Shirley's breath caught in her throat as she watched the figurine tumble down to the ground. 'No!' she yelled, bending to pick it up.

Its arm was missing and the rest of it was covered in cracks. For seconds she stood, speechless, nursing her precious figurine while the tears flowed.

She was upset but she was also angry. 'You bastard!' she shouted at Tommy in an uncharacteristic display of courage.

'Look what you've done to my mam's ornament,' she said, holding it up for him to see the damage.

Tommy swung his fist at Shirley's hand, launching the figurine across the living room. It landed in the corner and smashed into tiny pieces.

'Don't you fuckin' dare speak to me like that!' he yelled, gripping his hands tightly around Shirley's throat.

Shirley retaliated. 'Get off me!' she stormed, bashing his arms with her fists to try to loosen his grip. His hands continued to tighten around her throat until she was unable to speak. So she dug her nails into his hands.

Tommy drew his hands away in shock. He was still holding the cigarette and, as he pulled his hands away, the lit end singed his fingers. He dropped it instantaneously, howling from the stinging pain.

'I'll fuckin' teach you!' he screeched as he started raining blows on Shirley's face and torso.

Shirley held up her arms to protect her face but this incensed him more. As Tommy unleashed his full fury, Shirley was helpless. After a torrent of punches, she crumpled to the floor. Tommy wasn't finished. No longer able to thump her, he used his feet instead. His sturdy work boots were perilous and Shirley cried out in pain as blow after blow assailed her body.

When he had finished, he straightened himself up, panting for breath with spittle leaching from his angry mouth. Then he grabbed her hair, forcing her to face him.

'Fuckin' bitch,' he cursed then spat into her face before walking away.

Shirley lay on the floor in pain. She glanced up through eyes that were already beginning to swell. There in a corner of the room she could just about make out the shattered remains of her treasured figurine.

41

It had been several weeks since John had left for London, and Adele was still finding it difficult. Even though she was now in touch with him, and he had forgiven her rash behaviour, it wasn't the same as having him here with her.

At work she coped by pouring herself into her new supervisory role, which helped to take her mind off things. But the nights were the most difficult. As she glanced at the clock, she dreaded the long evening that stretched ahead of her.

She was presently occupying herself by listening to more sad ballads, but at least she wasn't drinking as much. Instead she consoled herself by eating. She'd always had a sweet tooth, which she had managed to keep under control until now. Shortbread, chocolate and cream cakes were now a nightly indulgence. To hell with the few pounds she'd gained; she had nobody to look good for now.

While she listened to her music, she relived the break-up again in her mind. All the whys and wherefores were never far from her thoughts. She couldn't help but beat herself up over it, and was almost relieved when the ringing phone gave her a change of focus. That was, until she found out who it was and what had happened.

'Adele, it's yer mam. I'm in hospital, love.'

Her mother's voice sounded weak and shaky, sending Adele into an immediate panic. 'What is it, Mam? What's happened?'

'I… I've had an accident. I fell down the stairs. I'm all right. There's nothing to worry about but I need some things from home.'

'Oh my God! Are you OK?'

'Yes, just a few bruises, that's all. But they won't let me go home till the doctor's seen me tomorrow morning so I'm going to need some stuff.'

'Sure,' said Adele. 'What is it you need?'

Adele knew immediately that the story about falling down the stairs was fabricated, probably for the benefit of eavesdroppers. While she took a note of the things her mother needed, the thought occurred to her that her father should have been taking her mother's things into hospital. This convinced her even more that something must have happened between her parents although she doubted whether he would have been that helpful anyway. He wasn't like normal husbands.

'What ward are you in and what time is visiting?' asked Adele. She wrote the details down on a piece of paper. 'OK,' she added. 'I'll bring your things tomorrow when I've had a chance to collect them but I can come and visit you tonight as well if you like.'

'No, it's OK, love. It's getting a bit late now. You won't have long by the time you get here.'

Adele looked at the clock. Ten past seven. She did a quick calculation in her head; five minutes to freshen up and a short drive that would only take fifteen minutes at this time of night. That meant she should have at least half an hour with her mother before visiting finished at eight o'clock.

'No, I'll come,' said Adele. 'I've got nothing else on and I can be there in no time.'

Adele was curious. She wanted to see for herself what sort of state her mother was in and the fact that she was trying to put her off didn't sound good. She guessed that if her mother hadn't wanted her to fetch some things then she would probably have tried to conceal her injuries from her altogether. The way her mother always tried to cover up for her father still puzzled Adele.

She raced around the house, and within just over five minutes she was ready to go and assess the latest damage her father had inflicted.

It took a while to find Ward 13 and, by the time Adele had traipsed through the extensive hospital grounds, it was twenty to eight. She rushed through the ward, passing beds surrounded by the families and friends of patients.

When Adele reached the end of the ward she still hadn't found her mother. She checked the details she had written down again. Yes, definitely Ward 13. She wondered whether she might have taken it down incorrectly but she was fairly certain that her mother had said thirteen. She remembered the irony of that particular number. Unlucky for some.

Adele decided to walk back down the ward and take it slowly this time. With all the visitors around, it was difficult to see the patients. But something told her that her mother probably wouldn't have any visitors.

There had been one patient without visitors but she'd passed her by. It couldn't be her. Surely? But what if it was? Adele felt a sense of doom. She made a point of looking at that patient as she approached.

Adele stopped at the end of the bed, trying to take in the woman's features. It was difficult to tell whether it was her mother or not; the injuries were so bad. In the end it was her mother's straggly hair that gave her away. When Adele was within a metre of her, she gasped in shock. Shirley attempted a lopsided smile from her swollen, misshapen lips.

'Oh, Mam,' said Adele, rushing towards her.

As Adele put her arms around her mother, she could feel tears of distress cloud her eyes. She forced the tears back, not wanting to upset her. She held her gently, careful to avoid the bruising to her arms and trying not to press too hard on the arm that was in plaster. Shirley's face was so full of bruises and red welts that there was hardly any unblemished flesh visible, and her lips were split and puffy. Her eyes were both swollen and coloured black and blue. It was no wonder she hadn't called out when Adele walked past; she probably couldn't see to the end of the bed.

She was wearing a flimsy hospital gown with a wide neckline, and Adele could see that the bruising also extended to her throat and shoulders. The marks on her throat looked like angry fingerprints and Adele baulked at the thought that her father had tried to strangle her.

Adele had a flashback to a few years previously when her father had given Peter a savage beating. She could relive the event even now. The fear coursing through her. A desperate need to help her brother. The blood spattering. Her brother's face a mask of pain and the stinging blows she received as she tried to form a human shield. Adele's breath caught in her throat. She could picture the scene only too well.

'What brought this on?' she asked.

Shirley's eyes flitted across to the visitors sitting around the neighbouring bed. 'I told you, I fell down the stairs,' she said.

Adele knew that her mother wouldn't confide in her while other people could overhear so she dropped her voice to a whisper. 'Why, Mam? I thought he wasn't as bad these days.'

Shirley glanced across at a woman who was watching them and shrugged her shoulders. The movement caused her to wince in pain.

'What about your arm?' whispered Adele. 'Is it broken?'

'Yeah,' Shirley replied. Then, noticing that the woman's eyes were still on them, she added loudly, 'That must have happened because I fell funny.'

There was nothing funny about this situation, Adele thought, sardonically, but before they had chance to discuss the matter any further a nurse announced that visiting time was over. Adele would have to wait until the next day to hear the horrifying truth.

42

Adele called at her parents' home once visiting had finished so that she would have her mother's things ready to take to hospital the following day. As she still had a key, she let herself in. She was surprised to find her father there as the pubs were still open. He was sitting in his armchair slurping from a can of beer.

As Adele walked into the living room, he glanced at her, grunted then carried on watching TV. Adele was incensed.

'Aren't you going to ask how my mam is?' she demanded.

'Oh, you've been to see her, have you?' he asked.

Adele noticed the way he refused to make eye contact with her. But he disguised his guilt with a display of apathy, which annoyed her even more.

'Yes, I have. And you should have been visiting her too! Or maybe you feel too guilty for what you've done.'

'What yer talking about? She fell down the stairs.'

'That's a load of crap, and you know it!' yelled Adele.

'Don't you speak to me like that, young lady, or I'll give you what for.'

'Oh, here we go again. You can't face up to what you've done so you resort to threats and intimidation.'

'Don't come here with yer big fancy words. I've done nowt wrong,' he said, then he turned his head towards the TV screen again, ignoring Adele.

She was becoming increasingly furious. How dare he just brush it off! She'd make him face up to it. It was about time he answered for his behaviour. Acting in anger, she stepped in front of the TV, blocking it from his view. 'If you're so bleedin' innocent then why aren't you at the hospital?' she challenged. 'You haven't even had the decency to ask how she is!'

'I'm warning you!' he shouted. 'If you don't fuckin' shift from that TV, I'll come and shift you.'

But Adele was beyond fear. Rage had taken over. 'You don't scare me anymore!' she yelled. 'You're just a good-for-nothing bully.'

'Right!' he bawled, rising from his chair and lunging at Adele.

She anticipated his move, sidestepping him so that she was now standing next to the fireplace. Before she could use her kickboxing skills, he was upon her, slapping her on the side of her head. She drew backwards, trying to recover from the blow. Then she advanced on him with a roundhouse kick. But he was fast despite his bulk. He grabbed her leg, sending her off balance.

Adele fell to the ground, her head hitting the stone hearth. Ignoring the dizziness that made her head swim, she swiped viciously at his leg till it went beneath him. He landed on top of her, his weight pinning her to the ground. Before she could wriggle free, he had his hands around her throat.

'I'll teach you, you stuck-up little bitch!' he cursed. 'Don't you fuckin' dare come in my house shouting the odds at me!

She deserved it. She's nowt but a useless, lazy cow. And you're not much better. That boyfriend soon pissed off when he found out what you were like, didn't he?'

She gasped for breath, her feelings of terror battling with the fury that raged within her. How dare he use John against her!

Just when she thought she could stand it no longer, he released his hold. 'That'll fuckin' teach you!' he sneered.

Adele struggled to throw him off but he was too powerful. He laughed at her failed attempts; he was toying with her.

'You bastard!' she cursed.

Adele glared at her despotic father and clawed at his face. He reacted by grabbing her hair with one hand while he slapped her hard across the face with the other. The stinging blow brought tears to her eyes. But she wouldn't let him beat her!

Her determination sent angry waves of adrenalin pulsing through her body. Adele's fight mechanism kicked in. She reached for something with which to hit him. Her hand settled on the smooth, hard surface of the brass cat. Adele raised it and brought it down forcefully onto his head and he collapsed on top of her. But she carried on pummelling him.

Hatred! Anger! Fear! They all combined. Driving her on.

Smash!

Years of neglect and abuse.

Bash!

A lifetime of terror and pain.

Smack!

Over and over she kept hitting him with the brass cat. Again and again.

Blood oozed from a gaping wound at the side of his head but still she kept going. Until she was exhausted. And her rage was assuaged. She dropped the heavy ornament and pushed him away from her. For a few seconds she sat back, panting. Relieved to have beaten him off.

But her relief soon turned to panic. She looked at her tyrannical father lying still. No longer a tyrant. His body was limp, his eyes dead inside a battered head that rested in a pool of blood.

'Oh my God!' she wept. 'Oh my God!'

She stayed rooted to the spot, too shocked to move for several minutes as she stared at the lifeless form of her tormentor. It was over.

Peter couldn't believe what he was seeing. There on his doorstep was his sister in an obvious state of shock. Her eyes looked like saucers; wide open, the pupils dilated. Her face was pale and drawn. She was breathing heavily and had a sheen of sweat on her brow.

He stepped back in surprise and noticed the state of her clothing, which looked bedraggled. Her jacket was slightly torn and there were spatters of blood on her face and body. The blood on her face was smeared and he guessed she had been crying. Then he noticed her hands; they were full of it, as though dressed in crimson gloves.

'Shit!' he said, pulling her into the hallway and shutting the door behind her. 'What the fuck's happened?'

Adele tried to speak but her voice broke and the tears flowed once more.

'Have you been attacked?' he asked but she still couldn't speak. The state of Adele suggested that she had been the perpetrator rather than the victim but Peter found that hard to believe.

'OK, come in,' he said, pulling her gently by the arm and leading her through to the kitchen. He sat her down on one of the wooden dining chairs. It would be easier to remove the blood from them than from the upholstered suite in the living room.

'Right, I'll make you a cup of tea for the shock,' he said. 'Then you can tell me what's happened.'

While Peter rushed around making tea, he kept a watch over his distressed sister who was now sobbing and shaking. He set the tea down next to her and opened the lid on a brandy bottle.

'N-no,' Adele muttered.

'Have it!' he ordered. 'We need to calm you down then you can tell me what the fuck's happened.'

His phone rang. Peter was tempted to ignore it but he was waiting for the heads-up on a job. He picked up the receiver. 'Not now,' he said. 'Something's gone down. I need to sort it urgently… No, nothing like that… just a bit of business. That's all. I'll get back to you once it's sorted.'

He turned to Adele who was drinking the brandy-laced tea. 'You ready to talk yet?' he asked.

Adele nodded and settled the cup back down on the table. 'Oh Peter,' she cried. 'I-I-I've killed him.'

'Killed who? What the fuck you on about?'

'Him. Our dad,' she spat the last word as though it tasted sour on her tongue. 'I've killed him.'

'What? How?' Peter asked, finding it difficult to believe what he was hearing.

'I… He… he put Mam in hospital,' she sobbed. 'You should see the state of her!'

She paused, and Peter stared at her, waiting for her to continue.

'I only went to get some things for her... the bastard was there! I was so angry. He didn't even ask how she was...'

'OK,' said Peter, trying to keep his voice calm. 'So, what happened?'

'I don't know! It all happened so quick. I got annoyed. He was calling her useless... and me too. I'd just come back from the hospital. Seeing her like that... and then him just brushing it off.' She paused again, her voice shaking.

'So you attacked him?' asked Peter, his calm façade now slipping as worry set in.

'No... not exactly. He went for me first. We were rowing... and... and then he went for me. He was strangling me and hitting me. He had me pinned down on the floor!' Adele broke off again and took a sip of the brandy-laced tea before continuing. 'I had to stop him, Peter!' she cried. 'So I hit him with that brass cat. And once I started, I couldn't stop!'

'Jesus!' said Peter.

'I couldn't stop hitting him, Peter,' she wept, looking at her blood-drenched hands.

'Jesus Christ, Adele! You don't fuckin' do things by halves, do you?'

She hung her head in shame. After a few seconds she raised her head again and looked at him. 'Oh, Peter. What am I gonna do?' she asked. 'What will happen to me?'

Peter took a tentative step towards his sister and rested his hand on her shoulder. 'It's OK, we'll sort it,' he said, in a flurry of words. 'Finish your drink. I'll go and run you a bath. Make sure you scrub every bit of that fuckin' blood off you. And leave your clothes outside the door. We'll need to get rid of them.'

She nodded.

Peter paced the room, trying to think of a plan. 'Give me your house keys,' he babbled. 'I'll go back to your place. Grab you some clean clothes. You stay here. Put my dressing gown on while you're waiting. When I get back we'll sort it. OK?'

Adele nodded and tried to force a smile from her trembling lips.

'It's OK, sis. Don't worry,' he reassured her, patting the top of her head before he left the room to go and run her a bath.

Peter wished he felt as sure as he was pretending to be. But, the truth was, Adele was well in the shit and, at the moment, he didn't know if he could get her out of it.

43

On the journey back to her parents' home, Adele tried to calm herself by taking deep breaths. But her heart was thundering in her chest, and her hands felt clammy.

Although they were in Adele's car, Peter was behind the wheel. He didn't want to get any blood in his car and Adele was too edgy to drive. He had covered the car seat with polythene to minimise the amount of blood that might transfer onto his clothing.

While he drove he explained what they were going to do. A sea of words floated around inside Adele's head. But she missed their collective meaning. She was finding it difficult to take everything in.

'Adele! Fuckin' snap to, will yer?' Peter ordered. 'I need you to concentrate. This is important. OK? As long as you do everything I say, it'll be all right.'

He outlined the plan. He'd already explained to her that they had to do it that night so that everything would appear as normal as possible by the time their mother returned from hospital the following day. They would remove the body first and put it inside the boot of her car. Then they'd clean up their parents' house and remove all traces of blood. They'd also have to get rid of the weapon: the brass cat.

'Don't worry about them,' he said, in reference to the body and the weapon. 'We're gonna put them somewhere where no fucker will find 'em. Then we need to go back to mine and clean your car out. It's important to remove every last trace of blood. We don't want anything that might fuckin' incriminate us. OK?'

Adele nodded and muttered, her mind picking up on the fact that Peter seemed to know what he was doing. It was as though he had done this sort of thing before.

Before long they arrived at their parents' home and parked the car in the next street so there was less chance of anyone spotting them. As they made their way to the house Adele's heart rate sped up even more. She could feel a cold shiver of fear zip through her body then settle in the pit of her stomach, clutching at her insides.

They stopped at their parents' front door. Before they entered, Peter scanned the street to see if there was anyone around. Fortunately the street was empty. He then looked across at her. 'Right,' he whispered. 'This isn't gonna be fun but I need you with me to make sure we don't miss anything. Brace yourself.'

'OK,' muttered Adele, taking a deep breath. But it wasn't OK; it was anything but OK and she dreaded what she would find on the other side of the door.

'You go first, unlock the door,' whispered Peter.

Adele looked puzzled and a renewed pang of fear shot through her body. She was hoping he'd lead the way. Somehow that made it feel easier.

'I don't wanna touch the door,' he said. 'Don't worry, I'll go in front once we're inside.'

As soon as they were in the hallway, Peter withdrew some disposable latex gloves from his pocket and put them on. 'You don't need any,' he said. 'You can explain your fingerprints but I hardly ever come here. The most important thing for you is to get rid of all the blood.'

Adele felt a huge hammering inside her chest when she heard the word 'blood'.

'Come on, let's get it done with,' said Peter.

She followed him through the hallway and into the living room where they could hear the television still blaring. After the shock of battering her father to death, switching off the TV had been the last thing on Adele's mind.

'Was the TV on all the time?' asked Peter.

'Yes,' she murmured.

'Good, that means there's less chance someone could have heard something.'

At first she couldn't see past Peter but when the sight of her bludgeoned father met her, she stopped in her tracks. He was lying at an odd angle. He didn't look like their father. More like a car crash victim. His body was limp yet contorted.

Adele approached cautiously, staying one step behind Peter. There was blood. Lots of blood. Coming from her father's head and scattering outwards. She edged closer. Drawn to the sight of his head. The blood more concentrated. Thick masses of it. Congealed around his head and clinging to his hair.

At first all she noticed was the blood. But as she drew closer, she took in the detail. A dense concentration of multiple head wounds. His head dinted with the force of the blows. Shards of splintered skull protruding through the crimson mass. Black hair, white bone, pink flesh; all splattered with various shades of red. And something else, which made her heave. Brain matter; squidging out beneath the bone in lurid shades of red and pink. Her stomach lurched and she forced down the bile that rose to her throat.

Adele felt light-headed. Her senses were vying for supremacy as fear and panic took a hold on her. She stepped back, her mind telling her she needed to get away. 'Oh my God! I can't,' she muttered. 'I can't do it.'

She began pacing the room, frantic. Her head was pounding as the blood pulsed around her body. It was as though she had seen her dead father for the first time. She hadn't fully taken it in before; she was too hyped up with anger. But now, the harsh reality hit her.

'I need to get some air, Peter,' she said as her chest tightened and her breath came in short gasps.

Before she could reach the hall, Peter grabbed hold of her arm, spinning her round and giving her a sharp slap across the face. The force of the blow brought her to her senses.

'Fuckin' calm down!' he ordered. 'Get a grip, Adele.' Then his voice became gentler as he gripped her by the shoulders, stared into her eyes and said, 'I know it's not easy but you need to stay calm. OK? We'll deal with it.'

Adele nodded. She could feel hot salty tears coursing down her face. 'Just give me a minute,' she said.

'OK, take some deep breaths. Compose yourself. Then we'll get on with it.'

When Adele had got over the initial shock, her breathing eased. Her muscles felt wobbly; the aftermath of the adrenalin rush that had assaulted her body. Peter was right. She needed to stay calm.

Adele approached the body once more. This time she was prepared for the horrific sight of her battered, dead father. She tried to keep a grip on her emotions and focused her eyes elsewhere as they did what had to be done.

Peter did most of the work, wrapping their dead father's body inside the fireside rug, which was so full of blood that it would be difficult to clean. The ghastly spectacle didn't seem to bother Peter, and Adele wondered again whether he had done this sort of thing before, but she decided she didn't want to know.

When they had the body wrapped securely they carried it outside and headed towards the car so they could put it in the boot. As they made their way down the pathway that skirted their parents' back garden their progress was slow. Adele could feel the weight of the dead body inside the rug, tugging at her overstretched muscles. It seemed to be getting heavier.

When the strain became too much, she slowed almost to a stop. 'I can't, Peter,' she gasped.

Peter glanced around. 'OK, ease it down a minute,' he whispered. 'We can't stay for long though. Someone might spot us.'

While she rested, she was conscious of Peter's stare until, eventually, feeling pressured, she nodded her head. Peter grabbed one end of the rug and heaved their father's body under his arms. Adele mimicked his movements.

She only had hold of it for a few seconds before her muscles screamed out at her again. But she persevered, knowing they had to get to the car as soon as possible.

When they reached the car, Peter checked once again to make sure there was nobody about who might see them. Although the body was well disguised by the rug, people were bound to wonder why they were carrying such a huge bundle at that time of night.

Adele felt shattered by the time they had heaved the body into the boot. But there was more work yet to do.

They returned to the house. All the time while they were in the living room, Adele could hear the drone of the TV in the background. Her head was now aching and she reached to switch off the TV.

'Don't!' ordered Peter. 'Leave it on. I don't want anyone to hear us. We'll switch it off before we go.'

The clean-up seemed to take ages but Peter insisted they were thorough. Adele was relieved when they had finished. She glanced around the room one last time. It looked odd. The missing rug and brass cat were bound to raise suspicions. Not to mention the clean smell of disinfectant.

Peter seemed to pick up on her thoughts. 'I know it looks suspicious,' he said. 'But no one can prove fuck all. As long as you keep your cool and don't tell the police nowt.'

Adele kept quiet. She knew her ordeal was far from over and she dreaded the police interrogation that she still had to face.

She was about to leave the house when Peter spoke again. 'Right, what things do you need to collect?' he asked.

Adele stared at him blankly until he elaborated. 'You were collecting some things to take to hospital tomorrow, weren't you?'

In the midst of all that had happened, it had slipped Adele's mind.

'Get the stuff you came for in the first place,' Peter continued. 'We've got to make everything look as normal as possible... And when you pick our mam up tomorrow, you've got to stay fuckin' calm. All right? Don't go giving the game away. As far as she's concerned, he's disappeared along with the rug and the cat. And nobody knows fuck all about what's happened.'

Adele's mind was in turmoil as they drove away from her parents' home with her father's body in the back of the car. For a while she stayed silent but thoughts were chasing around inside her head. If only she hadn't lost it. If only she'd ignored her father's scathing comments and just collected her mother's things. But she hadn't expected to see him there and the sight of him had infuriated her.

She'd always known she had a temper. It had been with her since she was a child. But she hadn't realised what she was capable of, and the realisation both shocked and frightened her.

Perhaps it would never happen again. Maybe it was because of what their father had put them through. But, nevertheless, she would have to live with the guilt and she didn't know whether she could.

She snapped to as they left the suburban streets behind and drove into the countryside. 'Where are we going?' she asked.

'The river,' said Peter. 'We're gonna sink him. Don't worry, no one will ever find his body.'

Adele gulped but stayed silent. She could feel her brother's eyes on her. 'What?' she asked.

'Listen, Adele,' he said. 'Once we've finished the job, you've got to put this behind you. Don't go beating yourself up over him. He wasn't worth it.'

Even as she nodded her assent, she could feel the bitter tears of regret clouding her eyes.

Peter stopped the car on a dirt track. She peered through the windscreen and saw that it led onto a bridge, which straddled the River Mersey. It was quiet. The only sounds she could hear were the flowing of the river and the hooting of an owl.

'Right, let's get him out,' said Peter, all matter-of-fact. 'We're gonna toss him over the bridge.'

Adele followed him to the boot of the car, taking in the smell of the country air, permeated by death. She tried to keep her emotions in check as she stared at the rolled-up rug, which contained her father's body.

'I'll grab the heavy end, you take his legs,' Peter said.

Again, Adele tried to retain control. While they struggled to carry his lifeless form towards the bridge, she blocked out all thoughts of her father, trying to remain as impassive as Peter, but it wasn't easy.

'Right, put it down a minute,' said Peter when they reached the bridge. 'Let's just have a breather before we chuck it over.'

Adele noticed his use of the word 'it'. Perhaps that was how he managed to be so detached, by thinking of their father as a thing rather than a person. Perhaps there was some truth in that view, she thought, sardonically.

'You ready?' he asked and Adele nodded.

They lifted him between them and heaved his inert body to the top of the fence that ran down the side of the bridge. Adele jumped when she heard the almighty splash as his corpse hit the river's surface. Then it sank to the bottom.

'Don't worry,' said Peter. 'This part of the river's deep. No one will ever fuckin' find him.'

A transient thought flashed through her mind. How did Peter know how deep the river was?

Adele stared down into the darkness. Her eyes settled on the water below, bubbling and eddying. She could see no sign of her father or the brass cat, both wrapped up inside the blood-drenched rug. And tomorrow, the river would add vibrancy to a picturesque countryside scene, for visitors to behold. No one would know the evil secret which lurked below its surface.

44

Adele was exhausted when they returned to Peter's flat. All she wanted to do was sit down, but they still had work to do.

'We've got to clean your car out tonight,' said Peter. 'We don't want to wait till morning. It'll be easier for someone to spot us then.'

Peter parked the car in a quiet side street. Then they crept through the street carrying cleaning equipment and set about the arduous task of scouring the car out. To enable them to see in the dark, they switched on the car's internal light.

Peter was the first to spot a man walking his dog. 'Quick, get down,' he said, flicking the light off before concealing himself in the footwell.

Adele was crouched down low in the footwell of the driver's seat. She could feel a cold sweat and a prickling sensation down her spine as they waited for the man's footsteps to pass the car. But the footsteps stopped.

Adele could sense the man hovering nearby. She tensed, expecting the man to peer through the car window or try the door. But then she heard him say, 'Good boy' to his dog, and the footsteps continued. When she could no longer hear them, she started to straighten herself up but she could feel Peter's hand on her back, pressing her back down.

'Not yet!' he whispered. 'We need to give it a couple more minutes until he's well out of sight.'

Once the immediate danger was over, Adele became conscious of the cramped conditions, which made her achy and uncomfortable. She was glad when Peter gave the OK and she could stretch out her limbs again.

'Shit! That was close,' whispered Peter.

They carried on scrubbing out the car until they had eliminated every last trace of blood. By the time they had finished, Adele was exhausted from the night's events. But she wasn't sleepy yet. Her senses were still on full alert, which added to her exhaustion.

Back in the flat, she felt edgy and unable to settle, her muscles twitchy. While they had done what they had to do, she didn't have much time to think, but now it hit her anew. Images of what she had done pervaded her brain. She'd killed her father and helped to dispose of his corpse. Adele could feel the tension throughout her body. Her chest was tight and her breathing shallow.

'Here, get that down you,' said Peter, handing her a liberal measure of brandy. 'It's for the shock. You can stay here tonight.'

Adele did as instructed and they stayed up till the early hours discussing the situation till they'd covered every angle. An ironic thought flashed through Adele's mind. It reminded her of their childhood days when she would help get Peter out of trouble. But now they were adults, and this wasn't just a bit of trouble. She was seriously in the shit!

It took several more measures of brandy before she was able to sleep. It was an eerie feeling. Despite being sickened by her own actions, she couldn't help reliving the ordeal over and over inside her head, and examining it in minute detail. It was like some form of misguided punishment.

At four in the morning she fell into a disturbed sleep only to awaken in a panic a few hours later. In the transitional period between sleep and consciousness she tried to shake off the bad dream she'd had until she realised it wasn't a dream. She really had killed her father.

Realisation hit her like a brick. She tried to calm herself, taking deep breaths and relaxing her muscles. But it was no use. Eventually, when further sleep escaped her, she rose from bed and made herself a coffee, passing the time watching breakfast TV until she heard movement from Peter's room.

'You OK?' he asked when he entered the lounge.

Adele shrugged. Did he really expect her to be OK?

'Listen,' said Peter. 'I didn't mention it last night but we need to talk about the police. They'll want to interview you and there'll be questions asked, especially when our mam tells them about the missing rug and brass cat. We need to get our stories straight.

'Tell them everything was normal when you went to pick up her things. That you didn't even go into the living room. Pretend to think about it. Say you would have noticed if anything was amiss. That way they'll think something happened after you left the house.

'Don't expect them to go easy on you though. They'll come at you with the same questions over and over, just from different angles. Don't buckle, whatever you do. They can't prove owt. And if you get upset, just make out it's because you're worried about him.'

Adele's spirits plummeted further.

'Try not to worry,' he urged. 'Just do as I say and everything will be all right. Oh, and wear something that covers up those marks on your neck.'

Adele instinctively raised a hand to her throat.

'Where he tried to strangle you,' Peter added. 'He's left marks. Wear something that isn't too obvious though.'

Adele wished she had Peter's confidence.

'Try and get some rest before you pick our mam up,' he added. 'It's gonna be a long couple of days.'

But Adele knew she wouldn't rest; her mind was too preoccupied, as well as hazy from the excess brandy the night before. She'd just have to cope as best as she could, and hope she didn't give the game away.

45

It was time to pick her mother up. Adele had taken the day off work and she had just received the call that she'd been waiting for. Her mother confirmed that the doctor had examined her and allowed her to go home. Adele checked one last time that she had everything her mother needed then she set off for the hospital.

This time when Adele walked up to the ward she knew where to find her mother. She was sitting on the edge of the hospital bed awaiting Adele's arrival. Although Adele had already seen her mother's injuries, they still shocked her. She winced as she took in her mother's battered face and plastered arm.

Then a strange feeling came over Adele. It took her by surprise. Like hatred suffused with justification. How could he have done this? The man was evil! Then she checked herself for thinking so badly of the dead; of her father who she had killed.

'How are you feeling today?' she asked her mother.

'Not bad, love. I'm sure I'll soon be a lot better,' Shirley said, rubbing the plaster on her broken arm. 'That'll teach me to go falling down the stairs,' she chuckled, for the benefit of the woman in the next bed.

Adele ignored the comment and concentrated on helping her mother get her things together. They both knew the truth even if Shirley didn't want to acknowledge it.

During the journey back, Adele tried to mentally prepare herself for her mother's reaction when her father didn't return home, and she noticed the missing cat and rug. But her mother's incessant chatter made it difficult to concentrate. She was like an excited schoolchild, returning home with tales of her day, as she prattled on about the other patients.

When they arrived at the house, Adele let Shirley unlock the door and walk in first. They made their way through the hallway and into the lounge.

'Thanks, love,' she gushed, flummoxing Adele. 'It was good of you to give the place a clean. I was going to do it but... yer know.' She sniffed the air. 'Ooh, it smells lovely too.'

'I didn't...' said Adele before her mother cut in.

'Where's the rug?'

'I don't know,' said Adele. 'I haven't been here apart from picking your things up, and I went straight upstairs. Are you sure it's not one of your neighbours?'

'Hang on,' said Shirley. 'The cat's gone missing too. What the bloody hell's been going on?'

'I've told you, Mam, I don't know. You'd best check with the neighbours. Hasn't one of them got a key?'

'Well, yeah. Her next door, but she wouldn't come in without asking. She just has it for emergencies... Eh, what if it's yer dad? D'you think he might have cleaned up to give me a surprise?'

Adele was amazed at her mother's gullibility but she kept her reply brief, not wanting to upset her. 'I doubt it,' she said.

Her back felt clammy and she sensed a slight quiver in her voice. It wasn't easy having to lie to her mother. To divert her, Adele offered to put her things away. Then she busied herself before making her excuses and leaving for home.

Adele could feel relief surge through her as soon as she was outside her mother's house. She was glad to get away. Lying didn't come naturally to Adele and she dreaded the charade that she would have to keep up in the coming weeks. It was going to be tough.

The ringing of the phone woke Adele from a troubled sleep. She glanced at the bedside clock before crossing the room and picking up the phone: 11.45 p.m. She'd been asleep for almost three hours, having dropped into bed exhausted after her sleep deprivation of the previous night.

'Hello,' she said half-heartedly as she held the receiver to her ear.

'Adele, thank God I've caught you!' said Shirley. 'I'm at my wit's end. Yer dad's not come home from work.'

It took Adele a few seconds to come to. 'Eh?' She looked at the clock again, planning her response. 'You sure he's not still at the pub?'

'I don't know, Adele. He's usually home by now. I asked the neighbours if they'd seen anything of him when he didn't come home from work but nobody's seen hide nor hair of him.'

'OK. Well, try not to worry. He's probably the worse for wear. He might have even stayed out at one of his mates'. He's done that before, hasn't he?'

'Well yeah, but not for a long time. And you'd think he'd be here, with me coming home from the hospital.'

Adele didn't furnish that statement with a response. Instead she said, 'OK, well I tell you what, Mam. You try and get some sleep. I'll ring you tomorrow and if you've still not heard from him I'll come round so we can decide what to do.'

It was several more minutes before Adele managed to get her mother off the phone. She took a lot of convincing that there was no point sitting up half the night worrying. In the end she accepted Adele's suggestion.

Adele sighed as she replaced the receiver. Although she'd expected her mother to call at some point, she could have done without it tonight. Once again her senses were on full alert and it took her several hours before she could get back to sleep. She only managed another three hours before the phone rang again.

'All right, Mam,' she said after Shirley had explained how Tommy still wasn't home. 'Let me have a shower and something to eat, and I'll be round.'

Adele quickly rang work and booked another day off, telling them it was a family emergency. As she got herself ready she was beginning to panic again. She didn't want to go back to her parents' house. To the place where it had happened. But she had no choice. Deciding that she would cope better with a bit of moral support, she rang Peter and asked him to join her there.

'OK,' said Peter. 'But don't forget, all I know is that he hasn't been home. You've got to keep your cool. OK?'

'Yes,' said Adele, then she put the phone down.

An hour later and Adele was ready to set off for her mother's. She was wearing a high-necked blouse, which disguised most of the bruising. The rest she had covered with make-up, taking care to wear a colour of blouse that wouldn't show any marks from the foundation cream.

Peter was already there when Adele arrived and she drew some comfort from his presence.

'I didn't know you'd rung our Peter,' said Shirley.

It suddenly dawned on Adele that Peter was the last person her mother would have expected to see. After all, he wasn't welcome at his parents' home. And if his father was still alive, he wouldn't have been there. She locked eyes with her brother and a look of acknowledgement flashed between them.

'Yeah, well,' she stumbled before collecting herself. 'I was worried.'

Peter quickly stepped in. 'Have you heard this, Adele?' he asked. 'The rug and cat are missing. Bit weird innit?' His blasé act was convincing even to Adele.

'Yeah, we noticed last night.' Then, turning to her mother, she asked, 'Did you check if any of the neighbours had been in?'

'Yeah. And they haven't,' Shirley was fretting again. 'I'm worried sick,' she said. 'Nobody knows owt and they've not seen anything of him either.'

'I tell you what,' said Peter. 'The pubs will be open for dinner soon. We'll go round his regulars and see if anyone saw him last night.'

When they had finished checking the local pubs and putting on a believable act for the customers, Peter turned to Adele and said, 'Look, I'm sorry sis but I've got to go now. I've got a bit of business to attend to.' Her face dropped and he immediately grabbed hold of her arm. 'Don't worry. It's all going OK so far. You've just got to carry it on when the police arrive.'

'Police?' In her anxious state she had forgotten that they would have to report the fact that their father was missing.

'Yeah, you'll have to ring them. Think. That's what you'd do normally, isn't it?' He checked his watch. 'I'm really sorry, Adele, but I've got to dash. You'll be OK though. Just do as I've told you and keep your cool.'

Then he was gone, leaving Adele to face things alone. She was disappointed but checked herself before her feelings turned to annoyance. He had helped her out, after all. And it was her problem, not his.

Shirley was waiting eagerly for news when Adele returned to the house.

'Sorry, Mam. Nobody's seen him.'

Tears sprang to Shirley's eyes. 'There's something not right, Adele. I just know it. Why would the rug and cat go missing too?' she asked.

Adele held her tightly, hoping her mother couldn't hear her own booming heartbeat. 'We're gonna have to ring the police, Mam,' she said.

After a few minutes of trying to calm her mother down, Adele picked up the phone and made the call.

The police seemed to take forever to arrive and Adele took the time to compose and prepare herself. She had to make this convincing.

The sharp knock at the door made her jump. 'You stay there. I'll get it,' she said to Shirley.

Adele led the two police officers into the house then busied herself making hot drinks while they spoke to her mother. When Adele returned to the lounge, her mother was still prattling, glad of somebody else to offload her problems onto.

'He's not been the best father,' she persisted. 'But he does have his good points.'

One of the police officers picked up on this morsel of information and continued to probe. Shirley was only too willing to give him all the facts he was looking for apart from how she'd sustained her injuries. But the policeman wasn't stupid; Adele could tell by the look on his face that he knew her story about falling down the stairs didn't carry much weight.

The policeman paused from writing in his notebook then turned to Adele. 'I'd like you to tell me about your last visit to the house, two days ago,' he began.

Adele nodded. She could feel a prickle of sweat underneath the high neck of her blouse.

'What time did you arrive at the house?' he asked.

Adele tried to control the tremble in her voice. 'Erm, it was after hospital visiting was over,' she said. 'I'd just been to see my mam at the hospital. About quarter past, maybe half past eight, I think.'

She was conscious of her harried speech, and tried to compose herself. But she could see the police officer watching her keenly.

'And did you notice anything unusual?' he asked.

'No, nothing. But I didn't come in here. I just went straight upstairs to collect my mam's things.'

As soon as she'd said it, she realised her mistake and could feel a rush of heat flood through her body. Why mention the living room? But the officer didn't pick her up on it; Adele didn't know that her mother had already told him about the missing cat and rug.

'When was the last time you saw your father?' asked the policeman.

Adele thought back to the previous occasion when she had seen her father. An image of his battered head flashed through her brain and she quickly quashed it.

'Er, last week I think.'

Her mother butted in. 'It was the Sunday before last. Remember?'

'Oh, yeah. Sunday,' said Adele.

'And did you notice anything strange about his behaviour?'

'No,' said Adele.

The officer turned to Shirley and Adele felt a moment's reprieve. Her shoulders sagged and she resisted the urge to let out a sigh of relief. 'What about you, Mrs Robinson? You say you last saw your husband three days ago. Did you notice anything unusual in his behaviour?'

'No,' said Shirley.

'Anything at all?'

'No. But the rug and brass cat are missing, like I already told you.'

The policeman looked over towards the fireplace and wrote something in his notebook. 'You say your husband wasn't home when you returned from the hospital?' he asked.

'Yeah, that's right,' said Shirley.

'So, did you last see him when you were taken into hospital?'

'Just before. He didn't come to the hospital with me,' Shirley answered, her face flushing slightly.

'Did he contact you during your time in hospital?'

'No,' said Shirley, and Adele noticed her lip curl. 'He's been busy with work though,' Shirley added.

'And you say he wasn't home from work when you returned from the hospital?' the officer persisted.

'No, I thought he'd just gone for a couple of drinks,' Shirley replied.

'Did he often go for a couple of drinks after work?' asked the officer.

'Yeah, but our Adele and Peter have been round the local pubs and nobody's seen him,' said Shirley.

'Peter? Is that your son?'

'Yes.'

'Very well,' said the officer, shutting his notebook. 'We'll want to interview your son and some of the neighbours, see if we can find out a bit more. Try not to worry for now. We'll come back to you if we hear anything. And if you think of anything, anything at all, that might help, please give us a call.'

He glanced from Shirley to Adele, and Adele felt a stab of guilt as she watched her mother's eyes fill with tears again. 'I'll show you out,' she said to the officers, and she headed to the hallway, leaving her mother in the living room.

Once the officers were out of the house, Adele turned around and leant back against the front door. This time she did heave a sigh of relief. Then she took a deep breath before she returned to her mother, ready to continue the charade.

46

Peter's appearance was casual when he answered the door. His shirt was untucked and his sleeves rolled up. He scratched his head and yawned as he held the front door open for Adele.

'You all right?' he asked once Adele was sitting down.

But it was obvious by Adele's appearance that she wasn't all right. He could tell that even before she spoke. She had dark circles under her eyes, her skin was pale and she was twitchy. He noticed the way she kept picking at her nails. The police questioning combined with a lack of sleep the two previous nights had taken their toll. She looked physically and emotionally drained.

'It was terrible, Peter! I'm sure they know,' she said, referring to the police interview.

'Don't worry. It's just par for the course,' he said, pouring brandy into one of the two glasses he had lined up.

'None for me, thanks. I've got to drive home,' she said.

'You sure? You're welcome to stay if you want.'

'No, it's all right. I don't want to get into that habit anyway.'

'OK, but if you don't mind me saying, Adele, you look like shit. You could do with a good night's sleep.'

'Cheer me up, why don't you? What do you fuckin' expect?'

She was wound up like a taut spring and Peter could tell that the slightest thing would set her off. It was worrying.

'They asked me about my visit to the house when I came to collect Mam's things. Like they were trying to trip me up. It was awful! I kept thinking I was gonna give the game away.'

'I told you what it would be like. They're relentless bastards. But, the important thing is, you didn't cave in and confess.'

'Yeah, but what if I do?' Adele asked and Peter could detect the tremble in her voice.

'Just stick to the story, Adele. Jesus! Don't fuckin' lose it now. You did well. Now try not to worry. The worst part's over. They'll probably be back again, asking more questions, but you've done it once so you can do it again.'

'Do you think the neighbours will suspect us?' she asked. Then she jolted her head as though something had just occurred to her. 'What if they heard something or saw us taking him out?'

'No, they won't have done. Don't forget, the telly was blaring and I checked around before we carried him out. There was no one in sight. So just sit tight and stop worrying. It'll all blow over in a few weeks.'

'I don't know, Peter. I keep reliving everything. It's really panicking me. I don't know if I can live with the guilt.'

'And do you think confessing to the police will make things any fuckin' easier, Adele? Think about it. Whether you confess or not, it still happened. The old bastard deserved all he got anyway so don't go beating yourself up! You've got to find a way of living with it. Because, I tell you summat, you start confessing to the coppers and things'll get a whole lot fuckin' worse. Have you ever been inside a prison, Adele? It's no fuckin' walk in the park, I can tell you.'

Peter was getting riled. The last thing he needed was for his sister to have an attack of conscience and confess to the police. That would land him right in it. And he had too much at stake to get banged up. Things were really taking off for him, but if he was out of the picture for a while, he might risk losing it all.

He tried to calm himself down. Shouting at her wouldn't help so for the next half hour he concentrated on persuading Adele to keep quiet. By the time Peter let her out of his apartment, she was looking a little more relaxed than when she had arrived. But he was still concerned about her.

Although he had tried to appear relaxed in front of Adele, he wasn't as laid-back as he seemed. A part of him was beginning to regret getting involved in the first place. But she was his sister and they'd been through a lot together. There was no one else she could have turned to.

Anyway, it was done now, but it didn't stop him worrying about the consequences of Adele making a confession. As he swigged his brandy, Peter tried to think of a way he could manage the situation. Like most jobs, there would be a way of dealing with things. He just had to think.

He continued to ruminate as he paced his apartment, crystal tumbler in hand. Then it came to him. Like a flash of inspiration. He'd thought of a way he could put Adele out of the picture with the minimum of consequences.

In the meantime he'd still have to make sure she didn't confess to the police or anyone else. But it was doable. And it would mean that he wouldn't have the worry of it anymore.

★

Adele was helping her mother prepare sandwiches for their lunch. It was typical of her mother to invite her for lunch then have nothing ready, Adele thought, cynically. As she buttered bread they talked. Or, rather, her mother talked and Adele listened.

'I do miss him, Adele,' Shirley sniffed. She glanced across at Adele who didn't comment, but it was as though her mother had picked up on what she was thinking. 'Oh I know he wasn't perfect. He had a bit of a temper, but he wasn't always like that, y'know?'

'I know,' said Adele automatically but she didn't really know. She had never seen that other side of her father, just the belligerence which he'd always displayed towards her and Peter.

'It's not easy being on yer own,' her mother continued.

As if Adele didn't know how that felt!

'I'd love to know what happened. It's bloody funny what happened to that brass cat, isn't it?'

Adele shrugged but she could feel her face flush at the mention of the cat.

'It was the only thing I had left of my mother's too. And what about that rug? Bloody funny if you ask me.' Shirley then sighed and stopped what she was doing. When she began speaking again, Adele could hear the crack in her voice. 'I wish he'd come back, Adele. He might be dead for all we know but it's not as if we can even have a funeral for him. Not without a body.' She sniffed and wiped a tear away with the back of her hand.

A tremor of guilt ran up Adele's spine. She walked over to her mother and kissed her on the top of her head. 'It'll get easier,' she said but her words were spoken through a stiff jaw. Combined with her feelings of guilt was irritation at the way her mother pined for the man who had made all their lives a misery. But she bit back her irritation. Part of her still felt sorry for her mother. He might not have been the perfect husband but her mother was clearly missing him.

Adele didn't know how she would get through today. The guilt was eating away at her. She was so tempted to confess all to her mother; to put her mind at ease. While Tommy's disappearance was a mystery, Adele knew that her mother would still hold out a flicker of hope that one day he would walk back through the door. And Shirley would welcome him heartily.

But Adele resisted the temptation to confess all. She couldn't trust her mother not to tell anyone, and she wouldn't have her mother's support as she did with Peter. Shirley's feelings about Tommy were far removed from those of her children.

'It'll get easier,' she had said to her mother. She hoped to God that it would get easier for her too. Because she didn't know how much longer she could live with this guilt.

47

Peter had invited Adele round to his flat for a few drinks and a chat. She was curious as she'd got the impression on the phone that the chat was about something important.

When she arrived at the flat, Peter welcomed her, brandy at the ready as usual. She sipped her drink, drawing comfort from the warmth of the brandy as it slid down her throat and radiated inside her chest.

'I got the feeling you had something important to talk about,' she said.

'Yeah,' said Peter, staring pointedly at her. 'I've had an idea.' He paused before carrying on. 'Look, sis. I know you've been finding it tough, and I'm a bit worried about you spilling the beans. I'm not being funny, but it will land me in the shit as well if you do and I can do without...'

'I won't,' Adele cut in.

Peter held up his hand to silence her. 'I can't take that chance, Adele. I need you out of the picture.'

Adele paled. What was he suggesting?

'You spoken to John lately?'

'Yeah, I managed to patch things up and we still keep in touch. Why? Why are you asking?'

'Well, now *he's* not around I get to see our mam more. So maybe it's a good time for you to go down to London and join John.'

Adele knew that the word 'he' referred to their father. 'Dad' wasn't a word that Peter often used. 'But she still needs me, Peter,' she said.

'She'll be all right. It's about time she learnt to stand on her own two feet. You're too soft with her. She plays you like a fuckin' fiddle.'

'But… I don't know.'

'You want to go, don't you? I know how you feel about the guy. You've told me.'

'But, you don't know her like I do, Peter. She'll go to pieces. Anything could happen.'

'Will she 'eck. I can go round there now he's gone, so she won't be all on her own. Anyway, you can always ring her.'

'It's not the same though, is it?' said Adele who could sense her brother becoming irritated.

'Look, Adele,' he said. 'I'm not fuckin' asking, I'm telling you!' He took a deep, calming breath before continuing. 'You *need* to go. I can't have you spilling the beans. Being with John will take your mind off what happened. But don't get a fuckin' attack of conscience when you're with him. You don't tell anyone. OK?'

'And if I don't go?'

'Don't ask me that question, Adele. You won't like the answer.'

Adele felt a stab of fear.

She nodded, knowing she didn't have much choice in the matter. 'All right,' she said, 'I'll do it.'

48

'It won't be long now,' Adele said, her face breaking into a smile.

She was on the phone to John who was overjoyed that she was coming to join him.

'Yes, and you know the first thing I'm going to do when you arrive, don't you?' he asked with a hint of mischief in his voice.

'No, go on, tell me,' she said, suddenly feeling much lighter. 'Does it have something to do with me arriving?'

'Oh yes, you're definitely going to arrive,' he said. 'Multiple times. I'm gonna chase you up to the bedroom. Then I'm gonna keep you there till you're begging for mercy and can't take any more.'

'Ooh, I can't wait,' Adele laughed.

Once she had finished the call she continued tidying some things away, the joy at hearing John's voice giving her some impetus to carry on with sorting the house out. She had a lot to take care of before her move to London, but it wasn't long before thoughts of her father's death clouded her brain once more. She shook them off and tried to concentrate on her future with John instead. But it wasn't easy. She prayed that one day, eventually, she would think about it less and be able to get on with her life.

The last few weeks had been trying ones. As well as finishing work and having to say goodbye to everyone, the persistent questioning from the police had put her constantly on edge. It hadn't been easy breaking the news of her imminent departure to her mother either. Shirley had sat there snivelling into a tissue as Adele discussed her plans.

'I don't think I can take much more,' said Shirley. 'First your grandma, then your dad and now this.'

The memory of Peter's words had flashed into Adele's mind. Yes, perhaps she was too soft with her. So she tried to stay strong and not let her mother dissuade her from following her heart.

'At least you've got Peter back,' she said. 'He comes round a lot now, doesn't he? He's always bringing you things as well.'

'Well, yes. But it's not the same as having your daughter by your side, is it? And just when I need your support as well.'

'You've got the neighbours too and I'm only a couple of hours away on the train. You can visit whenever you like. We'll go sightseeing together.'

But Adele knew her mother would never visit. She'd work herself into a state as soon as she contemplated the journey. Then she'd back out at the last minute, deciding she couldn't cope with it.

'I'll ring you too, all the time,' Adele added.

Again Peter was right. Her mother would cope, somehow. Adele needed to get on with her own life and try to put that nasty business with her father behind her.

Peter was having a night in with his latest conquest. One thing he was finding as he gained status in the world of crime was that there were always women available. They knew of his reputation and many of them couldn't resist a bad boy.

He'd planned a night watching TV then seduction later. But he'd become aroused as soon as he saw the outfit she was wearing: a tight-fitting top that clung to her curves and a short leather skirt. She certainly knew how to get a man going.

Within no time, she was lying on her back on the sofa, their clothing scattered around the room, and Peter was on top. As he thrusted away, the TV blared in the background. But Peter wasn't watching it; he was otherwise occupied. Until a news item grabbed his attention.

Peter quickly tried to sit up, extricating himself from the girl's legs, which were wrapped around his back.

'I've not finished,' she grumbled.

He pulled her legs away then grabbed at her panties, which were lying by the side of the sofa, and shoved them at her. 'Do yourself a favour, love, and fuck off!' he said. She was about to speak when he held up his hand to silence her. 'Shut the fuck up!' he ordered and something in his voice told her that she would be foolish to complain.

The girl collected her clothing and dashed, humiliated, from the room. Meanwhile, Peter was sitting naked, his penis now flaccid and his eyes riveted to the TV screen.

49

Adele was also having a night in. She was trying to relax with a glass of wine, reading a book, when there was a loud hammering at the front door. She looked at the clock, her senses on full alert: 10.50 p.m. Who could it be at this time of night?

She peered through the living room window before answering the door. At first she couldn't see anything; they were standing too close to the door, lost in the shadow of the house. But then she caught sight of Peter as he stepped back, peering up at the windows.

'Oh, it's you,' she said, to herself rather than Peter, in an attempt to calm herself down.

As soon as she answered the door, Peter fled inside the living room. But he didn't sit down. He was too busy pacing about and unable to settle, bouncing on the balls of his feet with his limbs primed for action. He was making Adele nervous.

'Shit's hit the fan!' he announced. Before Adele could ask what he meant, he added, 'A kid's gone missing. They're dredging the fuckin' river. I've just seen it on the news.'

'Oh no!' said Adele, her heart racing once more.

'They'll probably want to speak to you,' he continued. 'Especially if they find your fingerprints on that fuckin' brass ornament.'

For a few moments Adele couldn't speak. She was trying to process his words, which had bombarded her brain. She was too startled to think beyond those words and come up with a way to deal with things. But Peter soon took control.

'Right,' he said, taking in a deep breath. 'I've been thinking about it on the way here. This is what we'll do.'

As he spoke, Adele noticed that Peter was becoming calmer, his limbs less fidgety. It was as though he drew strength at the sight of her weakness. Where her mind had become fuzzy, his was alert and strategising. A tiny part of her couldn't help but be impressed by his resilience.

'For now I want you to carry on as normal. Act as though we know fuck all. The police might not even find him anyway. It depends how much of the river they cover. What day is your train to London booked for?'

'Saturday.'

Peter thought for a moment before carrying on. 'OK, that gives us a few days. Even if they find him, you were going to London anyway. Our mam knows that too. So, it won't look as though you're doing a runner. If they want you for questioning once you're down there, they'll get in touch. When they do, you're to deny everything no matter what evidence they've got. OK?'

'Yes, but… what if they can prove it?' she asked, panicking.

'Without a confession it will make the case against you weaker. I'm not sure how easy it will be for them to get prints off the brass cat, but if they do, make something up. You used to pick it up and admire it or you helped our mam with the cleaning. Don't worry, if it gets that far we'll sort out a brief for you. But there's something I need you to promise me, Adele...'

As he paused and took another deep breath, she remained silent, waiting for him to continue. An air of expectation hung over them until he spoke.

'You can't bring me into it, sis. They might have enough on you, but they've got nowt on me unless you tell them I was involved. And I won't be happy if you dob me in it.'

'No, I wouldn't,' she said.

'But you need to be prepared for their questions again. And it'll be worse than last time if they think they've got something on you. They're gonna know you can't have lifted the body by yourself and they'll be at you to tell them who else was involved.'

'OK!' she snapped.

Adele spoke sharper than she had intended but Peter's words were still swimming around in her head. She was in shock and was finding it hard to take it all in. Adele was also frightened and the rush of fear that stormed her body was making it even more difficult to process all this information.

'Sorry, it's just...'

'I know, sis. It's scary, I know that. But try not to worry. Things might not come to that. I'm just trying to cover all the bases just in case.'

She managed a weak smile before the tears began to fall.

Adele was almost ready to set off for the station. In the few days since Peter had visited her, she hadn't heard anything from the police and she was looking forward to her new start with John. She threw a few last minute things into her suitcase and zipped it up. Then she took one final look around her home. She and John had spent some happy times here and now they would hopefully continue, except they would be in a different part of the country.

Her mind began to wander; to a time when she wasn't so happy. To all the things their father had put them through. She thought fondly about Peter; how they'd always stuck up for each other as kids. Her relationship with him had changed as they'd grown older but he'd still been there for her when she needed him. He was the one person she knew she could count on to help her out of a difficult situation.

Her stream of thoughts led onto her father's death; an involuntary switch in topic, which she couldn't suppress. The memory was vivid and she shuddered as a mental image surfaced. The brass cat. Innocuous in appearance, yet deadly. Hammering it against his skull, time after time. The sound of its impact against bone. The sight of his skull splintering. And the blood on her hands. So much blood!

The recollection was so strong that she felt the bile rise in her throat. She swallowed down the bitter taste and carried on checking the rooms to make sure she hadn't left anything vital. Guilt was eating away at her but she was determined to put it behind and carry on with her life. It would be a new start and she would be happy; she knew she would. And maybe the flashbacks would go in time.

Nevertheless, Adele was hyped up. She found herself rushing around, subconsciously trying to get away before the past made a nasty assault on her. When the doorbell rang, she jumped, as though it represented a prophecy come true.

The sight of the police on her doorstep intensified her already heightened senses. Panic swarmed her body and, although they weren't here to arrest her yet, she was convinced they were. The officers wore plain clothes, but Adele still knew who they were even before they announced it.

There were two of them, both male. One was tall, middle-aged and a bit rough round the edges, as though he had seen a lot during his career and had become hardened to it. The other man was younger, somewhere in his late thirties, average height and build and with an air of intelligence.

The older-looking one of the two officers held out his ID. 'Hello, Miss Robinson. I'm Inspector Right and this is Sergeant Stewart.' He nodded his head towards the younger man. 'Do you mind if we come inside?'

Adele pulled the door back with shaking hands, allowing them to enter.

'Miss Robinson,' said the inspector, once she had led them through to the lounge. 'We would like you to come down to the station to answer some questions in connection with your father's disappearance.'

'Why, what's happened?' she said, trying to disguise the tremor in her voice.

'We'll explain down at the station,' said the inspector.

Although he wasn't telling her anything yet, she latched onto the word 'questions', trying to reassure herself that at least she wasn't being arrested. She quickly got ready, and within a few minutes she was sitting in the back of a police car.

By the time they arrived at the station, Adele was even more worked up. Her throat felt constricted, her mouth dry and her hands sweaty. The inside of the police station and the formal process of being brought in for questioning were strange to Adele. Although Peter had tried to prepare her for further police questioning, her panicked state meant she wasn't thinking rationally.

Adele tried her best to remain calm while she waited to be interviewed. Eventually she was led through to an interview room and invited to sit down opposite Inspector Right and Sergeant Stewart. The sound of Sergeant Stewart flicking the switch on a tape recorder underlined the seriousness of Adele's situation and she jumped.

The inspector then explained her right to silence, the fact that anything she said could be used against her in court and that if she withheld something which she later mentioned in court, she would be asked why. She nodded her understanding but could feel her heart beat even faster at the implications of those words.

Adele felt the room spin. Her head was hazy but she kept a grip, reminding herself of Peter's words, *Don't buckle, whatever you do. They can't prove owt!*

'Miss Robinson,' began the inspector. 'We have found your father's body.'

Adele gulped, then feigned shock. 'No!' she said. 'Where?'

'Some of our officers fished him out of the River Mersey earlier today. Would you happen to know anything about that?' he asked.

'N-no,' Adele stuttered. 'Why would I?'

'You sure about that?' asked Sergeant Stewart.

'Yes. I don't know anything.'

'You don't seem too surprised that your father is dead,' said the sergeant.

'I am, but I suppose I half expected it because of how long he's been missing.'

'You don't seem very upset either,' added the inspector.

Adele rushed to defend herself. 'I am. Course I am,' she said.

'From what your mother told my officers when he

disappeared, I gather you didn't get along with your father,' he then said.

Adele could feel the heat from the overhead light and she felt clammy. Although it was a statement rather than a question, Adele knew he was looking for a response. Despite the heat, her face blanched. 'I-I, not really,' she stammered. She didn't see any point lying as it might backfire. 'But that doesn't mean I killed him,' she rushed to add, feeling her heart throb at her own words.

'What about the rug and the brass ornament that disappeared from your mother's home?' asked Inspector Right before she had a chance to recover from his previous question.

She feigned bewilderment. 'What about them?'

'Have you any idea what might have happened to them?'

'No. Why?'

The inspector didn't respond to her question. Instead he continued to fire questions at her. 'And how did you feel when you saw your mother's injuries?' he asked.

'Well... concerned. Obviously.'

'And a little angry too?'

'N-no. Why would I be? She fell down the stairs. It could happen to anybody.'

The relentless interview continued in that vein for some time. As Peter had warned her, the police continued to ask the same questions repeatedly but came at her from different angles. Then, suddenly, Inspector Right nodded towards Sergeant Stewart who switched off the tape recorder and the officers got up and left the room.

Adele was now alone. It was a bit of breathing space, but she anticipated that they would be back soon. While they were away she tried to come to terms with the situation. They must have found the cat and the rug if they had found her father so why hadn't they mentioned it? Perhaps they were waiting for her to trip up. She realised that they hadn't mentioned any evidence so perhaps they hadn't got any fingerprints from the brass cat.

When they came back into the room she was a little more relaxed. She expected the same situation over again with the officers asking the same questions repeatedly and her denying any involvement. She was right. They repeated the scenario twice.

The officers left her alone for a third time. She was tiring now and not looking forward to the next round of questions when the officers returned. But she was determined to stay strong.

It was several hours before the door to the interview room opened again. Adele sat up straight and squared her shoulders, ready for whatever they were going to throw at her. But it wasn't the detectives; it was the custody sergeant.

'We're releasing you without charge,' he said.

Adele was astonished. She couldn't believe they were letting her go, and she had Peter to thank for helping her get through.

50

'Thank God that's over,' Adele said to Peter when she arrived at his apartment.

'Have they charged you?' he asked.

'No, but they've told me to stay in Manchester for now.'

'Do you wanna drink?' he asked.

'Yeah, I think I need one after that.'

Peter poured some brandy into a tumbler and passed it to her.

'Sit down,' he said. 'We need to talk.'

The serious tone of his voice frightened Adele. 'What is it?' she asked.

'You need to be prepared for more questioning,' he said.

'Jesus!' said Adele. 'I thought that was it.'

'It might not be. Why do you think they've told you to stay in Manchester? It's in case they need to question you again.' He paused then continued. 'Did they produce any evidence?'

'No, they just kept interrogating me.'

'They might have more to go on,' he said. 'It can take a while for it to come back from the labs.'

Adele stared at him open-mouthed for several seconds before speaking. 'Oh my God! I didn't realise… I don't know if I can go through that again. It was hell!'

'You might not have a fuckin' choice,' said Peter, taking a sip from his own tumbler. 'Best thing we can do now is make sure you're ready if it does happen.'

As Peter had predicted, the police called at Adele's home again, only this time she was placed under arrest in connection with her father's death. On hearing the police officer's words Adele gasped. Then her adrenalin kicked in, the blood pumping ferociously around her body until she felt lightheaded.

'I would also like to inform you that we have a warrant to search the premises,' said Inspector Right, and Adele flinched as she noticed his eyes settle on her suitcase.

Despite Peter's previous advice, Adele was in such a state that it didn't occur to her until later that she needed a solicitor with her. She spent the journey to the station trying to quash her panicked thoughts and focus on staying relaxed.

Once they arrived at the station, Adele was booked in by the custody sergeant. She was then led to an interview room where she was told to wait. Eventually Inspector Right and Sergeant Stewart arrived. When he had outlined Adele's rights to her, Inspector Right began by questioning her again about the evening when she visited her parents' home to collect her mother's things for hospital.

'So, take me through the events of that night again,' he said.

'There's nothing much to add. I went in…'

The inspector interrupted her. 'And that was at around 8.15 to 8.30 p.m.?' he asked, looking at his notes.

'Yes,' she said.

'How did you get in?' he asked.

'I-I've got a key,' she replied, a look of curiosity on her face.

'OK, carry on.'

'I went upstairs to get my mam's things.'

The inspector cut in again. 'So, you went straight upstairs?' he asked.

'Yes.'

'Which rooms did you go into?'

Adele pretended to think. 'My parents' bedroom, and the bathroom.'

'Is that it?'

'Yes.'

'So, you didn't go into any of the downstairs rooms?'

'No.'

'OK, so what did you do then?'

'Once I'd got her stuff I let myself out.'

Then Sergeant Stewart spoke. 'Did you notice anything while you were there?'

'No.'

'What about sounds? Any indication that there was anyone else inside the house? Movement from any of the other rooms? The sound of the TV?'

Adele had already thought about the TV. She would deny hearing it because, if she admitted hearing it, the police would want to know why it wasn't still on when her mother returned the following day. Then she would have to say she entered the living room to switch it off. And that would implicate her.

'No,' she said.

'Then why did your parents' neighbour notice that the TV was still on when she went to bed at 11 p.m.?' asked the inspector.

Adele felt a rising panic. They knew. The police knew! But they still didn't have any proof. So, she would keep denying it like Peter had advised and hope they couldn't detect the rush of fear that shot through her body.

'I've no idea,' she said.

When they had questioned Adele for a while, the police left her alone again. She was worried. Something was going on but she didn't know what.

It seemed like an age before the inspector and sergeant returned and took their seats opposite her. The sergeant was carrying a box, which he put down on the table. From the other side of the table, Adele couldn't see what was inside it. Then the sergeant began to remove plastic evidence bags from the box.

It was difficult to identify what the first evidence bag contained; it was something small, perhaps a fragment or a hair. But the second bag contained the blouse that she had been wearing when she killed her father. Shit! The relevance hit her. But, before she could react, the sergeant put his hand into the box again. He withdrew another evidence bag.

Inside it was the brass cat. The sight of it made Adele's breath catch in her throat. A cold chill ran down her spine and she suppressed a shudder. Then she felt an urge to vomit and tears flooded her eyes. 'I-I think I need to make a phone call,' she said.

'Very well,' said the inspector. 'But, before you do, I think you need to know that we're charging you for the unlawful killing of your father.'

Peter had been back home for two hours following a lengthy and gruelling session at the police station. He'd rung Adele to find out if she had also been taken in for questioning but the phone line was dead. Of course! Realisation dawned on him; she had been planning to leave so she'd probably still have the phone disconnected.

Next, he rang his mother to find out if she had heard from Adele but she hadn't. She told him that she had been questioned again too and it took him all his time to calm her down so he could get her off the phone.

He was concerned about Adele. All he could do was wait for her call but when he still hadn't heard from her a while later, he knew it wasn't a good sign. If they had kept her in longer than him then perhaps it was because they knew they had something on her.

The hours dragged on, but Peter stayed calm and mentally prepared himself to deal with whatever situation arose. By the time the phone rang he was ready.

'Peter, they've charged me,' Adele cried down the phone.

'How come? You've not spilt the beans have you?'

'No, I think it's because I visited the house that night. And they've got evidence. My blouse and that bloody cat!'

As soon as she mentioned the evidence he knew she was up against it. And the fact that she was there on the night of their father's death didn't help either. The police had also questioned him about that night but he had made sure he had a stern alibi, and friends to back up his story.

But despite having all the odds stacked against her, he'd still do his best to get his sister out of the shit. 'I know it sounds easier said than done, but try not to worry,' he said. 'I'll get a brief round to the station as soon as possible. Don't answer any more questions till then.'

'OK, thank you,' she wept.

Peter continued. 'The brief will tell you what to do. Wait for him to get there, and don't let them break you.'

'OK,' she replied weakly.

'Oh, and Adele?'

'Yes.'

'Don't forget what I told you. Not a word, OK? No matter what happens.'

'Yes, I know. I told you I wouldn't do that.'

'Shhh,' said Peter, worried that she'd mention something on the phone that might implicate him. 'Just do as I say and listen to your brief, and everything will be fine. OK?'

He put down the phone and sighed. There was no doubt Adele was in a state. He just hoped she didn't break, but something told him she would keep to her word and not say anything about his involvement. She owed him that, at least. After all, he had stuck his neck out in trying to get her out of the shit. There was nothing else he could do now other than provide the best solicitor he could afford, then sit back and hope.

51

Peter was entertaining David round at his flat. After the events of the last couple of days, he needed a stiff drink and he didn't fancy sitting alone getting maudlin. When it came to the law, it was always good to chat to someone who knew the drill.

'So, how's it going with your kid?' asked David.

'They've fuckin' charged her with manslaughter,' Peter replied.

'How come? I thought they'd released her without charge after they took her in for questioning?'

'Yeah, that was before they found the evidence.'

'What have they got?'

'Fingerprints, material and one of her hairs under his nails, and her hair on his clothing. The fuckin' lot!'

'Jesus!' said David. 'What's the material?'

'A blouse she was wearing, apparently. The dozy cow had it packed in her case ready to go to London. I told her to get rid of her clothes. I shouldn't have fuckin' left it to her! I should have got rid of them myself. She got rid of the jacket she was wearing 'cos it was full of blood but she kept the blouse. She told me it was one of her favourites; though why she'd want to wear it again after what she'd just done is a fuckin' mystery. I'm cursing myself that I didn't make sure she got rid of it.'

'Fuckin' hell! I'm glad she wouldn't go out with me, now. No offence, mate, but your sister sounds like a right fuckin' psycho,' said David.

Peter gave him an evil stare before saying, 'Don't push your luck, Dave!'

'OK, just saying,' David replied. Then he asked, 'Is she in custody now?'

'No. They've charged her with manslaughter and released her till the trial. She's lucky they're going for manslaughter and not murder with the fuckin' job she did on him. But they've taken account of all the circumstances; the fact that it was in self-defence and the shit childhood we both had 'cos of him.

'Apparently there were plenty of fingerprints on the brass cat that she used to batter him and they could tell from the wounds on his head that he'd been hit multiple times. The shape of the cat matched the fuckin' big hole in his head too.'

'Shit!' said David. 'I hope things go her way at the trial.'

'I hope so too,' said Peter. 'But don't hold your fuckin' breath.'

He was seriously worried. Things were looking bad for Adele and her brief would have his work cut out. But there was something else that was secretly bothering Peter; the possibility that even at this stage she could implicate him. Still, she'd kept her word up till now so he could only hope she didn't cave in at the trial.

★

Adele had had plenty of time to reflect since the police had charged her for the death of her father. She still replayed the scene over in her head, wondering if there was anything she could have done differently. Perhaps she shouldn't have goaded him. She could have taken a step back at any point but she hadn't. A force within her had taken over and now she had to bear the consequences.

It was as though a strange calm had come over her now that she had accepted what she had done. The worst had happened; she had killed her father and been charged, and now she was awaiting trial. It didn't get much worse. She knew she would go to prison for what she had done, but she had come to terms with it. Although she was frightened, she would deal with the situation as best she could.

In the hours in which she had mulled over the situation in her mind, she'd also thought about her future. All her life she had struggled to rise above her circumstances. And she had done well, all things considered. She'd got herself a good job and a wonderful boyfriend. But now she'd thrown it all away. She was a common criminal; no better than Peter and his friends.

At first she had avoided seeing her mother. She'd heard from Peter how badly Shirley had taken the news, and Adele didn't feel up to facing her. Shirley had sent a message with Peter telling her to stay away. But Adele couldn't stay away forever; she felt she had to face her mother eventually. And now she was ready.

When Adele arrived at her mother's home, she felt everyone's eyes on her, saw curtains twitch and children stop playing while they gawked at her. Some even ran back indoors. But Adele stood tall outside her mother's front door and took a deep breath before going inside.

'Oh, it's you,' said Shirley who was sitting in the kitchen drinking tea with one of her neighbours. 'I sent a message for you not to come here if what Peter told me is true.'

Shirley seemed to gain strength from the presence of her neighbour but when a painful silence followed Shirley's words, the neighbour announced that she had to go home. She gave Adele a scornful look before stomping out of the house through the back door.

'I needed to see you,' said Adele.

She pulled up a chair, and noticed how her mother flinched as she sat down next to her.

'Is it not true?' asked Shirley, her eyes filling with tears and her hands gripping her mug of tea. 'Is that why you've come here; to tell me you didn't do it?'

'I can't discuss it, Mam. Not until after the trial anyway. My solicitor's told me not to.'

'But I'm yer mam. Surely you can put my mind at ease?' Shirley's tears flowed freely as she grabbed Adele by the wrist. 'Surely you wouldn't do a horrible thing like that, love?' She then gulped and took several seconds trying to calm down before she said, 'The police said his head was a mess.' Her voice broke on the last word and, as she bowed her head forward, a fat tear dripped into her tea, making a plopping sound.

Adele kept her gaze fixed on the mug of tea, trying to postpone the painful confrontation that was bound to follow. Her mother wanted answers and Adele felt obliged to give them despite her earlier resolve not to say anything.

She needed to justify her actions and was about to tell her mother how it had happened but, before she could speak, Shirley sobbed, 'Who would do a bloody awful thing like that, Adele? His head was smashed in, for God's sake! Why did the police charge you? Surely you wouldn't do something like that.'

Adele spoke slowly, the words jarring in her throat, but even as she spoke them, they didn't sound convincing. 'It was self-defence, Mam. I didn't have a choice.'

Shirley looked up and drew her hand away from Adele's as though it was contaminated. 'So you did do it?' she asked, backing away in her seat.

'He was strangling me, Mam. He was hurting me... You know what he was like,' she pleaded.

Shirley stood up and moved away from where Adele was sitting. Drawing courage from the distance she had placed between them, she yelled, 'Get out!'

'Mam, have you forgotten what he did to you?'

'I said, get out! He might have been a bit free with his fists at times but he would never have done what you did. You disgust me!'

'But, Mam.'

'You've taken my husband from me and I can never forgive you for that! Now, please go, Adele. I don't want you here.'

'Mam, I told you it was self-defence.'

'I don't care!' Shirley shouted, becoming hysterical. 'No matter what he did, he didn't deserve to die like that. What you did was sick!'

Shirley's bitter words cut through Adele and left her reeling. She was shocked at her mother's strength of feeling. Although Adele felt remorseful for what she had done, she also felt betrayed. Yes, what she did was wrong. She knew that. And if she could turn the clock back, she would do. But she'd done it for her mother. For years she had tried to protect her. Yet here she was ordering her to leave her home out of some sense of misguided loyalty.

Adele attempted to speak again but no words came. There was no point in pleading with her mother any more.

The neighbour dashed back into the house. Adele got the impression she had been listening close by. She rushed to Shirley and took her into her arms, smoothing her hair and patting her back alternately. By this time Shirley was sobbing profusely.

The neighbour locked eyes with Adele. 'I think you'd better go,' she murmured. 'She's in a state and you being here is only making her worse.'

Adele nodded silently, her own tears now flowing. Then she left her childhood home, wondering if it was for the last time.

52

It was several months later and Adele was being tried for the manslaughter of her father, at Manchester Crown Court. In the months since she had been charged, Adele had come to terms with what she had done. Although she was still afraid of what lay ahead, she was determined to stay positive and strong.

It helped having a brother who had spent time inside. Peter had spent many hours coaching her on how to handle life behind bars, just in case she was found guilty.

Adele watched her mother take the stand. She was surprised at her appearance. Although she appeared timid and out of place, as Adele would have expected, it was her clothing that stood out to her. She was wearing a well-fitting cream trouser suit with matching top, and her hair looked recently washed, although it still hung about her shoulders in limp strands. Adele wasn't used to seeing her mother look so smart. She would have been touched if it wasn't for the reason why she was taking the stand.

Her mother was a witness for the prosecution.

'Hello, Mrs Robinson,' the prosecutor began. 'I realise how

distressing this must be for you but I'd like you to start by taking me back to when you first realised your husband was missing.'

'It was when I came back from the hospital,' she said, her shoulders stooped and her voice barely audible.

'I know this must be difficult, Mrs Robinson, but if you could please speak up and address your replies to the jury, I would be grateful.'

Shirley raised her head, the look on her face one of absolute terror. 'It was when I came back from the hospital,' she repeated.

The prosecution barrister consulted some notes. 'Would that be on Wednesday twenty-fourth August 1983?'

'Yeah, I think so,' said Shirley.

'The hospital records show that Wednesday twenty-fourth August was the day you were discharged,' said the prosecutor.

'Yes, that's right then,' said Shirley.

'And what did you notice on your return from hospital?'

'Well, Tommy wasn't home and I thought he'd be there because I'd just come out of hospital.'

'Anything else, Mrs Robinson?'

'Yeah, the rug was missing, and the brass cat. I couldn't understand it.'

'Was that all or did you notice anything else? Any strange smells for instance?'

'Oh yeah,' said Shirley. 'There was a strong smell of disinfectant.'

There was a rising din amongst the public gallery and Adele noticed one of the jurors lean over and whisper something to the person sitting next to her. The judge called for order so that the prosecution barrister could continue examining his witness.

'And who was with you when you returned from hospital?'

'Adele,' said Shirley.

'Adele Robinson, your daughter, do you mean?'

'Yes,' replied Shirley, her voice dropping once more.

'Could you please speak up, Mrs Robinson, and tell the jury how Adele Robinson reacted when she noticed the missing items? Was she shocked?'

'Not really. She didn't seem too bothered. She said summat about it probably being to do with the neighbours.'

There were further whispers from the public gallery and the prosecutor waited for them to subside before continuing.

'And what happened next, Mrs Robinson?'

'Well, our Adele went home and I waited up for Tommy. I thought maybe he'd just gone for a few drinks.'

'Then what did you do?'

'I rang Adele and told her he hadn't come home.'

'What time was this?'

'After the pubs shut. Getting on for twelve, I think.'

'And what was her reaction?'

'She told me to wait till the next day and then she'd come round.'

'And what happened on the following day, Thursday twenty-fifth August, Mrs Robinson?'

'I rang our Adele and she came round... Oh no, hang on... our Peter came round first, after I'd rung Adele.'

'Did you think that was a bit strange?'

'Yeah, I'd not seen him for ages. Him and his dad had had a bit of a falling-out.'

Again there were whispers amongst the public gallery. Adele noticed the faces of most of the jury; they were fixed on her mother, engrossed in what was being revealed.

'So, what do you think prompted your son to put in an appearance?'

'He said our Adele had rung him.'

'Very well,' said the prosecutor, pausing to give the jury a chance to absorb this piece of information.

'Can you tell us what happened next, Mrs Robinson?'

'Yeah, Adele… no, no Peter it was. He said we should check the local pubs to see if anyone had seen him.'

'Seen who? Your husband, Mrs Robinson?'

'Tommy, yeah,' Shirley replied faintly.

'And then what?'

'Adele came back, said no one had seen him. And then she called the police to report him missing.'

As Shirley finished speaking, Adele could see the tears welling up in her eyes. She gazed across at the jury and saw the expressions of concern on their faces. They'd noticed her mother's tears too.

'Very well,' said the prosecutor. 'That will be all for now.'

By the time Peter was called to the stand, Adele was thankful that at least somebody seemed to be on her side. She'd managed to keep the police off his trail, even though they had asked her repeatedly who had helped to shift the body, and Adele knew Peter was grateful to her. Like his mother, he was dressed smartly in a silver grey, stylish suit with fashionable wide lapels and a black T-shirt underneath but, unlike her, he exuded an air of confidence. Adele guessed that his confident air was probably all front, but nobody else would have known that.

Peter took the stand, his head held high and shoulders back as he gazed around the courtroom. His eyes lingered on the jury until the defence barrister addressed him and began his questioning. Peter seemed to be doing well until the prosecution barrister cross-examined him.

'Mr Robinson, isn't it true that you were convicted of burglary and…'

'Objection!' cried the defence barrister, rising from his seat.

The judge allowed the objection and asked the prosecution not to make reference to Peter's criminal record. But the damage had already been done.

Adele had a sinking feeling. Despite the judge's words, the jury now knew that Peter had a criminal record. In their minds that made him an unreliable witness and they would probably dismiss everything he had said in her defence.

53

It was now the last day of the trial. All the evidence had been presented to the jury; most of it was damning, although Adele's solicitor had made a good attempt at defending her. Now all she could do was wait patiently for the verdict. The hours dragged and she did her best to occupy herself and try to stay calm.

When Adele was called back into court she felt her pulse quicken and a shiver ran down her spine despite the fact that she was sweating profusely. But she was determined not to lose control.

Adele had been preparing for this moment for the past few months. She took a few deep breaths to calm herself and tried to relax her tense muscles before she set off for the courtroom.

As the court official led Adele through the tiled corridors of the court, her footsteps echoed in tandem with her pounding heartbeat. She told herself that the trial would soon be over and then she would deal with the outcome, whatever the verdict was.

Adele entered the courtroom and noticed all eyes in the public gallery switch from the jury to her. She spotted John but his facial expression was impossible to read. He'd stuck by her up to now, convinced that the police had got it wrong and that she couldn't possibly have killed her father. She hadn't had the heart to tell him otherwise.

The judge addressed the jury and asked the foreman of the jury to stand up. Adele continued taking deep breaths, willing her frantic heartbeat to return to normal.

The judge's next words echoed around the courtroom. 'Ladies and gentlemen of the jury, do you find the defendant guilty or not guilty of manslaughter?'

The foreman squared his shoulders and looked around him before delivering the verdict. 'Guilty,' he said, loud and clear as though proud of the fact that he was putting Adele behind bars.

Adele felt the impact of that one word, then a hissing in her ears. She became light-headed but fought to maintain control. Once more she spotted John in the public gallery. His facial expression flitted through a series of transitory phases. From shock, to disbelief, to something else she couldn't quite fathom.

She then looked to Peter for support. His eyes met hers and, while the rest of the public gallery was in uproar, he stayed silent. The judge called for order so that he could pronounce sentence, and Adele braced herself. She kept her eyes locked on Peter waiting for his reaction as the judge spoke.

Adele's heart was pounding. The blood was pumping fiercely around her body and her head felt fuzzy. She found it difficult to concentrate on the judge's words. Everything was a blur, but she heard his most pertinent words: seven years' imprisonment. Seven years!

Peter still held her gaze, his expression steely and

determined. It was as though he was willing her to stay strong. She realised that, no matter what else happened, her brother was still on her side.

Her eyes flitted back to John whose face had changed again. She wasn't sure whether his look was one of disgust or loathing. Either way, it wasn't good. In that moment Adele knew that, unlike her brother, she had lost John and would probably never see him again.

Once Adele had been taken away Peter and David remained seated amidst the din in the public gallery.

'Shit!' Peter kept repeating, even though the outcome wasn't unexpected. 'Seven fuckin' years!'

'Cheer up, mate. She probably won't serve all of that if she keeps her nose clean.'

'It's still a fuckin' long time! I just hope she can hack it.'

'No fuckin' choice now, has she, mate?'

Peter glared at David who quickly backtracked.

'She'll be all right. You've been preparing her, haven't you?'

'Yeah,' sighed Peter. 'Let's just hope she keeps her cool and does as I told her. One sign of weakness and the other cons will be all over her. They'll make her life a fuckin' misery.'

'Ain't many gonna try it on with a violent killer though,' said David. His comments were starting to annoy Peter.

'She needs to use that to her fuckin' advantage then, doesn't she?' A tense silence now stood between them. They left the courtroom and made their way to the nearest pub.

Adele blinked at the glare of the flashbulbs as she stepped outside the court. The press! They were everywhere.

As she was led to the waiting van, the crowd surged forward, hurling questions and taking snapshots. The insistent chatter and piercing light assailed her senses. Her accompanying officer bowed her head and two others flanked her, then they plunged her into the van and locked the doors.

She glanced at the two women sitting across from her and attempted to make eye contact. But their hardened faces remained impassive, their vacant stares hovering somewhere in the middle distance.

Eventually, as the lengthy journey gave way to boredom, the women began to chat. Their conversation revolved around prison lifestyle, past experiences with the law and speculation about which prison they were being transported to. Adele tried to join in but as soon as the women found out it was her first crime, she instantly became a spectator to the conversation rather than a participant.

The van juddered to a halt and the officers unlocked the back door of the van, and led the prisoners into a large yard. Adele looked around at the imposing Victorian building and the high walls bordering the yard.

As the other women chatted, Adele was besieged by panic. Overwhelmed by the constraints of the prison. The muscles tightened around her chest and she drew in shallow gasps of air. She felt dizzy. Claustrophobic. Petrified! What was familiar to the other women was alien and threatening to Adele.

She tried to control her feelings of fear as the officers led them into the building and then to a holding room. The tense wait inside the room was punctuated by visits from prison officers who summoned individual prisoners at intervals.

When Adele's turn came she was led to a smaller room where her details were taken. Then she went to see the doctor who also took some details from her. Once that was done she went back to the holding room where she awaited the next stage of the process.

'Adele Robinson!' called a grim-looking female prison officer with cropped blonde hair and an attitude.

It was the second time Adele had been summoned from the holding room. On this occasion the officer led Adele to a different room.

'Right, now we're going to search you,' said the officer who had accompanied Adele to the room.

Adele braced herself while the blonde officer gave her a thorough pat-down, her hands lingering for a few seconds too long on the most intimate areas of Adele's body. Then it was over and Adele was forced to wait once more in the holding room until she was finally called out again.

This time Adele was issued with her bedding and crockery before being led to a cell. She followed the female prison officer along the lit corridors clutching her bundle. The officer looked friendlier than the blonde one but, nevertheless, she remained tight-lipped as she led Adele through the prison.

There were three levels inside the building but they were open, their balconies looking out onto the floor below. Adele glanced up at the dome-shaped ceiling, its skylights and additional lighting casting an eerie glow on the cream-painted, coarse brick walls. Each of the levels was lined with cells along one side and a barrier on the inner side, which overlooked the ground floor.

Everything about the interior of the prison was menacing, from the ceiling height to the profusion of metal. Adele felt unnerved as she took in the metal stairways, metal handrails and metal gates separating different areas of the prison. But the most daunting was the wire mesh leading from one side of the first floor level to the other; presumably to stop prisoners from leaping over the upstairs corridors in a suicide attempt. The thought made Adele shudder.

Despite the amount of electric lighting, the corridors felt draughty and cold; perhaps because of the sheer size of the interior and the abundance of metal.

It was night-time by now and the prisoners were locked in. Nevertheless, Adele was aware of their presence as she heard their screams and shouts echoing around the open corridors. Some were even engaged in loud cell-to-cell conversations.

Although Peter had spoken to her at length about life behind bars, the reality was more cutting. Adele was frightened of this strange environment and worrying thoughts raced around inside her head. What types of people were ensconced behind the cell doors?

After they had spent a while walking through the corridors and up and down the squeaking metal staircases, the officer came to a halt. Adele followed suit and waited while the prison officer sifted through the large bunch of keys, which hung from a chain attached to her uniform.

When she had found the right key, she lifted it up to the door. Adele tensed at the grating sound of metal against metal as the key turned inside the lock. The officer swung the door open and nodded her head in the direction of the cell's interior.

'Here you go,' she said, and she gave Adele a gentle nudge in the back.

Adele stepped inside the cell and her eyes adjusted to the dimness within. The officer slammed the heavy door shut and turned the key once more. She shivered as the banging of the door echoed around the tiny cell.

Once inside, Adele presented a pitiful, almost Dickensian character as she hovered close to the cell door, her body language painting a picture of fear and abhorrence. Adele's body had closed in on itself; back rounded, knees bent and head bowed. Her arms were turned in against her torso, clutching the bundle tightly to her chest.

She spotted movement to her right and peered across at the bunk beds that dominated most of the cell. A huge woman was splayed across the bottom bunk, wearing only her bra and pants. The woman's ample flesh was hanging about in voluminous folds, spilling over the sides and top of her ill-fitting bra. Her stomach formed an apron, covering most of her briefs. A pang of fear zipped through Adele.

The woman rose from her bed and lumbered towards her; a heavy, aggressive movement, which made Adele flinch.

'Well! What have we got here then?' she asked. 'You're a tasty piece. I think this might just be my lucky day.'

She then stuck out her tongue through fleshy lips, narrowed it to a point and flicked it provocatively up and down. Adele felt a tug of repulsion in her gut as she eyed the woman's features. She had a square jawline, which was far too masculine to be considered pretty, her hair was dark and cropped short, and her skin was pockmarked. She wore an earring in one ear and had a tattoo of a swallow at the top corner of her right cheek.

'Well, aren't you going to come inside then?' she asked.

Adele took a tentative step, noticing the woman's eyes drinking her in.

'I don't bite... Promise,' she grinned. Then she snorted loudly before sticking out a manly hand and declaring, 'I'm Anna Tomlinson, by the way. You'd do well to remember the name 'cos I carry a bit of clout around here.'

Adele returned the gesture, enabling Anna to crush her fingers in an effusive grip.

Then, nodding towards the bunks, Anna said, 'You're on top,' chuckling at the double entendre.

Adele stared back at the woman, a look of barely concealed contempt on her face as her brother's words rang in her head. *Whatever you do, don't show any sign of weakness or they'll fuckin' have you.* She straightened herself up, crossed the room and placed her things on top of the bed.

'I'm Adele,' she said. 'Adele Robinson. You might have heard of me in the news, so I think *you'd* do well to remember the name. I'm Peter Robinson's sister.'

Adele watched with satisfaction as the woman's face dropped in horror at the realisation of who she was dealing with. The news story of Adele's violent killing of her father must have reached the prison. She also had no doubt that Peter's reputation as a hardened criminal preceded him.

She continued to put her things in place around the cell while her cellmate did her best to accommodate her. The woman's attitude had changed from intimidating to ingratiating and Adele smothered a smirk.

She had won a small battle in what was to become a protracted war against both prisoners and prison officers. Adele would heed all of the advice her brother had given her during the past few months. Nevertheless, she knew she was going to have to call on all her reserves, both mental and physical, if she was going to survive this place over the coming years.

Acknowledgements

I have many people to thank for helping me bring this book to market. This is my first novel with Aria Fiction and I have found the whole team helpful and great to work with. In particular I'd like to thank my publisher Caroline Ridding for support and advice, Sarah Ritherdon for her invaluable input at the editing stage and Yasemin Turan for her marketing efforts.

For help with the research for this book, I am grateful to the following people: Jim Coulson, Olwyn Taylor, Alan Dyde, Sara Cox, Haseeb Waheed and Pascoe Mannion regarding matters of law and police procedure, and Diane Wilson and Vicky O'Neil regarding banking procedure.

I would like to thank all the readers who continue to buy my books and recommend them to friends. Thanks also to Kath Middleton and Sophia Carleton for offering to take part in my blog tour.

And last but not least, I would like to thank all of my family and friends who have stuck by me and have always been there to offer support.